dog dish of doom

Also by

E. J. COPPERMAN / JEFF COHEN

dog dish of doom

E. J. COPPERMAN

Minotaur Books

A Thomas Dunne Book
New York

A THOMAS DUNNE BOOK FOR MINOTAUR BOOKS.
An imprint of St. Martin's Press.

www.thomasdunnebooks.com
www.minotaurbooks.com

Library of Congress Cataloging-in-Publication Data

Names: Copperman, E. J., 1957– author.
Title: Dog dish of doom : an Agent to the paws mystery / E. J. Copperman.
Description: New York : Minotaur Books, 2017. | "A Thomas Dunne Book."
Identifiers: LCCN 2017008617 | ISBN 978-1-250-08427-9 (hardcover) | ISBN 978-1-250-08428-6 (ebook)
Subjects: | GSAFD: Mystery fiction.
Classification: LCC PS3603.O358 D64 2017 | DDC 813/.6—dc23
LC record available at https://lccn.loc.gov/2017008617

Our books may be purchased in bulk for promotional, educational, or business use. Please contact your local bookseller or the Macmillan Corporate and Premium Sales Department at 1-800-221-7945, extension 5442, or by email at MacmillanSpecialMarkets@macmillan.com.

First Edition: August 2017

10   9   8   7   6   5   4   3   2   1

For Gene Wilder

dog dish
of
doom

CHAPTER ONE

"Can he whimper?" Les McMaster—yes, *the* Les McMaster: Broadway director, visionary, and musical-comedy hit maker—was concerned about my client Bruno, whom he was auditioning for a featured role in his latest Broadway smash.

"Sure, he can whimper!" I piped up from my seat in the front row of the Palace Theater. "Bruno, cry!"

Bruno, trouper that he was, let out some pitiable sobs that would cause a statue of Simon Legree to break down in tears. Bruno was a pro. I almost broke down myself, and I knew he was faking.

"You can do better!" I heard Trent Barclay call from the seat three rows behind me. "Bruno! Cry!"

Bruno, now a little confused because he *had* been crying, stopped and looked to Trent for direction, the last thing Les wanted. "Look at *me* Bruno," he said to the talent. "I'm the director."

"Well then, direct!" Trent was desperate to mess up this deal for me, I decided. The part had been Bruno's for the asking before Trent had piped up. Trent stood up and started walking down the aisle toward the stage. "Let him know you *mean* it!"

Les looked down at Trent and cocked an eyebrow. "He knows I mean it," he said. "Don't you ever think otherwise."

It's my job to settle down situations like this. Well, actually, it's *not* my job to do that; it's my job to negotiate the deal for Bruno and my other clients. But when a problem like this arises, I have to step in and restore some order.

I stood up. "It's fine," I said, my voice an unconvincing singsong. "Bruno knows what to do, Trent. Let's just sit and watch, okay?"

"No, it's not okay!" Trent looked into the otherwise-empty theater for his wife. "Louise! Don't you think Bruno can do better?"

"Um, I don't know," Louise answered, her eyes darting from Trent to Les and back again. "He was crying, right?"

"It doesn't matter what Louise thinks," Les informed him. "It matters what *I* think, because I'm the one casting the part." His voice was irritated and impatient.

I clenched my teeth. "Please, Trent," I hissed. "Let's just *sit down*."

Trent pouted like a petulant four-year-old and plopped himself into a seat on the aisle next to me. He glared up at Les and folded his arms: *Go ahead, show me.* Perfect.

Bruno, to his credit, lay down on the stage and waited for the argument to end. He even had the degree of professionalism necessary to avoid peeing into the orchestra pit.

Bruno was a brown shaggy dog of indeterminate breed. As far as I could tell, he was a mixed breed. Bruno was a mutt.

He looked sort of like a hairy ottoman, but he could act better than any dog I'd ever handled before.

I'm Kay Powell. I'm a theatrical agent specializing in animal actors.

"It'll be fine," I whispered to Trent once Les had turned his attention back to the dog. "He likes what he sees. Bruno's killing it. If we just let him be, he'll get the job."

"I'm sorry; am I directing too loud for you?" Les called from the stage. Directors can be, perhaps, a little dramatic. And don't get me started on human actors. There's a reason I deal with clients who don't talk back. In words.

Unfortunately, that doesn't always pertain to their owners. "The guy's a hack," Trent whispered back, not as quietly, drawing a look from Les. "I could direct better than this, and I've never directed anything in my life."

Louise, who had moved down to a seat right behind Trent and me, added, "It's true. Never."

"Well, Les has," I said. "Just let Bruno show him what he can do. Bruno is a natural."

I'd only been representing Bruno for a week, literally, when the call came in that Les McMaster was looking for a dog to replace the dog playing Sandy in his current huge hit revival of *Annie*. Word was that if the dog given the part worked out, he might be considered for the film version, which Les was also set to direct. This was the kind of opportunity that an agent like me—or even one with human clients—can't possibly pass up. I had considered passing over Bruno, a dog I hadn't seen really work before, but I'd taken a shot and it seemed to be paying off.

If only Trent Barclay could keep his yap shut.

After a few more minutes of audition, with me watching Trent, not Bruno (as I should have been) and resisting the impulse to dig my fingernails into the back of his hand as a warning, Les walked to the skirt of the stage and talked directly to me. "This is a really smart dog," he said.

"Of course he is," Trent said, usurping the agent (that's me) and worse, annoying the director. Again. "He can do anything."

Les didn't move his gaze from mine. "So I'd like to talk to *you* about him."

"Of course," I said, not giving Trent time to react. "Let's talk." I stood up and started up the steps to the stage.

"Shouldn't we be there?" Louise asked. "He's our dog, after all."

I should have seen that coming, I'll admit. Louise was the "creative" end of the team, having rescued Bruno from a shelter and taught him any number of interesting "tricks." Trent, on the other hand, was the "business" end, keeping the appointment calendar for Bruno and, one assumes, the books once he started earning a salary. The fact that a dog as good as Bruno hadn't yet gotten a job in show business was the reason they'd come to me in the first place.

"Don't worry, Louise," I said as sunnily as I could. "Nothing happens unless you agree and sign on later. But for starters, this is something Les and I do by ourselves. You take Bruno home now, and I'll call you later, okay?"

"Oh, we'll stay here," she answered. "So you can get to us right away. Why wait, right?" She and Trent sat down in their theater seats, looking at the set, which was made up as the orphanage from which Annie would eventually be rescued by Oliver Warbucks. They looked unmovable. Nobody made so much as a gesture to Bruno, who was sitting on the stage looking at his owners and probably wondering if Daddy Warbucks was going to come rescue him too.

I turned away from them, gave Les a look of conspiracy, and walked onto the stage, toward Bruno. I gave him a liver treat from my pocket and rubbed the especially smooth fur on the top of his head. Bruno sat happily and made a satisfied sound in his throat.

"Look, I think the dog is perfect," Les said. "But I'm not sure I'm going to cast him."

"Why not?" I asked, scruffing Bruno under his chin.

"Do you really have to ask?" Les countered, looking out into the house.

"I'll keep them away from you," I promised.

"Yes, you will," the director agreed. "Because I'm going to have it written into the contract."

I stopped petting Bruno for a moment, and he tilted his head up at me. *Hey! Lady! You're supposed to be paying attention to me, remember?* "You're going to . . . Les, why not just trust me?" I asked.

"Because it's too big a risk. We've only worked together once, and that was, well, it wasn't your fault, but still." It was true; I'd found Les a monkey for one of his rare misfires, a musical of *Around the World in 80 Days*. The monkey had stolen Phileas Fogg's glasses, which normally wouldn't have been a problem. But the respected British actor (let's just say his first name is "Sir") playing Fogg had been slumming in this tawdry musical and had written his lines on various pieces of paper he'd cleverly concealed around the set. Without his glasses, he had no idea what to say next.

And the sad part was, that was the highlight of the show.

"I can handle Trent and Louise," I assured him.

"It'll be in the contract, or I'll look for another dog," Les said. "That's it."

And that was it. He walked off the stage. I got Bruno's leash from the chair we'd dropped it on when we'd entered, and Trent bounded up without helping Louise, who lagged behind pretty badly.

"So?" Trent demanded. "Do we have the contract? Let me take a look at it; I went to law school for a year." That was interesting, since I knew he'd made what money he had funding Internet businesses that usually folded in a year or less.

I went to law school for all three years and actually passed the bar in New York state, but hey; why quibble? "Well, he's offering Bruno the role," I said. "We just have to go over some of the particulars."

Trent's eyes narrowed to slits and Louise's took on the emotional depth of a great white shark. "Particulars?" he said with a tone I didn't care for and at a volume I preferred he not reach.

I didn't know if Les was still within earshot, and empty stages have a tendency to echo. So I assessed the situation and made a decision. "Let's go backstage and see where Bruno would be most of the time," I said. "Every theater is different."

Before either of them could protest, I took Bruno's leash and led him toward the wings, from which we could access the backstage. The two other humans had no choice but to follow me; their moneymaker was literally walking away from them.

We walked toward the dressing rooms, and I found one whose door was unlocked, and opened it. Bruno walked in. I let go of his leash, and being the excellent dog he was, he sat down next to one of the two makeup tables and looked attentive. Trent barreled in behind us, and Louise, looking like a headlight-caught deer, followed.

"What's this about particulars?" Trent snarled. A Broadway director was going to cast his dog in a hit musical and he was upset about details.

"It's very simple, and not a big deal," I began. "Les wants to be able to direct Bruno in a way that makes all the actors comfortable and lets them keep the blocking they've already established, and he needs to do it quickly, because the dog playing the part now is leaving on Tuesday." This was Thursday. There really wasn't much time.

"So?" Trent led me. He wasn't being taken in by my assertion that this wasn't something for him to get upset about.

"So he wants time with Bruno alone. And that means he wants me to bring Bruno here every morning and pick him up after rehearsals and performances." That sounds reasonable, doesn't it? I mean, I'm asking you.

I wasn't asking Trent or Louise, because I knew what their response would be, and that's what I got back. "You mean he doesn't want us around?" Trent's voice was rising in pitch and volume.

"We can't even be here when he's rehearsing?" Louise threw in. I got the impression she was less disturbed than confused.

"It's a simple request he's making in the contract," I said in my calmest tone. "It's something I'd advise you to accept, because this can launch a career for Bruno. Les McMaster—"

"Les McMaster is a *hack*!" Trent's voice echoed through the crowded room to the degree that Louise took a step back, dislodging a jar of cold cream from one of the makeup tables. It fell to the floor, but luckily was made of plastic. A little cold cream did spurt out the top and land on the floor, though. "He couldn't direct a grade-school production about dental health!"

"Please keep your voice down," I said, noting a change in the light at the foot of the closed door. "He might be able to hear you."

"*Let* him hear me!" Trent was drunk with whatever power he'd decided he had. "My dog wouldn't work with him if he were the last director on Earth!"

"Trent." Funny, I didn't remember saying that. Oh! That was because the voice was Louise's. "Get off your high horse. The man's offering us money for a dog to sit and stay."

"That dog is talented!" Trent was on a roll. "That dog is an *artist*."

"Oh, knock it off," his wife responded. "This is all about you, as usual. You don't want to give up control to someone who actually knows what he's doing."

Trent stared at her with an expression that might as well have had daggers and nuclear warheads emanating from his eyes. He raised his hand reflexively, as if to strike her, but stopped when I gasped. Louise simply glared at him. But he said nothing. He turned and walked out the door.

Louise turned toward me. "Don't let this spook you, Kay," she said. "He does this all the time." Swell. I couldn't wait to work with him more. "I'll handle him."

"You sure?" I asked. "That looked . . ." My voice trailed off.

"He'd never really do anything like that, believe me. Just give us a call tomorrow. I'll get him to sign the contract." She took Bruno's leash from the floor, and the dog, a total trouper, got up and followed her out with a serene look on his face.

I left the dressing room (after picking up the jar of cold cream and putting it back on the table) and went into the hallway leading toward the stage door. I thought I saw a man's leg turning the corner as I walked out. Trent? Les? Could Les have heard all the screaming? Was it possible he hadn't?

It's not often I talk to myself, but this was one such occasion.

"Well, that could have gone better," I said.

CHAPTER TWO

On the drive home from Manhattan, I did everything I could to avoid thinking about Trent, Louise, Les, and especially Bruno, who deserved better guardians than the ones he had, I was afraid.

I got into the business of representing animals in an attempt to join the one area I knew something about with a business in which I could make a decent living. My parents, of course, had been against it from the start.

"Veterinary school?" my mother asked. "Why would you want to go to veterinary school and break up the act?"

Maybe I'm getting a little ahead of myself here.

I was born into a showbiz family: My father met my mother at the Nevele, a Catskills resort, in 1975. He was a waiter, and my mother, the former Eleanor Rey, was a dancer in one of the revues. By the time my father, Jay Powell, worked up an act of comic patter and a few song parodies, they were dating pretty seriously. It's never been clear to me whether they formed an act together or got married next; the chronology is a little shaky. So is the chronology of when they got married versus when I was born, which was in 1979. Sometimes it's better not to ask questions around my parents.

In any event, they had become one of the house acts at the Nevele by 1983, which is when I made my debut. Sometimes I suspect they named me Kay strictly to bill us as "Jay, Kay, and El" (which they did), and other times, I'm absolutely sure that's why they did it.

I wasn't an awful dancer and I could sing for a little girl, so by the time I was ten, I had my own spot in the show to solo, a segment my father couldn't resist calling "Oh, Kay!" And after the glamour of it gave way to the reality that we were a second-rate act in a second-rate resort playing in the smaller of two ballrooms, I had come to hate performing. So when I suggested that I might want to go to college to pave the way for a career in veterinary sciences because I'd always loved animals (there was a dog act in the revue one summer, and some guests brought their pets), my parents saw it as a betrayal of not just our show-business heritage, but of them personally.

"Veterinary school?" my father parroted. He's great support for Mom, because he knows she's the real talent in the act. "Do you know how many girls would kill to be in the position you're in now? To have a paying job in show business?"

"A lot of parents would be happy their daughter wants to get an education," I protested. Hey, I was seventeen. A little melodrama is par for the course, and in my family, well, drama is what we do when we're not doing musical comedy. "I want to help dogs and cats and birds and other animals. I want to help people be happy with their pets. It's the same thing as what you guys do—it's taking their minds off their troubles. Isn't that what you've always told me is the most important thing?" Man, I was good in those days.

To their credit, my parents listened, and conferred. "It's what you want," Mom told me finally. "What kind of parents would we be if we didn't help you go after what you want?"

So off to Ithaca College I went, bent on getting the grades I'd need to attract attention in vet school applications. Until the first day of organic chemistry class my freshman year, when I realized I was in miles over my head, and I'd better find another way to fulfill myself.

I did what every student with no particular ambition does—I became a history major and went to law school. And once again to their credit, my parents did not develop an I-told-you-so attitude; they supported me as much as they could and I worked for the rest.

But the truth is, I'd never intended to practice the law. If I couldn't fix sick pets, I could at least work with animals. I got the law degree to learn how to negotiate contracts. And my first year out of law school, having passed the bar exam, I opened Powell and Associates (there were no associates, but I did have an assistant), Theatrical Agents. But I solicited only nonhuman clients.

The first couple of years were rough. Mom and Dad had seen the writing on the wall when the Nevele was sold in 1997 and had taken their act on the road—or more specifically, on the high seas. They were now wowin' 'em for a line of cruise ships, playing the lounges while larger, more elaborate shows were being done at night. Mom and Dad got to travel, they got to see the big shows and hobnob with the name entertainers and guests, and they got paid. Not a bad retirement plan.

My business was sporadic—you have to build a reputation for yourself. Luckily, I had a mentor, Lou Romano, one of the few animal only agents working Broadway. Lou had actually done a Learning Annex lecture that only I and three bored twentysome-things attended, and I had dominated the question-and-answer session afterward. I'd given him my card, and occasionally Lou would throw me a bone, like when a local car agency needed a dog or cat for a TV ad. The national spots, which made tons of money, he kept for himself. Lou was a sweetheart, but no fool.

Little by little, my clients started to get work, and that gets you word of mouth. Now, five years in, I'd inherited some of Lou Romano's clients when he passed away. Apparently he'd been recommending me from the time he'd gotten the diagnosis he knew would turn out badly for him. A gent to the very end. Literally.

I pulled up to the driveway of my little house in Scarborough, New Jersey, a forty-minute drive from the George Washington Bridge. Sure, I still had thirteen years to go on the fifteen-year mortgage, but I had two bedrooms, a kitchen, a living room, a "den" (converted dining room), and a little backyard. Not bad for a beginning.

Right now, it was a little crowded. Mom and Dad, between gigs on the cruise ship, were in residence, working on their act. Dad was writing new material and Mom was keeping limber with ballet and tap classes a couple of times a week. It was April, and they figured to be back on the boat by June (although the phone hadn't rung yet, which was worrying), so it was important to keep those creative muscles stretched and healthy. I knew the drill.

I wasn't entirely prepared for the scene I found when I walked into the living room, though: Mom was at the spinet piano they'd bought for me (so they could rehearse and entertain when they were in town) playing "Over the Rainbow" for a lady of about eighty years, sitting in a wheelchair with a younger woman, dressed in medical scrubs, standing next to the TV table. Dad was sitting backward on one of my kitchen chairs, a baseball cap on his head (Staten Island Yankees) and a clipboard in his hand. The lady was singing enthusiastically, if not entirely melodically.

I knew better than to interrupt; I made my way around my own coffee table as if I were afraid I'd awake a sleeping giant. Finally, I got to Mom, who could play and converse at the same time. "Okay, I give up—what's going on?" I asked.

"We're holding auditions," she answered. Sure. That explained it.

"For what?" The sweet lady in the wheelchair was doing her best to sound like a twelve-year-old girl from Kansas, and it was possible she was getting the Kansas part down, but the rest was, well, not in her wheelhouse.

"Dad has agreed to write and direct a revue for the Scarborough Senior Center," Mom said. Her tone was not judgmental; she wasn't acting like I should have known. "We want to see what kind of talent we have available to us."

"And this lady?" I asked.

Mom gave a half nod to one side. "Maybe she can tell jokes," she said.

The song ended, mostly because Mom stopped playing (our guest had more or less given up on singing a few lines earlier, but looked pleased), and Dad made some marks on the form he had on his clipboard. "Very nice, Vanessa," he said. "We'll be in touch."

No sooner was Vanessa out the door than a tall African American man was standing in the doorway. He had white hair, what was left of it, and carried sheet music. I didn't want to know.

"I'm taking the dogs for a walk," I said to no one in particular, and went into the kitchen, where I knew I'd find my two pals.

Steve, the dachshund, was cowering in a corner, traumatized by the commotion around the house and, worse, the loud piano playing. I went over to him first and stroked his fur, then scratched him behind his ears. He perked up, wagged his tail, and followed me to the door, where Dad had put up a baby gate to keep the dogs out of the living room.

Eydie, my rescued greyhound, was standing at the gate, barely acknowledging my presence. She was appalled at having to stay out of the living room, since there were people there who clearly had not been treated to her company. She wanted badly to correct that error.

Instead, I got the two leashes and led them both out the kitchen door to the backyard. I have a chain-link fence around the yard, but that's just for the times when the dogs want to go out on their own. On our walks, we traverse the neighborhood.

I resisted the urge to check in on a couple of clients, especially

Trent and Louise, and concentrated instead on living in the moment. That's always been a problem for me.

The dogs were happy to be out on such a fine day, so we walked for a long time. I find it relaxing to walk with them; they don't ask for very much and they never talk back. "You should have seen the owners I had to deal with today," I told them as we walked past the borough hall. "You wouldn't believe me if I told you." I did not mention how lucky they were to have been adopted by someone as wonderful as me; I felt that should remain unsaid. I am nothing if not modest.

We stopped for a moment while Eydie decided to sniff a particular patch of grass more carefully than most, then moved on. We got to the main drag of Scarborough, West Roosevelt Avenue, and walked up toward the Carvel, which was not a logical destination with two dogs, but a sort of perfect goal, since I knew it was exactly a half mile from my house. Turn around, go back, complete the mile.

"Do you guys think I should drop the Barclays?" I asked the dogs. "I mean, they seem really sort of creepy, but Bruno is such a nice dog."

"I don't know," said a low voice, almost a growl. "Do you think they're being mean to the dog?"

I turned to see Sam Gibson behind me. Sam, who runs Cool Beans, the local coffee shop—which just sells coffee and pastries—was wearing an apron and an amused expression. "Ruh-row, Ray," he said. "Rooks rike rouble."

"You're incredibly amusing, Sam." Steve went over and sniffed Sam's leg. He loves Sam. Eydie, being a little less obvious in her feelings, licked his hand discreetly.

"You know, talking to your dogs is one of the first signs, Kay." Sam said.

"Of what?"

"Needing someone else to talk to." Sam asked me out once, and I turned him down because I had a client meeting. He'd been hinting he might do so again, and I thought I might have to have another client meeting. I like Sam, but not that way. He's so . . . Sam.

"You're never lonely when you have a dog," I told him. "Or two."

He chuckled, probably taking the hint and deciding to postpone any talk of dating for another time when he imagined I'd be more receptive. "You need anything while you walk?" he asked. "Iced coffee? Bottle of water?"

"No thanks, I'm good."

"You say that, but can you prove it?" He was gone before I could answer.

Scarborough is the kind of town where you don't know everybody, but you always know somebody. I wasn't in the mood to talk to people, so the dogs and I decided (after a quick conference) to head home the back way, off main streets where we were less likely to be engaged in conversation. The dogs didn't feel like talking either.

When I'd gotten into the agency business, it was largely because I love animals. But I hadn't considered the fact that the clients (dogs, cats, parrots, and, one time, a pig) would come with human owners. I don't do as well with people.

It's not that I don't *like* people; I grew up in a resort hotel and got to know the staff and some guests, and found them all fascinating. But people always seem to have me at a disadvantage, as if they all know the rules and haven't bothered to tell me. I've learned to negotiate contracts and I know how to talk to people in a business atmosphere, but one-on-one interaction with people I don't know *very* well has always been a challenge for me.

We got back to the house without any further incidents and I gave Steve and Eydie treats when we walked inside. The auditions in my living room seemed to have been concluded for the day; there was no more piano music and no unfamiliar faces I could see.

The dogs and I breathed a sigh of relief.

"I've been thinking," I told Dad while we made dinner that night (Mom is an awful cook and knows it, so she was putting the living room back together). "You and Mom have been spending more time here lately."

"It's because the cruise ship doesn't book acts until the last minute these days," Dad explained. "We're not cutting-edge, but I'm going to write us a new act and we'll get back out there, I promise you."

I have been told that a person is supposed to tear, not cut, lettuce for a salad. I do not subscribe to this theory, as a knife is much quicker and requires less touching of food. "That's not what I'm trying to say, Dad. I love having you guys around. But this is a pretty small house, and you don't have the freedom you need. How can you rehearse a new act in that living room? It's too small."

Dad looked up from the pasta he was stirring. "You want us to get our own place?" he asked. "I'm not sure if we could . . ." I knew they didn't have enough money to buy a house. They'd spent a good deal of their savings putting me through college, and hadn't completely recovered yet.

"No, not exactly. I'm thinking maybe I should start looking for something bigger. With a separate apartment for you guys, like a mother/daughter house. Then you could still stay here when you're not working, but you could feel like you had your own place."

Dad rested the wooden spoon he'd been using on a cutting board next to the stove. He came over to me and gave me a hug, which I hadn't expected. Some lettuce landed on the floor. Steve walked over, tail wagging, sniffed it, lost interest, and walked back to his bed next to the pantry. He stretched out and yawned. No meat. What was the point?

"You're a good daughter," Dad said.

"Well, I have good parents." I'd been thinking about a larger house for six months. The agency was doing pretty well, and home prices had stayed fairly low. The problem was, that meant I'd get less for this place, and that might make a new purchase more difficult. I'd have to talk to a real-estate agent.

If dealing with strangers was as easy as dealing with my parents, life would be a lot easier. We spent that evening eating and talking—and laughing at some of Dad's new jokes for the cruise-ship act. Mom said a couple of the auditions for the senior-center show were actually very impressive, and she thought the show, to be staged in a month, had a chance to be something special. We enjoyed one another's company well into the night.

And the next morning, I found out Trent Barclay had been murdered.

CHAPTER THREE

I don't usually wait by the phone for a client to call, but that morning I was anxious about Bruno's chances in *Annie* because a hit Broadway show pays nicely and suddenly I was thinking about a move to a larger home. Yeah, it's all about the art, but a girl's gotta make the mortgage payment too.

After putting together some scrambled eggs and toast—I'm not the most creative cook on the planet, especially at eight in the morning—I sat down with a cup of coffee at the minuscule kitchen table I'd bought thinking it would be cozy, when in fact it just squeezed into the corner of the room I needed it to fit.

I had not, of course, made any breakfast for my parents. They are veteran show-business professionals, and as such don't wake up before eleven a.m. at the earliest. This has been going on for all of their adult lives, and there is no point in trying to change it now, even if I wanted to.

So, with my phone out on the table for maximum call-receiving speed, I was reading the *New York Times* before moving on to *Backstage,* which admittedly I read on my laptop now. The *Times* still gets delivered in actual paper form because I am respectful of enduring institutions, even the ones that will probably die out in ten years so we can read our news on a three-inch screen. I will hold out on reading any publication on my phone for as long as I can, and then I will inevitably cave in and squint at the news every morning, tailored to my preferences, as it would be an awful thing if I just stumbled across an article on a subject I hadn't expected. Progress is a funny thing.

The phone didn't ring, but the *Times* shook me up pretty well.

A small article, barely three paragraphs, on page A26 (where once again efficiency had reduced the Metro section to three pages) just happened to cross my eye because the headline included the word "dog." It's second nature now, a professional talent cultivated over years.

MANHATTAN MAN FOUND WITH FACE IN DOG DISH, it read.

It took just a few seconds for me to read through the description of the incident, in which a man described as a "local entrepreneur" had been found dead in his SoHo apartment, facedown in a dog's water bowl.

Only in the second paragraph did the reporter mention two pertinent facts: (1) The man had been stabbed in the back with a carving knife and landed in the dog's dish; and (2) His name was Trent Barclay.

The noise I made in my throat was so instinctive and unusual that I didn't immediately recognize it as coming from me. But Eydie heard it and walked over to see what was wrong (and to see if there was any bacon with the eggs and toast). Steve, having heard my guttural gargling, looked worried and curled up a little tighter in his dog bed.

Without thinking, I petted Eydie on the head while my mind reeled. Maybe the paper was wrong. (Confronted with horrible news, like when my grandfather died, my initial response is to assume that some awful mistake has been made. So far, that has never been the case.) Maybe Trent wasn't dead. Maybe it was the wrong Trent Barclay (surely there must be dozens of Trent Barclays in the Manhattan phone book, if there still is a Manhattan phone book).

Maybe my chance to place Bruno in a great big Les McMaster musical *hadn't* just splashed into a dog dish in SoHo.

Yeah, I admit it: My concern was about my business, and not about poor Trent. For one thing, I hadn't known the man for very long, and had interacted much more with his dog than with him. Besides, Trent was kind of a jerk.

But the fact was that now I was sizing up the little kitchen I had and thinking maybe Mom and Dad could just get another extended gig on a cruise ship and I didn't have to think about a bigger place.

My mind didn't exactly clear, but I realized I had to form a plan of action. First, I picked up the phone and found Trent in my contacts. I called his number. It was not a huge surprise when the call went straight to voicemail. Probably a lot of people were calling Trent to tell him he was dead.

Failing that, I dialed Louise. Again, it didn't exactly shock me when her line wasn't answering either. But since the tiny *Times* article didn't mention anything about Trent's wife being discovered in Bruno's crate, there was a somewhat better chance she'd get back to me, so I left a message.

"Hi, Louise. Um . . ." (What do you say to a woman whose husband just got stabbed in the back—literally—and did a face-plant into the dog's water bowl?) "I, um, read about Trent, and I'm so sorry to hear it. Please give me a call back and let me know if there's anything I can do for you or Bruno, okay? I just feel awful about it and hope there's something I can do. So give me a call back as soon as you can."

I disconnected, then immediately pushed the button to redial Louise's number. "Um, Louise? This is Kay Powell. I don't think I said that before. So, um, call me." I hung up because I couldn't think of a way to make myself sound even stupider.

Now what? Who do you call when your client ends up murdered and humiliated at the same time? Is there a proper mourning period during which a victim's dog can't actually go out on auditions? You don't see that sort of thing in advice columns, and the *Times* doesn't have an advice column anyway. Or a comics page. Two of the paper's few failings.

When you get really upsetting news, there's a strange impulse to immediately share it with someone else. For one thing, it makes the news seem realer, somehow. For another, you get sympathy (if that's what you're looking for) and a sense of control, since you now have power over the information and get to decide about its dissemination.

The problem was that at the moment, I didn't have anyone to tell about Trent Barclay's murder.

Sure, I could have told Mom or Dad, but they were asleep and I hate to wake anyone, especially two old hoofers whose bones creaked a little before they limbered up for the day. They'd have sympathy for me, all right, but first they'd have to remember what it was like to be awake. No, telling my parents could wait until later.

I hadn't made a horde of friends in Scarborough since I'd moved here. Sure, there was Sam and one or two others who ran businesses in town, but they were acquaintances, even if Sam hoped otherwise. I had clients, but they were generally nonverbal and their owners were not the type of people I'd found especially ingratiating. Trent and Louise were not atypical of the "stage parents" my clients tended to have.

My college and law school friends were scattered about the country, and it'd sound weird for me to contact them out of the blue to tell them a total stranger had gone facedown in a two-inch dish of water.

I'd basically decided to get on Facebook and tell any of the random 126 people with whom I was "friends" there about Trent when the doorbell rang. Knowing Mom and Dad could essentially sleep through a marching-band competition held in their bedroom, I took my time getting to the front door and looked through the convenient peephole while the bell rang a second time.

A woman in business clothing, tall and of Latin descent, stood there looking far too stern for a Jehovah's Witness. She looked, in fact, like a bill collector, but I wasn't aware of any delinquencies in my payments. So there was no choice but to open the door.

"We're not holding any auditions right now," I told her, figuring this was another of my father's "discoveries" for the senior pageant. "I don't know what they told you, but you're best off trying somewhere around three."

The woman reached calmly into her jacket pocket and produced what looked like a very slim leather wallet. She flipped it open to reveal a badge.

"I'm Detective Alana Rodriguez of the NYPD," she said with almost no inflection whatsoever. Clearly she'd gotten in line twice when they were handing out indifference. "I'm here to discuss the murder of Trent Barclay last night."

I've done better at first impressions.

"Of course, Detective," I said. Then I stood there and we looked at each other for a long moment. Detective Rodriguez did not move a facial muscle. I got the impression you couldn't get her to move one without dynamite.

"May I come in?" she monotoned finally.

Idiot. "Of course," I said. "Sorry about that." I stood to one side and let the detective into my front hall, which doubled as the living room. She came in and towered over me just for effect. She wasn't as tall as the Chrysler Building, but she had a couple of stories on me easily.

I ushered her toward the sofa, which was crammed next to Dad's rehearsal piano, and she sat, so we were just about eye-to-eye. Until I sat on the facing armchair. "I read about Trent in this morning's paper," I told the detective. "It's an awful thing."

"Did you know him well?" she asked.

There was a tone about the question, prepared and ready, that I can't say was my favorite thing. "Not really," I said. "He and his wife were clients of mine. Actually, their dog, Bruno, was the client."

Rodriguez's eyes narrowed. "The dog is the client?" she said. She must have known that, since she knew to come talk to me.

It was a way to elicit a response. I was going to be careful about all the ones I gave her, I decided.

"Yes. My agency specializes in nonhuman talent." I considered giving her a business card, but didn't, figuring she could ask if she really wanted one. "Of course, Trent and Louise would have gotten all of the money Bruno earned, but he would be doing all the work."

"You went with them to an audition for the dog yesterday," the detective said. That was not a question; it was a directive to continue talking.

"That's right. Les McMaster is looking for a dog to play Sandy in the Broadway revival of *Annie,* and I thought Bruno would be very good for it." And that was all I was going to say until someone asked me a direct question.

So she did. "Did anything unusual happen at the audition?"

"Unusual?" All right, so I was buying time. I knew what she meant. But this was getting into uncomfortable territory, where I might have to implicate a very major theater director in the death of a dog owner. That wouldn't really sit well with any potential clients. It's not easy being a one-person business.

"Yes," Rodriguez said. She'd produced a voice recorder, one of the slim ones, from her jacket and was holding it in my general direction. But hey, no pressure. "Anything at all?"

"Not really," I said. The whole scene backstage where Trent had accused Les of being a no-talent hack whose career was hinging on his—that is, Trent's—dog had happened *after* the audition. That was how I was justifying my response. Sue me.

Rodriguez, who clearly had heard another story somewhere in her investigation, raised her eyebrows. "Really," she said.

Now I seemed to be withholding information from a New York City police officer, and that couldn't be good. "Well . . ."

"Ms. Powell," Rodriguez said, "it's a really bad idea to lie to a cop. Right now I have no reason to think you were involved in the murder of Trent Barclay. But if you give me one . . ."

Whoa! Back up, lady! *Involved?* I spouted. "What do you mean, 'involved'? You think *I* killed Trent? What possible reason would I have to do that?"

"I said no such thing," the detective countered. She had the most bland expression on her face since Pia Zadora gave up acting, if you could call that acting. "So why don't you stop playing games with me and tell me what you know that might help me solve this case and leave you alone?"

I thought about that. I had no loyalty to Louise Barclay, and Trent certainly didn't have any use for my scruples anymore. The only one to whom I had ties was Bruno, and I was pretty sure *he* hadn't stabbed Trent in the back with a carving knife. So who was I protecting?

"There was a . . . I wouldn't even call it an incident; it wasn't that big, backstage after the audition," I told her. "Trent was going on about how Les McMaster was a terrible director because Les had asked me to keep Trent and Louise away from him if he hired Bruno to work on *Annie*."

Rodriguez's expression never changed, but I'm pretty sure her hair flattened out while she was listening. I can't be sure it was a conscious thing, but it gave her the look of someone who was hearing things she either couldn't or didn't want to believe.

"The director wanted you to let him work with their dog but not to let them near him?" she asked after a moment.

Les McMaster was a prominent theater director and could make me a pariah in the business if he decided to put his mind to it. Worse, he could make sure nobody ever heard my name again, and I'd have to find some actual legal work to keep up the payments on my house. But I was talking to a cop about a murder, and my options seemed sort of limited.

"He wanted it written into Bruno's contract," I said.

"Theater people," Rodriguez muttered.

"What?"

"Nothing. So was McMaster in the room when Trent Barclay made all these disparaging comments about him?" Rodriguez was back to being unflappable. You couldn't flap her no matter how hard you tried.

"No. Trent, Louise, and I—and Bruno—were in a dressing room backstage. I had done my best to make sure Les was nowhere near because I knew Trent could be, um, passionate about his opinions, and he'd already questioned Les's ability to direct his dog. Would you like a cup of coffee or something?" Maybe I could ingratiate myself to Rodriguez and she could keep my business from being completely destroyed because I'd dropped a famous director's name while being questioned about a murder.

"No thank you," the detective said quickly. "So McMaster didn't hear Trent's tirade about him, is that right?"

This was the part I really hadn't wanted to talk about, because if I said what I really thought, Les could be incriminated and I could be looking for work representing something more disrespected than animal performers. And I couldn't begin to imagine what that might be.

"Do I need to talk to a lawyer?" I asked. I've seen enough

cop shows (and have cast two Siamese cats named Bridget and Sprinkles in one) to know that the word "lawyer" is supposed to stop all questioning in its tracks. Of course, I *was* a lawyer, but never a criminal attorney, and I didn't really know any who did that kind of work. I should have kept up with more of my law school class on Facebook.

"No you don't," Rodriguez said. "You're not being arrested or charged with anything. Not yet."

Not yet? "I can't say I'm crazy about that answer, Detective," I said.

She didn't even shrug; that's how unconcerned she was. "I understand, but I can't rule anything out. You're not telling me everything you know, and that raises some suspicions. Now. Did Les McMaster hear what Trent Barclay said about him, or not?"

"The truth is, I don't know," I said.

Her eyes narrowed a little. "And where were you last night between ten and two in the morning?"

I didn't care much for *that* question. "Here, and I can wake up my parents to vouch for me if that's necessary," I said.

The detective shook her head. "Not now," she said.

"Okay . . ."

Rodriguez stood up and snapped the voice recorder off. "That'll do it for now." She did not reach out to shake my hand. "I'll see myself out." That was no big thing, since the second she stood, my front door was four feet from her right hand. She opened it and left.

Steve, who had been lying on his bed in one corner of the room the whole time Rodriguez had been there, stood and walked over to me, offering a nice smooth dachshund head to stroke. So I did.

"I'm hoping that wasn't the highlight of my day," I told him.

But never think a bad situation can't decline quickly. Before I could process the situation I was in, the door to my parents' bedroom opened and my father emerged in what he called his "backstage robe," a smoking jacket that had probably looked a lot like satin in 1987. Behind him was my mother, who is more the flannel pajamas type. It was hours before either of them should have been awake and I stared at them with a sense of impending doom.

"We want to help," Mom said.

I was right. Things could always get worse.

CHAPTER FOUR

My first impulse—to tell my parents that they'd had a dream about me being questioned by the police in a murder investigation—had been quickly discarded. I might be able to convince one or the other, but telling them they'd both had the same dream was pushing it even for me.

I came clean instead, but not before asking them exactly why they were awake at what was for them an ungodly hour.

"I can sleep through a world war, you know that," Dad said. "But if there's the slightest bit of trouble for you, your mother wakes right up, and when she's awake, I'm awake." They're like the same person, only with two bodies because they're a double act and get paid more that way.

"Tell us exactly what's going on," Mom said. "And did you eat?"

I explained not only Trent's death, Rodriguez's allegations, my concerns about Les and my reputation, but also the fact that I'd made scrambled eggs and toast for myself but not them because I wasn't expecting my parents to be awake before lunch.

"Don't worry about that, Kay," my father said. "It's the police thing that's bothering me. It's never good to see a cop at your door."

My mother gave him a special smile. "Except in the fire-hydrant sketch," she reminded him.

It's a long story.

"Well, then, but I mean real cops." My father stood up and walked into the kitchen. "You want coffee, El?" he called back.

"No thanks," Mom said, then she turned her attention to me. "Do you think the detective really thought you killed that man because he was messing up your chance to get his dog a job?"

I shook my head. "She just sounds that way naturally, I think," I told her. Dad walked back into the room with two mugs of coffee and handed me one. He knew I'd need it. "I really don't think she suspects me so much as she doesn't know enough to rule me out yet."

"We should get on this case," Dad said, looking at Mom. "We should investigate and clear Kay's name." My father, like so many show people, has a thirst for the dramatic and a real talent for blowing things wildly out of proportion.

I fixed a stern glance and pointed it at him. "You're not doing anything like that," I said in my best schoolmarm tone, stopping just short of calling him "young man." "My name is just as clear as it was yesterday. It doesn't need clearing. You're going to stay away from anything in the least connected to Trent Barclay's murder. Got that?"

He held up his hands, palms facing me, in a gesture of surrender. "I got it, I got it. Is it okay if I watch the news to see if they say anything about it?"

"No."

"Man, you're strict," Dad said, and I did my best not to laugh, which wasn't very good. My father has always been able to get on my good side by being silly. Say what you want, but when your adolescence includes going out in front of a bored audience and singing "Take Me Home, Country Roads" eight times a week, a little thing like that can go a long way.

Mom, however, is a tougher audience. "I'm still concerned," she told me. "What if whoever killed this Barclay man has a grudge against you too?"

"The only connection I have with Trent Barclay is his dog, Bruno," I assured her. "He doesn't seem the homicidal type."

Mom's lips puckered. "There's his wife and the director, both of whom make very good suspects, and they know you."

I stood up. "But they don't have a reason to be mad at me," I said. "Now, I'm going into my office, and you two should go back to sleep. It's not even ten."

"We have auditions," Dad told me. He got up too. "I should shower and get dressed."

Mom looked at him. "The auditions don't start until one," she said.

"I know. I want to be ready." They exchanged a look, and both headed for their bedroom.

I chose not to think about that.

Instead, I got myself into my 2012 Prius (laugh all you want, but I pay less in gasoline bills than you do) and headed back into

Manhattan. Okay, East Harlem. I can't afford office space in Midtown.

It took about forty minutes to get into town because there was more traffic than I'm used to. I rarely drive during anything approaching rush hour, but Rodriguez's visit had thrown off my usual schedule. By the time I got to 118th Street, I was already running a half hour behind the schedule I had pushed back mentally when I woke up that morning.

But Consuelo, the lovely fifty-year-old I'd hired as a receptionist and kept on as an office manager/assistant/entire staff, had organized me within an inch of my life. Short and trim with hair that hadn't naturally been this dark in fifteen years, she was on her feet and carrying her iPad toward me even before I had both feet in the tiny office.

Maisie, the macaw we'd appropriated in lieu of payment from an owner who had been, let's say, less than kind to the bird, flapped her wings in the cage over Consuelo's desk. Maisie is in a constant state of irritation and thinks everyone should just go away and leave her alone. She hasn't yet worked out the part where she gets food and the cage gets cleaned without people coming by to help.

"You have an appointment with that parakeet at eleven thirty, then a phone call with a bear cub and a callback for the calico cat," she was saying as I took off my jacket and hung it on a hook over my not-very-large desk. Consuelo always refers to the clients and not the owners, because she knows I won't remember the names of the people but I will recognize the animals.

"All today?" I said. "That's a lot. Did you hear about Trent Barclay?"

"That's Bruno the dog?" Consuelo said. "Yeah, I heard. The cops called and I gave them your home address. That wasn't wrong, was it?"

It figured, though. I shook my head. "No. As long as you know they're real cops, always cooperate and always tell the truth."

"You sound like a sixth-grade video in civics class," she said. She has a slight accent, but her syntax is completely New York.

Consuelo had been widowed six months before I opened the office in East Harlem. Her husband, Roberto, had keeled over with no warning and had been dead of a heart attack before he hit the floor, she said the EMT had told her. They hadn't had health insurance and he hadn't had a checkup in six years, but he hadn't been sick.

"It was just his time," she'd told me at the interview. (I should explain that I figured anyone who applied for this job could do it. Some could probably do it very well. I like to work with people I connect with, so I asked each applicant to tell me her—there were no men—story.) "There's nothing you can do about that."

I don't buy that particular sentiment. Now, don't get me wrong: I don't believe that Consuelo could possibly have saved her husband's life by watching him more closely. I don't think anyone in particular was responsible for his death. But I do believe that his demise was caused by buildup in his arteries and not the strange, inexplicable ringing of a cosmic alarm clock that had simply sounded when the time was right.

Consuelo had been the person with whom I had bonded most immediately during the interviews, and my instinct had turned out to be well founded. She was very good at her job. That meant she organized my time and handled my clients and kept track of their health, their coats (except the birds), their bookings, and their owners. And she managed to keep everyone from getting mad at me, which is the biggest accomplishment of all.

I gave her a look now. "Either way, if a police officer calls you about anything involved in this, you tell them exactly what you know every single time no matter what. We're good?"

"I like to think so," Consuelo said.

She had an interesting look on her face. "What else did you tell them?" I asked her.

"The truth," Consuelo answered, a sharp expression aimed at me. "That I didn't know anything about this at all because didn't *nobody tell me*."

"There wasn't time," I said. "I met with them late yesterday; you know that. Bruno did his audition, there was some drama afterward, which is not terribly unusual, and then I drove home. I didn't know Trent was going to end up snorkeling in a dog dish."

"And of course you don't own a telephone, so you didn't have to call and tell me that the wheels were coming off, right?" She had a twinkle in her eye that showed both affection and defiance.

"All right, I apologize, Consuelo. I'll make sure to tell you every time I think that one of my clients' owners might just find a stray knife in his back. Okay?"

"Is that too much to ask?" She sat down behind her desk, which is larger than my desk because she runs the office and all I do is pay her.

Before I could continue this scintillating banter, the phone rang and Consuelo picked up. "Powell and Associates, Agents to the Paws," she said.

That was new. *Agents to the Paws?* I mouthed back. Consuelo waved a hand to tell me to shut up.

"Of course," she said into the phone, her face indicating this was a serious matter. "Let me connect you." She pushed the Hold button and looked at me. "Louise Barclay." With great significance.

That was unexpected. "Louise! What does she want?" I asked.

"You'll know the minute she tells you."

I picked up the phone, giving Consuelo the latest in a series of dirty looks. But with love. "Louise," I said. "I was so sorry to hear about what happened."

"I know," Louise answered, in a tone that indicated surprise, like she was gossiping with a friend, not preparing to inter her husband. "I'm still pretty stunned."

I thought that was a safe bet. "Is there anything I can do for you?" I asked. "Do you need someone to watch Bruno for a few days?"

There was a moment of silence—you should pardon the expression—on the other end of the conversation, like Louise was considering what I'd said because she'd never thought about it before. "I don't think so," she said in a little-girl voice. "Let me get back to you on that."

"Sure. What else can I do?" Better not to give her suggestions, or this conversation would go on past Trent's funeral. I wrote *Ask about Trent's funeral* on the pad in front of me, which also bore a note reminding me about Mom's doctor appointment the previous Monday, which she'd missed because I'd forgotten to remind her, the beginning of a grocery list (okay, the word "pretzels"), and a doodle for a new company logo that was supposed to be a cat playing Hamlet and looked more like Donald Trump's toupée growing arms.

"I was wondering if you could come here to the apartment," Louise said. "The police were here. They seem to think I killed Trent, and showing them I didn't is going to take up a lot of my time. If Bruno is going to make the callback audition for *Annie,* I'm not going to be able to take him."

"Sure, I . . . um . . ." *Callback audition? What callback audition?* "Les McMaster wants a callback? Why didn't I know about that?" I said. Consuelo looked up, her eyebrows lowered in thought. Maisie squawked in contempt.

Louise, mistakenly thinking I'd been talking to her, said, "I don't know. His office called about dinnertime last night before all this happened. They said he wanted to see Bruno again before he decided. Is that good or bad?" She was asking me about her dog's acting career and I was wondering if they'd managed to clean her husband's blood off the kitchen floor yet. People have different priorities.

I pressed the Mute button and asked Consuelo if Les McMaster's office had called to ask about a callback for Bruno. She did not have to refer to notes and simply shook her head. If Consuelo said it hadn't happened, I could bet my last dollar, which was probably in my wallet right now, on it.

"What time is the callback, Louise?" I asked after I took her off Mute.

"Two this afternoon."

"I'll be there in an hour. So sorry about Trent."

"Yeah," Louise said. "Me too."

As soon as the conversation was over, I asked Consuelo to get me Les McMaster's office on the phone, but she was already punching the number into her keypad. She waited perhaps four seconds. "Kay Powell calling for Mr. McMaster," she said into the phone. "Sure." She punched Hold and looked at me. "On two."

We have two phone lines because theater is still an old-fashioned enough business that a fax line is a sporadically used necessity. I punched the button and nodded thanks to Consuelo as I said, "Les?"

"This is Akra, his executive assistant," the woman's voice said from the other end of the line. "Mr. McMaster is not currently available. How can I help you?"

It has been my experience that people who ask how they can help me usually are capable of doing so, but often aren't willing. I decided to test my theory with Akra, whose name in third grade I would bet was Alice or Alex.

"I brought a client to see Les about the role of Sandy in *Annie* yesterday," I told her. "I've just been told that he requested a call-back with my client for today at two. Can you tell me why your office didn't call mine to request that callback?" The agent always gets called about auditions. It is never okay to contact the client (or in this case, the person who walks the client three times a day) directly. That is a breach of professional protocol.

"Oh my," Akra said, her voice trying desperately to sound like it had the capacity to convey emotion. "I'd really have to ask around. I have no idea how that happened, Ms. Powell." I pictured the screen in front of her, where she had consulted my contact information before using my last name.

That made no sense. "Did you place the call?" I asked. "If you're his executive assistant, I assume Les would ask you to do that."

"I'm sure I didn't, or I'd remember, Ms. Powell." Akra was mentally patting herself on the back for remembering my name for six seconds without having to look it up again. I have an active fantasy life.

"Do you know which client I'm referring to?" I asked.

Silence. Consuelo grinned on the left side of her mouth. Maisie looked pissed off. Which was the way Maisie *always* looked.

Akra, having taken enough time to Google the entire population of Lichtenstein by last name, said, "I'm sure you mean Bruno Barclay. I see that audition scheduled for yesterday at four and then the callback today at two, but I don't know who called about today's meeting or why you weren't consulted."

"Can you find out?" I asked. "It's pretty unprofessional, and I want to make certain that it doesn't happen again."

"Of course," Akra said. She'd do it as soon as she had her battery recharged and her software updated. "Can I reach you at this number?" She read my phone number back to me.

"That's the number," I said. "Please let me know why it wasn't dialed." And I hung up. I'm not big on taking one's frustrations out on the culprit's assistant, but in Akra's case, I was making an exception. It was something about the way she hadn't had any idea who I was. Petty? Moi? It's been suggested. I disagree.

I have a parking space rented at a garage just three doors down from the office, and I pay enough monthly that I prefer not to move the car (and pay to park elsewhere) in Manhattan when I don't have to. So I took the 6 train from 116th Street to Grand Central, changed to the 7 to take me crosstown, and then the 1 train to Christopher Street, where a walk to Louise and Trent's— well, Louise's—apartment took only a few minutes.

And sitting on the front stoop waiting for me when I got there was my father, dressed in his "official" clothes—a pair of khakis from the early '90s and a denim shirt with the logo of a cruise line on it. Dad was nothing if not a loyal company man when he thought it could help him get another gig.

"What are you doing here?" I asked when I regained the ability to compose sentences in English.

"I'm helping," he said. "Consuelo called Mom to tell her you had an unexpected audition at two and couldn't take her shopping, and she called me. I was in the city on an errand, so when I heard you'd be here, I took the subway down."

"And you got here before me. What errand? You didn't mention coming into the city this morning. I would have given you a ride."

He found an invisible piece of lint on the denim shirt and meticulously removed it. "It's not a big thing," he said. "I'm meeting with a few booking agents, that's all."

"You're firing Morrie?" Mom and Dad have had the same agent since before the Nevele closed.

"Baby, Morrie died six years ago. I've been doing it on my own, but . . ." Dad doesn't like to let me know things aren't going well for the act.

"Why didn't you tell me?" Although I had mentally answered my own question already.

Dad avoided eye contact. "I didn't want you to feel bad," he said. "We need a new agent and we didn't ask our own daughter."

"Dad, I'm an agent for animal performers. You and Mom are, unless there's some horrible secret you haven't told me, humans."

My father looked at me sideways and grinned. "You're funny. Ever think of going on the stage?" he said.

"I thought about it and then I started representing dogs who want to go on the stage. Now, what are you doing here? I thought you had auditions."

The sideways glance turned once again into an evasive look up the street. "Your mother is better at those than I am, and she can play the piano. I thought you might want some help on this meeting, so I came by in case you wanted me to come up. I know it's hard for you to deal with situations like this."

"Situations like this?" I said. "How often during my childhood did I have to cope with the widow of a man who fell down in his dog's water bowl because he had a knife sticking out of his back?"

Dad's mouth flattened out. "You know what I mean. Situations that involve death."

He had me there. Ever since I was a little girl, I've had a hard time coping with the idea of death. It's always seemed hideously unfair to me that life ends, that we have no control, and that there's no Reset button. You're dead, and that's it. When I was small, I'd lie awake trying to reconcile the facts and invariably end up crying.

Actually, I'm still not that crazy about the whole business to this day. But it's more my death and those of my loved ones that bother me.

"I really didn't know Trent very well, Dad. He was a client's owner and that's it. I just met him for the first time last week. So I actually do think I can handle this one on my own." Frankly, if Dad hadn't brought it up, I wouldn't have equated Trent's death with my own fear of the inevitable. Trent was a guy who was paying me to represent his dog, and if the truth were told, I really hadn't liked him very much. He was loud, unnecessarily assertive, obnoxious, and annoying. So this wasn't really hitting me in the solar plexus.

Luckily, I thought it unlikely I'd be asked to speak at his funeral.

"You sure?" Dad looked up at the building like he was trying to figure out which apartment might be Louise's. I knew it was in the back of the building and the windows couldn't be seen from here, but I didn't think that was the point anyway.

"I'm sure. Go find yourself an agent, but don't sign anything until I read it, right? I'm a lawyer and an agent, so I'll catch anything they try to sneak by you." I have to keep reminding my parents about the law degree they helped pay for.

But Dad kept looking up at the building, apparently waiting for it to divulge all its secrets to him. It seemed the building was being especially stubborn about such things. "I really don't mind if you want me to come up," he said.

I felt my arms cross in a gesture of impatience that I had probably learned from my mother. "What's this really about, Dad?" I asked.

He looked sharply at me, the actor in him no doubt deciding to feign outrage at the perceived impugning of his character, but he saw my face and realized who he was up against. He shook his head a little and smiled sadly. "I never could put one over on you," he said.

"Well, there was the whole Tooth Fairy thing. Come on, what's up? Why do you want to go upstairs so badly?"

Dad sat back down on the stoop, and his age seemed to catch up with him all at once. My father doesn't look as old as he really is, especially when he doesn't want to, but now he seemed to shrivel a little and he let out a breath.

"The fact is, sweetie, the act hasn't been going so well for a while," he said weakly. "You know we haven't gotten the bookings we're used to, and even the cruise-ship stuff is starting to dry up. That's not even a joke."

I sat down next to him. "Things will pick up, Dad. They always do."

He shrugged. "I don't know. The act itself is a little outdated. Who wants to see a couple of old codgers singing and dancing up on a stage?"

"Works okay for the Rolling Stones, and they're older than you," I tried, but Dad wasn't buying. He shook his head again.

"I'm just saying. We're not getting booked, and frankly the travel is starting to get to your mother a little bit." He looked away and I was afraid he might be crying softly. "She wants to stay close to home more often, and I can't get us anything in the city. So I thought if I could meet this woman with the dog, and the dog got the job on Broadway . . ." He didn't finish the sentence.

"You thought Louise was a way to get to Les McMaster about being in *Annie*?" I said. The idea was so beyond logical I considered the possibility my father was just kidding.

"It's stupid, I know, but I'm grasping at straws here, Kay. Do you think maybe that would work?" He kept looking away. I didn't study the part of his face I could see too closely. My father is a man of dignity, even when he's performing what some would consider corny comedy on a stage to a half-empty house. I had no desire to puncture that dignity now.

"I'm insulted," I told him, and Dad looked at me in surprise. Luckily, his cheeks were dry. "You want an in to a Broadway director, your own daughter is representing the performer in question, and you think you have to go to a woman whose husband was murdered this morning so she could put in a good word for you with her *dog*?"

Dad opened and closed his mouth a couple of times. "I don't intrude on your business, sweetie," he said.

"This is show business," I reminded him. "If there's one thing you taught me, it's that you use every possible connection you can find."

Dad shook his head, seemingly in amazement at the creature he had helped create. "You're a peach, sweetie," he said. He looked up at the building again. "Let's go."

"What do you mean, 'let's,' kemosabe? I just told you I'd give you an in with Les. You don't need Louise Barclay now."

He was already starting up the stairs to the front door. "I'm here to help you, Kay. I want to see how you operate, and maybe I can be of use with the lady and the dog. Besides, it's going to be pretty grim up there. You'll need some moral support."

I knew better than to argue with him when he started talking that fast; it was how he'd once convinced a club owner to take the three of us in for a full month despite the fact that I was a minor and the only shows this establishment usually booked featured women who weren't always fully dressed. Hey, we needed the gig.

We walked up the four flights of stairs to Louise Barclay's palatial apartment, whose stairwells didn't smell and whose stairs were freshly painted. You'd think there'd be an elevator in a relatively upscale building like this one but in Manhattan, where the average price of a co-op apartment is over a million dollars, "upscale" is a relative term. This one was clean and well appointed, no doorman but working buzzers. We got to the landing (Dad wasn't even breathing heavy) and found the brightly lit door to Louise Barclay's home, which at the moment included yellow crime-scene tape on the front door, admittedly hanging down where it had once been stuck up in an intimidating fashion, I was certain. I knocked on the door because there didn't appear to be a doorbell.

Louise opened the door after a moment. She was wearing a "silk" robe that I'll bet she thought of as a dressing gown and fuzzy pink slippers that were open in the back. Without makeup, she looked about five years older than she had when I'd seen her the day before.

Of course, her husband being stabbed might have had something to do with her somewhat less polished appearance.

"Oh, it's you," she said by way of greeting. And sadly, that was not the worst reception I'd ever gotten from a client. There was this one chimpanzee who wasn't happy to see me, and let's not discuss what he tossed at my head to express this displeasure. Louise stood to one side. "Come on in. Bruno's in the back."

The apartment appeared to contain a living area, a bedroom,

a bath, a tiny "lanai" that was basically large enough for one person to smoke a cigarette on, a galley kitchen (also fitted with drooping crime-scene tape), and a small nook that had probably once been a walk-in pantry and now had been fitted out as a home office with computer equipment, a tiny desk, and a telephone with actual wires coming out of it and plugging into the wall.

Louise didn't ask me who the sprightly gentleman with me was, so I decided not to mention my father unless she brought him up. It was sort of a game designed to help me understand just how oblivious Louise was right now. The more she was out of it, the better for my dealings with Les when I brought Bruno to see him again.

But Dad had other ideas. Once inside the apartment, he stuck out his hand in Louise's direction, smiled his best ingratiating book-me-now smile, and said, "I'm Howard Mancuso, Ms. Powell's attorney."

It took all the effort I could manage not to swivel and holler, "WHO?" at the top of my lungs. Instead, I felt my mouth tighten up, my throat dry up, and the moisture from there apparently migrate to my palms, which started to sweat. "You're just here as a friend, *Howard*," I said. I was striving for a pleasant tone and managed to sound more like a flamingo being run over by a garbage truck.

"Of course," "Howard" said. Dad continued to hold out his hand until Louise, looking dimly aware of her surroundings, took it. He leaned over and kissed her hand, which I thought was overplaying the role, but Louise smiled after a moment. "Charmed," my father said. Apparently in the role of Howard Mancuso, he was channeling the spirit of Charles Boyer.

"Thanks," Louise answered. Which actually seemed sort of appropriate. She showed us into the living area, which was something of a relief, as looking into the kitchen and seeing the outline of the body on the floor was getting a little uncomfortable for me.

I don't know if I would have reacted that way had my father not brought up my problems with the concept of death, but I'll admit it was spooking me to be in the apartment where Trent had died. My immediate mission became to get Bruno and blow this popsicle stand as quickly as I possibly could. My stomach was queasy and my palms were no drier. I probably looked as white as a sheet.

"Is Bruno ready to go?" I asked as we walked back into the living area. Bruno was not visible there, and given that Louise had pointed in this direction when she'd mentioned where the dog was before, that was troubling.

"He's in the bedroom," she said, as if I should have known that "in the back" meant one of the bedrooms, probably the master bedroom. "He's been in there since Trent got killed, and he doesn't want to come out."

Bruno hadn't been walked since late last night? That wasn't okay. "Maybe I should take him out for a walk before we go. Where's his leash?" I asked.

But Dad had his own agenda. "We'll take the dog in a moment," he told Louise. "Tell me what happened last night. As an attorney, I'm always curious about this sort of situation."

I started to say, "Dad!" but remembered the role he was currently playing. "Howard, that's not our business. Louise has been through enough." I turned toward her. "I'm sorry, Louise."

She waved a hand at me like a rag doll does when the little

girl playing with it isn't terribly well coordinated. "I don't mind," she said. "The doc has me on enough Xanax that really nothing bothers me right now."

"So what can you tell us?" my father persisted. I gave him a look that was not my usual adoring-daughter gaze. He chose to ignore me.

"I was asleep." Louise didn't sound all that awake even now, and she drifted toward the entrance to the little kitchen and gestured vaguely with her left hand. "I don't know what woke me up; it must have been something to do with what was going on in here. But I got up when I saw Trent wasn't next to me in bed."

"Was he already . . ." Dad did not ignore my look this time, probably realized what he was doing to Louise, and stopped talking. But Louise seemed unperturbed, dreamy, staring at the floor in the kitchen. I'm not even sure she knew Dad had said anything.

"I came out to see if he was in the kitchen, and he was," she went on, seemingly in the same thought. "But he was on the floor, facedown, and his nose was in Bruno's water dish. I thought he'd just fallen down, but there was blood on the floor, so I called his name, you know, Trent. He didn't answer. I took another step forward and that's when I saw the knife handle."

She burped.

"And you didn't hear anything?" This time it was me asking, because Louise didn't seem to mind and what the heck, I'm naturally nosy. I get it from my father. "No struggle, no yelling? Wait." The thought had just occurred to me. "Bruno didn't bark?"

Louise shook her head. "He was in the bedroom with me, and I guess he just slept through it," she said.

Dad had wandered away and was now standing by the apartment door, looking at it the way a stray cat might look at a cappuccino machine: as if it was an interesting object the like of which he'd never seen before.

"The lock isn't broken," he said. "There's nothing wrong with the chain. Was it on when . . . this happened?"

Louise looked dreamier, and I thought she might very well fall asleep standing in the kitchen and strangle herself accidentally with crime-scene tape. I took her arm and led her to a chair in the office nook.

"No," she said in answer to Dad's question. "It was weird. We *always* lock the door all the time, when we're here and when we're not." Her voice was taking on a singsong quality. She wasn't going to be a reliable witness for much longer until she had a long nap.

"Why don't you come in and put your feet up for a few minutes?" I said. "Show me where Bruno's leash is, and I'll take him out so you can sleep."

Louise pointed vaguely at the desk and Dad walked over to find the leash, a pistol-grip model with extendable lead (I prefer the old-fashioned nylon leash) sitting next to a legal pad. He brought me the leash and I led Louise into her bedroom.

I found Bruno there, being the good-natured guy that he is, not whimpering or crying. He wagged his tail when he saw me and walked over when he saw the leash. He had been waiting patiently for far too long.

Dad and I managed to get Louise to lie down and I think she was asleep before she made it to the bed. She snored loudly as I latched the leash onto Bruno's collar and led him out of the room. We didn't even bother to keep things quiet; Louise would sleep for hours if I was any judge of narcotics-driven slumber. And I'm not.

"What was on the legal pad?" I asked Dad as we walked down the hall to the stairway.

"Les McMaster's phone number," he said. "How'd you know I was looking?"

"Whose daughter do you think I am, *Howard*?"

CHAPTER FIVE

"It was a simple screwup," Les McMaster said.

Back in the Palace for Bruno's callback audition, we were the only two people in the 1,700-seat auditorium. And Les was trying to explain to me how my client had been called back and I hadn't been notified.

"You called Trent and Louise directly," I said. "You know perfectly well that's not the way things are done. You don't bypass the agent."

"And I'm telling you it wasn't intentional," he protested. "I asked Akra to take care of calling you, and for reasons I don't know, she didn't. But you're here now and you're getting your commission. I'm going to hire the dog."

Bruno, who didn't speak human, didn't know the job was his. He sat beautifully at Les's feet, the perfect dog for little

Annie to adopt at the end of Act Two. Nobody had given him any direction, but he was very much in the role of Sandy. The dog was a natural.

Neither Les nor I had mentioned Trent's death. Dad had suggested this course of action when we'd parted at the Port Authority Bus Terminal. Dad had decided against meeting this potential new agent—he said—and was heading home. But he thought it would be best if I waited for Les to say something about what had happened to Trent, to see if he was doing the overly upset mourning thing that show-business phonies (and most other phonies) do when someone they don't like dies. If that's what Les was doing, he'd missed his calling as an actor, because I was convinced.

"Bruno gets the job?" I said. "No provisions in his contract?" I'd have to tell Dad how cleverly I'd brought that up, to see if Les admitted he knew Trent wouldn't be coming in and disrupting rehearsals with protests of his dog's great talent at the expense of everyone else in the company.

But Les turned and looked at me. "Oh no, the provisions stay," he said. "I thought we'd settled that yesterday."

Bruno, perhaps confused that no one wanted him to perform some amazing feat of dog acting, stood and trotted toward Les, whom he could see was clearly the alpha dog in this pack. He whimpered a little, still auditioning, but got no response. To Les, this was a done deal. He didn't need to see Bruno work any harder.

Les's silence on the subject was odd: It didn't make sense that he had no idea Trent was dead. If nothing else, Detective Rodriguez must have contacted him after I'd blatantly ratted him out during my interview. "Yesterday was yesterday," I told Les. "Things have changed since yesterday."

Les's eyes got smaller. "You know about Trent Barclay, don't you?" he asked.

The swine! He was playing the same game!

"No," I said casually. "What about him?"

"Perhaps I shouldn't say," Les mused.

Say, I thought, trying to send the message telepathically. *Say.*

I'm not sure why it was important to me that Les mention Trent's death before I did, but it mattered. I continued sending my thought messages.

"Well, if it's not important," I said, "don't worry about it."

He bit on his lips. Show people are notorious gossips, so holding back any information he considered significant was a concerted effort on his part. "It's important enough," he said.

"What?" *Here it comes. . . .*

"Trent is having an affair," Les said.

I knew he had heard about . . . wait. What?

"An affair?" Maybe Les really *didn't* know about Trent's death. But the idea that Trent was cheating on Louise created another whole motive situation that could easily make her—with no sign of forced entry in her apartment the night her husband was stabbed in the back (literally)—a very serious suspect. I wondered if Detective Rodriguez knew about Trent's dalliance.

"Yeah," Les answered. "Word is he's doing it with his dog walker."

Wow. There are all sorts of terms for acts these days that I've never heard of. "His dog walker?" I was reduced now to simply repeating whatever Les said.

Les nodded. "I hear he has someone walk Bruno when he and his wife aren't around, and maybe all the service isn't for the dog. You know?"

Maybe I knew and maybe I didn't. "Trent Barclay was cheating on Louise with a random person walking his dog?" I said.

"That's what I hear," Les said. "What do you mean, 'was cheating'? Did Louise find out?"

It just came out. "Trent's dead," I told him. There. He had the upper hand now. So I was a rung lower on the show-business ladder. I'd live with it. Besides, I knew something Les didn't and that seemed more important right at the moment. "Somebody stabbed him in the back and he landed in Bruno's water dish."

Les looked stricken. He paled and staggered back onto an easy chair on the set that Daddy Warbucks usually called his own. He put his hand to his forehead (Les, not Oliver Warbucks). His mouth dropped open. "What?" he croaked.

Nobody is better at being theatrical than a theater person.

"Yeah," I went on. I thought I sounded more unconcerned than I should have. "Didn't the detective come and talk to you about this?"

Bruno, finally convinced nobody wanted him to whine, beg, whimper, roll over, or otherwise play a role, lay down next to the sofa on the set and went to sleep.

"No. No, of course not. I would have said something," Les said, his voice shallow and his breath coming in gulps. The man could work a room. His focus sharpened and he looked at me. "Why didn't you tell me?"

"I thought you knew," I answered, which was true but seemed inadequate. "I figured you were trying to see how much I knew and you were waiting for me to say something." That was sort of it. If you looked at it charitably.

Les didn't look at it charitably. "You were playing me," he said, his voice sounding authoritative again. "You wanted to see if you could use the information in your negotiations about Bruno."

That wasn't entirely true. "Well, I wouldn't say that."

Les smiled. "You're a much tougher agent than I thought you were, Kay," he said.

Um . . . thank you? "It just never occurred to me that you wouldn't know," I answered. "You're always at the center of everything." One thing an agent really does know how to do is stroke egos.

"So there's a police detective questioning people?" he asked. "That should be interesting." He stopped. "I wonder why he hasn't come to talk to me yet."

"*She,*" I corrected. "I'm sure Detective Rodriguez is building up to you."

"Maybe." Les seemed distracted. He was probably thinking of commanding Akra to call the NYPD and demand to be interrogated in Trent's murder. "But maybe I'm just not that big a figure in Trent's life. I only met him once and I immediately wanted never to see him again."

Time to tackle the tricky subject, I thought. Bruno snored a little, so he clearly wasn't going to ask the question. "Les," I said, "Trent was a little . . . agitated . . . after the audition yesterday."

Les waved a hand. "If you think you can convince me he was really a wonderful guy, save your breath, Kay. I have an excellent sense of people, and Trent Barclay was an idiot."

"Well, I didn't know him that well, but maybe he was just having a bad day."

He smiled a smug grin. The game of I-Know-Something-You-Don't-Know was clearly tilting in Les's direction. "I heard what he said in the dressing room yesterday," he said. "He said I was a hack who couldn't direct a grade-school pageant about STDs."

"Dental health," I corrected. Who thought they had pageants about STDs in fourth grade?

"Whatever. I heard it. I was right outside the dressing-room door. So I know exactly what kind of guy Trent Barclay was, and I know exactly what he thought of me. Don't try to defend him, Kay."

This probably wasn't the time to ask him to add my parents to the ensemble.

"How mad were you?" I asked. Subtle, huh?

Les gave me a smirk. "Kay, if I got homicidal every time someone gave me a bad review, there'd be a string of corpses from here to Peoria, Illinois, my childhood home."

That sounded just like something a guilty party would say.

Suddenly Les was leapfrogging Louise as my favorite suspect. "It wasn't exactly a . . . wait a minute. How do you know about this supposed affair Trent was having with Bruno's surrogate walker?"

Bruno looked up at the mention of his name. Dogs can sleep but still be sort of in the room. I winked at him on impulse and he lowered his head and closed his eyes again.

"Louise told me. She called me last night to apologize for the way Trent had been acting at the audition, and that's why she knew about the callback and you didn't. She sounded like she'd been drinking. A lot. And she said Trent was getting it on with the dog walker."

"Getting it on?" What was this, 1977?

"You'd rather I quoted her directly? Because she was using the colloquial term."

I tilted my head in agreement. "Okay. But they have a dog walker?"

Les nodded. "A lot of people in the city do."

"Most of them aren't in the dog-in-show-business business," I pointed out. "You'd think they'd be more interested in his welfare and do it themselves."

What I was really annoyed about was that Les knew about the dog walker and I didn't, but these owners had been really serious about selective information for selected people. Which reminded me: "But how come Louise opened up to you so much?"

Les shrugged. "Like I said, she sounded like she was drunk. She probably would have opened up to the pizza delivery boy if he'd called looking for directions."

"How'd she get your number? I didn't give it to her." It was like I was trying to convince Les that he *hadn't* gotten a phone call from Louise the night her husband was killed, complaining that he was sleeping with his dog's surrogate parent.

Maybe Louise was still at the top of the list after all.

"I have no idea," Trent said. "She didn't get it from me. Maybe she tracked me down through the union or the theater. But she called me on my cell, and I don't give out that number if I don't have to."

"You should have had Akra call me after you told Louise about the callback," I said. I was determined to get back some of my own, although I wasn't sure what quantity of my own would be sufficient. Since it was already my own. And how had Les gotten my own? Am I rambling?

"I promise, from now on there will be no communication between Bruno's handlers and me; I'll always go through you." Les stood and walked over to Bruno, who looked up at him. "Because Bruno's going to be working very closely with all of us here, isn't he?" He chucked the dog under his chin. Bruno wagged his tail, but it was hard to tell if he meant it. Actors.

"Good enough," I said. I stood up and walked over to Bruno, leash in hand. Bruno understood and stood, a little shakily, which is not unusual when a dog has been asleep or close to it. He stretched and shook himself, then stood perfectly still while I attached the lead to his collar. "When will Bruno start rehearsal?"

"Tomorrow," Trent said. "We want to get him into the show by a week from Tuesday."

That was soon, but not impossibly soon. "Can I get a script?" I asked. "Maybe I can teach him a few of the moves before we start."

"I'll get Akra to give you one on the way out," the director, all business again, told me. He looked up toward the back of the theater. "Okay, Akra?"

The tall, dark woman called back. "No problem, Les. This way, Ms. Powell." I hadn't even realized she had been in the auditorium, and wondered how long she'd been watching the scene playing out onstage.

As I walked up the aisle toward her, Bruno at my heel without my having to give him a command, I looked back at Les McMaster and considered how that scenario had played out.

With Akra there as a witness, he'd made sure he was "shocked" when I'd delivered the news of Trent's death. Then he'd made sure to drop some very suggestive and persuasive evidence that made Louise seem like an unstable, angry wife who'd just discovered her husband was cheating on her. Les had, in other words, directed the scene beautifully.

He was back at the top of my suspect list.

CHAPTER SIX

I called Louise with the good news of Bruno's employment, but her number went straight to voicemail. So I decided to take Bruno home and then head back to my office to deal with the parakeet, the bear cub, and the calico cat. Except I didn't do that.

Instead, I took Bruno back to my house to meet Steve and Eydie.

As a professional theatrical agent, it's important that I never become too emotionally attached to any of my clients. Any one of them could decide to change representation, quit the business, or go to stud at any time, and if I had gotten involved with that client, it would hurt. This was a business, and I understood that.

And as a professional theatrical agent for *animals,* I had the added complication of not falling in love with every furry face I met. There's a reason we love pets and other animals so much, and part of why I get work is that people love to see animals in movies and plays and television shows. They're darn cute, many of them. So I'd resolved when I started the business never to fall for a pair of doe eyes, even if they were on a real doe.

So my decision to take Bruno home—just for the day—was a departure from the routine. And it was simply born from the idea that his owner had died the night before, his other caregiver was high on any number of narcotics and probably alcohol, and I wasn't crazy about going back to the apartment where Trent Barclay's blood had mostly been cleaned off the kitchen floor the last time I was there.

Truly, it was a completely logical and rational choice.

I called Consuelo, who routed the call with the bear cub's handler to the Bluetooth in my car. I spoke to the parakeet's owner and handled that issue in the car as well (it had to do with the size of the birdcage backstage at the nightclub where the bird was to be employed) and asked Consuelo to handle the calico's callback because cats are her absolute favorite and she wants to be an agent herself someday.

I tried calling Louise again and got the same response. She hadn't seemed especially concerned about Bruno's whereabouts, and I'd bring him back as soon as she got in touch. I left a message on her voicemail and kept driving, listening to an audiobook all the way to Scarborough. Bruno did not comment on the story, but lay on the backseat looking like this was just the most interesting adventure since *Raiders of the Lost Ark*.

Once we got home (my home, not Bruno's), we had barely made it to the back door when Eydie had stuck her snout out to see what was going on. She didn't care for dividing my attention, and had only put up with Steve because I'd adopted them together so she knew him. Most of the time she snubbed him when she could, but now with Bruno approaching and the smell of another male dog in the air, she was howling at Steve to come see the atrocity being committed by their subservient human (that's me).

Mom appeared directly behind Eydie just as Bruno and I were pushing our way through my own back door. "Well now, who's this fellow?" she asked, bending down to say hello to Bruno. Eydie snarled a bit, but Steve, on his pillow at one end of the kitchen, barely moved. Steve is cautious to the point of abject terror in the face of anything new.

"That's Bruno," I said. "He's just spending the afternoon until his person decides to call me back. Dad back yet?"

She pointed toward the living room. "Auditioning a stand-up comic."

"How bad?"

Mom made a point of eye contact. "Pretty bad," she said.

"I'll leave him to it. Did anybody call the house?" I got a bowl from the cabinet and put some water in it, then put it on the floor by the sink and showed it to Bruno. Eydie gave some thought to drinking out of it to show him who was boss, but I simply said, "No," and she walked over to her dish and drank heartily. That was who was boss.

"Nobody called," Mom said. "Don't they usually call your cell?"

I went to the refrigerator to get something for, believe it or not, me (after giving Bruno a liver treat, and then one each to Steve and Eydie, so they knew he wasn't getting special treatment). "Yeah, but I thought maybe Louise had called here looking for Bruno because she hadn't called my cell."

"Louise is the one with the husband?" Mom asked. She had processed the information about Trent, probably done some on-line research into it, and no doubt knew more than I did by now. She was drawing me into a conversation with an agenda, but I didn't know what it was yet.

"Yes, Louise was married to Trent Barclay and you know it," I said to my mother. I found an apple that probably hadn't been in the fridge for too long, and took out some cheddar cheese I had in a block. Mom finished petting Bruno, watched the dogs scout one another out, and then sat down at the kitchen table while I got a knife and a cutting board to put there. "So tell me what you've found out."

"Found out?" My mother is a fine entertainer but a lousy actress.

"I'm too tired to go through the first six minutes of the conversation, Mom. Can't we get to the part where you admit you've been looking up Trent Barclay all day and then you tell me what you've discovered?" In my family, direct talk is considered the norm. Well, it is when I do it. My parents are more civilized, but that takes up a lot of time.

Mom did look slightly disappointed. She likes to show off how computer literate she is and to have people "discover" her intelligence, but I had known her pretty much since birth so she didn't have to show off for me. "Okay," she said. "Did you know that this Trent guy's real name was Moshe Berkowitz?"

That was news. I sat down and put some cheese on a slice of

apple. "Nope, didn't know that. I'm used to people changing their names for business, but that's a pretty big change."

"The funeral home where his service is scheduled is called Anshe Emeth, and in lieu of flowers, people are asked to donate to something called Chai Lifeline," Mom reported without referring to notes. "The funeral's going to be tomorrow morning."

"Does this have some significance in his death?" I asked.

"No, I don't think so. Are you investigating his death?" Mom responded.

That was an interesting question. I'd been acting like I was either Cagney or Lacey when in fact I was the dog's agent. "No," I said. "I'm just curious."

Mom nodded. "That's natural. I did all this research today because Dad was with you in the city or auditioning acts for the show, but I have to admit I do want to know what happened to Moshe."

I wasn't used to calling him that yet. "Was he really in the software business, or was that something else he made up?"

"From what I could tell, that was real," Mom told me. "He didn't actually write code or invent anything, but he knew talent when he saw it and invested in people who made programs run better. He didn't get super rich, but he could afford to live in Manhattan."

"And then suddenly he decides his dog is Sir Anthony Hopkins."

"That part wasn't in the obituaries, or anywhere else," Mom told me. "There was no mention of him trying to get Bruno into show business."

"No reason there should be." Bruno was sniffing Eydie in one of her more sensitive areas, and she was not pleased, but she knew better than to snap at him; this was not the first time I'd brought a client home for a quick visit. "It's not like he was Lassie's trainer."

"The other thing is that Louise, his wife, was once an actress. Small roles on TV, one national commercial for a soup mix. That could be where they got the idea to audition Bruno out." Mom looked up, apparently noticing a quiet in the living room, because she said, "I think your father is finished in there." She stood up and walked to the door, looked out, and nodded. "Be right back," she said.

Suddenly I had a lot to think about. Trent Barclay (whose name was in my mind going to stay Trent Barclay) had made his money by exploiting other people's work. To be fair, that was what I did, but for animals.

Trent had also married a woman who had been an actress, and the two of them—but from the surface of it, mostly Trent—had decided to try to get their dog on the stage. Lucky for them, the dog was really talented.

But what Mom had asked me had hit home—why was I so interested in Trent's murder? Sure, Detective Rodriguez had vaguely treated me like a suspect, but cops tend to treat everybody like a suspect, so that was probably unimportant. I didn't need to clear my name with the cops; they'd find someone who had a real motive and could have been in Trent and Louise's apartment at three in the morning.

Of course, if what Les had said was true, Louise would have had a fairly classic motive to kill her husband, and she was certainly in their apartment at the time the stabbing had taken place. Why *not* think she was the killer?

And then I noticed I was sorting the facts in my head like an analytic detective when I should have been poring over Bruno's contract for any strange provisions Les would have included restricting him from lifting his leg on a fire hydrant during the production because it would have created bad press for *Annie*.

Why *was* I acting like an investigator when being Bruno's agent should have been more than enough?

Maybe it didn't matter. All I had to do was stop. The police were investigating Trent's murder and they had, you know, experience and training on their side. I had the ability to negotiate favorable terms for a cat who was eating scraps out of a dumpster three weeks before being tapped to play Angelina Jolie's pet in a biopic about Marie Curie. If I just stuck to my job and let the cops do theirs, I could have a normal life and they could catch the killer, whom I had now decided was probably Louise.

That left me with one serious problem, which was determining who would take custody of Bruno when his remaining extant owner was carted off to jail for perforating the not-so-extant one.

Better not to think about that now. I looked over at Bruno, who now seemed especially interested in Steve. The dachshund was peering at the interloper with an expression of barely concealed terror. Steve is afraid of everybody until he discovers there is no danger to him, after which he becomes the most submissive dog in recorded history. Steve is endearingly neurotic.

I reached down for my briefcase and moved the cheese to one side in order to rest it on the table. Inside was Bruno's contract, which Akra had been kind enough to provide. I'd told Les that I'd look it over for issues and consult with Louise before getting back to him with (hopefully) a signed copy for processing.

There wasn't anything especially unusual in the contract, aside from the language regarding Trent, which was now moot. Louise had been included as well—Les wanted both of them absolutely prohibited from attending any rehearsal at which Bruno would be working—and now I would try to excise the whole paragraph, seeing as how Trent was unquestionably not showing up to rehearsals and Les had probably just included Louise because she hadn't spoken enough at the first audition for him to determine whether he needed her to be absent when he was working with the dog. Better to be safe than sorry.

Everything else was pretty standard. I made a few notes in the margins for small points that needed to be tweaked (Bruno could not be walked during performances by anyone in the theater company; only Louise or a representative of her choosing would be allowed to deal with the dog alone). And I was about three-quarters of the way through when Mom and Dad came in from the living room.

"I think we should investigate the murder," Dad said without so much as a segue.

I was hip-deep in legalese about Bruno's health insurance and looked up, probably with an expression of total and complete confusion. "Huh?" I said eloquently.

"Moshe Berkowitz's murder," Mom said, as if my problem lay in remembering which of my clients' owners had turned up with a nose full of water and a back full of knife. "Dad and I have been discussing it. We need to make sure your name is clean in the business, and the only way to do that is to find the real killer." Theatricality is a trait that runs deep in my family.

"No," I said, and went back to checking subordinate clauses in Bruno's contract. Bruno, for his part, had made friends with Steve and was now lying next to the dachshund in Steve's fluffy bed, sniffing his neck. Steve's tail wagged.

"No?" Dad asked. "What do you mean, no?"

"How is that unclear?"

He looked at me strangely, as clearly I didn't understand him. "I'm saying your mother and I are going to help you find out who killed this Berkowitz guy so that you can go back to being an agent for dogs and cats."

I nodded. "Right. And I'm saying no, you're not. I'm not investigating Trent's murder because I'm not an investigator, and neither are you. I don't have to 'go back' to being an agent because I'm already an agent and nobody's trying to make me stop that. I'm not a suspect in the killing, nobody is threatening me, and I have no reason to believe that the police are doing anything except putting handcuffs on the killer right now. So don't tell me what you and Mom are going to do, because none of us is going to be looking into a murder that's none of our business."

Mom and Dad stared at me a moment. I don't think I'd ever been quite so defiant, even when I—and this is how my father still refers to it—"broke up the act."

"Someone has to do it," Dad said. He looked embarrassed that he couldn't come up with anything better.

"Someone is. They're called the police."

Bruno and Steve were lying on the fluffy bed, best of friends, when the doorbell rang. Eydie barked, which she usually does not do, but the two males just stood up, shook themselves, and headed toward the door to see who their new closest friend on the planet would be. I followed, since it seemed opposable thumbs would be necessary to turn the knob and open the door.

Once I did, I wasn't so thrilled to have the thumbs. Louise Barclay (Berkowitz?) was standing outside my door, looking angry. My first thought was to wonder how she'd gotten my home address; I never give that to a client's owner.

My second thought was to wonder exactly why Detective Rodriguez was standing behind Louise, also not seeming terribly amused.

Bruno and Steve, having walked all this way for the spectacle of the door opening, were remarkably unexcited. Bruno especially did not appear to be particularly thrilled to see the woman with whom he'd been living for quite a while. I'm told marriage can be like that too.

There wasn't time to consider much else. Louise pointed at me accusingly and said, "That's the woman who stole my dog."

"Stole your . . . what?" That was the best I could manage.

My parents showed up behind me at that moment. Because I had once again assumed that things couldn't get worse, and that's always a mistake.

"What's going on?" Dad demanded. He saw Louise and said, "I'm this woman's attorney, and . . ."

"No, you're not." I cut him off before he could do any further damage. "These are my parents. Now, what's this about a stolen dog?"

Bruno started licking my feet. He wasn't helping.

Rodriguez raised one eyebrow and looked down at Bruno. "Is that this woman's dog?" she asked.

"Yes, but I called her and told her that since I couldn't get her on the phone, I'd be taking Bruno back to my house and waiting for her call. She didn't call." I was in the right here, but even I thought I sounded like a fifth-grader trying to explain why she hadn't finished her social studies homework.

"What has this got to do with the murder investigation?" my mother asked. It was a good question, as I assumed Rodriguez did not handle all the crime that took place in New York City, even if this one was committed in Scarborough, New Jersey. Wait. There was no crime. Here. In Scarborough.

You know what I mean.

"I was questioning Mrs. Barclay when she complained that your . . . daughter? Your daughter had stolen her dog," Rodriguez said with the same inflection she'd use if she were explaining how to change a flat tire, only with less raw emotion. "Since I wanted to interview her again, I decided to come out here with Mrs. Barclay and see what was going on with the dog. Now, everyone agrees that's Mrs. Barclay's dog. What about the other two?"

Two? Eydie had ambled in through the kitchen door just because it would be more confusing to explain three dogs than two.

"Those are both my dogs," I said.

"Do you have any records that can prove that?" Rodriguez asked. "If you've stolen them too . . ."

"I didn't steal *any* dogs!" Can a person sound more pathetic? I'll bet not. "I am Bruno's agent, and Mrs. Berkowitz here asked me specifically to take him to a callback audition with Les McMaster this afternoon. I did. Then I tried calling her after the audition to tell her Bruno had been offered the role in question, and I got no answer. I couldn't leave Bruno alone, so I brought him here until such time as I heard back from her. Is that hard to understand?"

"Mrs. Berkowitz?" Rodriguez asked. She turned toward Louise.

"It's been legally changed to Barclay," she said.

"Did you ask her to take your dog to this audition?" Rodriguez asked Louise.

"No."

Mom and Dad gasped. I was aware of my eyes narrowing because I couldn't see the top of Rodriguez's head anymore.

"Think carefully, Louise," I said. "I have Les asking you to have Bruno at the theater at two, which can be verified through his office. I have my father here as a witness that I picked up Bruno at the time you asked and that you were happy to have me take him. And I have the contract that you and Moshe signed that named me as Bruno's agent. So do you want to change your answer to that question?"

Rodriguez was watching Louise's face closely.

"All right," Louise said. "I did ask her to take Bruno to the audition. But I didn't ask her to take him to *New Jersey*." New Yorkers are so superior.

Rodriguez put her hands on her hips, perhaps trying to decide whether or not to draw her gun just to make herself feel better. She didn't, but you could see the conflict in her eyes.

"I'm really investigating the murder of Trent Barclay," she said finally. "I have a few follow-up questions for you." She indicated me. "May I come in?"

I didn't say anything, but Mom, Dad, and I created a path

and gestured Rodriguez inside. She started in, then looked back at Louise.

"There's your dog," she said. "Take him if you want him that bad. Walk him around the neighborhood. I'll be out in fifteen minutes."

Louise looked as if she'd been slapped. Here she had tried a perfectly good plan to get me arrested for dognapping—for reasons I couldn't begin to imagine—and now she was being told that I was a valuable witness and she was the dog walker. It was a swift and terrible comedown for her, and she had to take a moment to digest it.

"I . . . I can't come in?" she pleaded, as if staying outside in my front yard was a certain death sentence.

"No," Rodriguez answered sternly. "I don't want you hearing the questions or the answers, and I don't want you influencing them. You're staying outside until I come out. You can have your dog for company." She gestured toward Bruno again.

"I don't *want* the dog!" Louise wailed. "I *never* wanted the dog!"

Rodriguez didn't shrug, but her shoulders gave it some thought first. "Suit yourself." She closed the door behind her. Bruno and Steve walked over to the corner of the room, tails wagging adorably, and lay down again. Bruno went down on his front paws, tail up, signaling to Steve that he wanted to play. They ran around the room once, then lay down again.

To show what a nice woman I am, I went into the kitchen and got each of the dogs a very healthy rawhide-free chew chip. I gave one to Eydie, who was haughtily refusing to fraternize with those other two animals by staying in the kitchen. Then I walked back into the living room to distribute chews to Steve and Bruno, and found my parents in enthusiastic conversation with the NYPD detective.

"So you see, we believe that we should do some investigating on our own," Dad was saying as I entered.

"No," I said without hesitation. "We don't believe that. We have never believed that. We believe the police are professionals and should be allowed to do their job without any interference. We're going to be excellent witnesses—or actually, I'm going to be an excellent witness and you're going to be my parents—and we will cooperate in any way the detective thinks we should, but we are decidedly *not* going to investigate on our own." Dad's mouth pursed, but I didn't give him a chance to protest as I sat down and faced Rodriguez. "Now, Detective, how can I help you?"

"I'd like you to do some investigating on your own," Rodriguez said.

CHAPTER SEVEN

I believe to this day that Detective Rodriguez said that because she had a dry, subtle sense of humor and saw an opening for a really good joke. That's what I think, and I'm sticking to it.

At the time, however, my mouth dried out and I remember wheezing a bit. Mom leapt up to head into the kitchen, where I knew she would find a bottle of water for me and bring it back before I could make such a sound again. Dad, on the other hand, was clearly vindicated in his investigative fantasy, and was grinning.

"What?" I managed to croak. Sure enough, Mom was at my side with a bottle of spring water, which had been properly chilled in the refrigerator. Room-temperature water is a crime against the human digestive system.

"Let me be more clear," Rodriguez suggested. "I want you to ask a few questions that you would normally ask in your usual work with the people in the theater, and then I want you to immediately tell me what they said and take absolutely no more action than that."

But the winds of this conversation were swirling around me and I wasn't yet able to comprehend those sounds coming out of the detective's mouth. So I fell back on an old favorite and said "What?" again, this time with a bit more clarity in my voice.

"I've spent the day talking to people who work in the theater," Rodriguez said. "I'm also talking to friends and relatives. This is a weird murder that doesn't seem to have a motive yet, and I'm having to straddle the two sides of it. Frankly, I'm not doing that well on the theater side. Mrs. Barclay showed up there when I was asking around, and everyone seemed more open to talking to her than to me."

This was not explaining why Rodriguez was looking at me but seeing Nancy Drew, but I hadn't yet regained the ability to form complete sentences, so she went on as if I understood how all that was relevant.

"It's clear to me that people at the theater, especially the director, Mr. McMaster, and his assistant, Ms. Levy, know more than they're telling me. There seems to be an odd sort of code that goes on there. You're either an insider or you're not, and outsiders don't get told the juicy stuff. I don't think anybody's lying, but they're holding some things back."

Dad was chewing on his lower lip. "But this Barclay guy, the one who used to be Berkowitz, he was only at the theater once, and that was yesterday," he said. "Do you really think his murder is tied to the audition for his dog?"

"I don't know what I think yet," Rodriguez replied. "What I

can see is that there's information I'm not getting, and since that's my end of the case, I'd like to find out what it is." She turned toward me. "So I want you to talk to some of the personnel at the theater and report back."

Now, you'd think that would be a no-brainer. And if you were anyone but me (which you undoubtedly are), you'd probably be right. But I'm me, and no matter how inconvenient it is at any given moment, I have to act like myself.

Before I could, Dad was acting like himself. "We'll be happy to," he said. "The Powell family is always glad to help out our men and women in uniform." Forget that Rodriguez wasn't in the military; she was a cop, and a plainclothes one at that.

"Just a second," I interjected. "Don't go volunteering me for anything yet, Dad. I have to work with these people. My agency is just starting to get a reputation. If they find out I'm dropping dimes on people in the theater to the police, my name is no good anywhere in the live theatre community in New York. I'm not sure I can risk that."

Rodriguez nodded. "I understand that. I can assure you that I'd do everything I could to keep your secret from getting out, but you know as well as I do that there are no guarantees with this kind of thing."

Dad stood still, his eyes wide at my impudence. But Mom, suddenly standing behind him, put a hand on his shoulder and he turned to look at her. "El," he said.

"Kay Powell," my mother said, looking at my father and not at me. "The New York City Police Department is asking for your help in solving a murder. You are not going to put your own concerns ahead of that."

My mother sees things very simply; she has never actually experienced a gray area in her life. "Mom," I said gently, "I don't think you're getting exactly what I'm risking here."

"You're risking your business by risking your reputation," my mother said, her voice as cool as a lemonade with extra ice. "You are going to be duplicitous with people whose trust is essential to your continued success in your chosen field. You're going to have to lie to people you like and you're going to tell their worst secrets, which might get them sent to prison for life, to a police detective. If you're found out, they could easily blackball you out of the community and you might very well have to sell your house and move to California to agent for the occasional cow in a movie that takes place in the Midwest. That means your father and I would have to move out too and we really don't have anywhere else to go for an extended period of time. So you'd have that on your head as well. Does it sound like I understand what you're risking here?" She put her hands on her hips and looked at me.

I wet my lips because it was a thing to do. "Yeah. Sounds like you have a decent grasp of the situation."

"Then just look at the detective and tell her that's what you're going to do," Mom said.

I turned toward Rodriguez. "That's what I'm going to do," I said.

Never underestimate a mother.

Rodriguez, whom I think didn't really believe what she'd just seen, said she couldn't leave Louise outside for too long and feel comfortable with the security of the conversation. She handed me another of her business cards.

"I'm not going to call you," she said. "Don't enter my number into your cell phone, so my name won't come up if we have any contact. You call me when you have something to tell me, so if you don't have something to tell me, don't call. This will work or it won't, but I'm going to do my best to keep you out of trouble, okay?"

She was gone before I could even think straight.

As soon as the door closed behind her, Steve and Bruno walked over to me as if to ask exactly what was going on. I wondered if Louise was going to come in for her dog, but then I heard Rodriguez's car drive away and I got the impression Louise had forgotten she had a dog. Until the *Annie* salary checks started coming in.

I looked over at my parents as I stroked the two dogs' heads. "Well. Another fine mess you've gotten me into."

They protested and eventually I gave in and told them I didn't blame them for my predicament. It was a lie, but sometimes that's the best way to move on. I ordered a pizza for the three of us and gave the dogs their food ahead of the major walk they would expect later in the day. I'd have to see if I had another dog bed for Bruno.

"We'll be with you the whole way," Dad said after the delivery guy brought our dinner. My father seemed practically giddy with the idea of informing on colleagues for the police.

"We?" I said. "You and Mom just have to audition some senior citizens for a revival of *The Ed Sullivan Show* and wait for me to come home from my new job as a snitch." I threw the dogs a piece of crust and Eydie, with the longest neck, caught it. She put it down and sniffed at it, decided it was not juicy beef, and turned up her nose. Bruno, whose tastes I was finding were less specific—he was a gourmand and not a gourmet—picked it up happily and laid it down on the pillow between himself and Steve. Bruno was good at sharing.

"Don't be silly," Dad answered. "We wouldn't let you do something this dangerous by yourself. I'm canceling the auditions and coming with you."

Now I knew how things could get worse, but this time I wasn't going to back down. "You are absolutely not doing that," I told my father. "I'm questioning theater people. The worst thing that can happen is someone tells the company I'm wearing last year's shoes."

"It will look a bit suspicious if Kay has her parents following her around when she's rehearsing with Bruno," Mom pointed out gently.

Dad considered that, chewing lightly on the inside of his cheek. "We could wear makeup and costumes," he suggested, but everybody—even Steve and Bruno—knew his heart wasn't in it.

"I'm taking the dogs for a walk," I said. "I'll start my undercover work in the morning. Remind me to call Consuelo and get her to clear off part of my calendar."

It was starting to get dark, so I took my phone with the flashlight app and I changed into sweatpants with a reflective stripe down the side before leashing up my three charges. They seemed happy to be outdoors, but of course Eydie was too sophisticated to let on such an emotion. She sniffed at the grass as if she'd never sniffed it before, looked up, considered, and sniffed again.

Walking three dogs at the same time takes a certain amount of skill, and I didn't have it. The leashes kept getting tangled up as Bruno and Steve inevitably wanted to go one way, while Eydie would choose the other. They all knew not to pull on the leash, which was helpful, but Steve especially, with that dachshund nose, was intrigued by every new aroma very close to the ground, and wanted to investigate each one.

At one point Steve got a whiff of something especially exciting, and wanted to go to the left to track it down. Bruno, whose olfactory sense was average for a dog, didn't pick up on that so he was moving forward and not noticing the path his new pal wanted to take. Eydie, I believe, was simply moving right because she felt someone should show these two ridiculous males who was in charge here.

All of that would have been fine except that Steve was on my right and Eydie on my left. So when they decided to move in the opposite direction at the exact same moment, they crossed the leashes right in front of my legs and I went down sideways on the pavement, scraping my right elbow.

I shouted something I'm not proud of and tried to get myself back into shape. The first priority was to grab the two leashes I'd dropped—Eydie's was still firm in my hand, although she was pulling now in what was for her a panic. I reached out with my left hand and caught Steve's, which was fairly easy because he had stopped in his tracks to look at me.

But Bruno, spooked by the sudden movement and my unfortunate language, was running away at a very high speed. Toward the street.

Bruno's life flashed before my eyes, but mostly what I saw was a future where I spent my remaining time on Earth guilt-ridden and possibly in jail for causing harm to an animal I did not own.

Rodriguez would have to find another snitch, because she'd be too busy arresting me and locking me up to use me effectively.

"Bruno!" I yelled, but he either didn't hear me or was too shaken. He kept running. I scrambled to my feet and took off at full speed after him, holding the other dogs' leashes. They, thinking this was a great game, matched my speed easily.

To be fair, a turtle with a torn ACL could have matched my speed easily. I'd just gotten up off the concrete.

I shouted his name again but there was no point; Bruno wasn't going to stop and turn around. He was only a few yards from the curb now, and there were some cars in the road. I wanted to turn away but I felt an obligation to watch in case a miracle happened.

And then one did.

Just before he was going to bolt into the path of an oncoming Hyundai Sonata, Bruno's leash pulled him back and stopped his progress. He looked quite surprised, then a little embarrassed, and walked gently back in my direction as I continued to run (or my version of it) toward him.

His leash was under a man's foot, and the man was Sam Gibson. He casually reached down and grabbed the loop of the leash before taking his weight off the lead, then led Bruno back toward me with a satisfied smile on his face.

"You shouldn't practice gymnastics when you're walking three dogs, Kay," he said as I stopped and gaped gratefully at him. "I'd think a person in your line of work would know that."

"Sam," I said, a little out of breath. All right: a *lot* out of breath. I made a mental note to get more exercise than simply walking dogs around suburban New Jersey. "Thank you. You saved Bruno's life."

"No charge," Sam answered. "I was just flying back from Krypton and saw there was a problem."

"I'm not kidding," I said. "I was afraid something awful was going to happen."

"I know." Sam didn't offer me Bruno's leash; he just started walking along with us as I tended to Steve and Eydie. "How's that arm feel? Looks a little scraped up."

There was a little blood on my arm, but the adrenaline from the hideous moment I thought something was going to happen to Bruno hadn't worn off yet, so I didn't really feel any pain. "It's okay," I said. "I'll clean it up when I get home."

"You sure? We're right by the store, and I have a first-aid kit." He pointed to Cool Beans, which was just up the street. I looked at the arm and decided cleaning it off wouldn't be an awful thing. We headed for the coffee shop.

Once inside, Sam closed the door so I could let the three dogs off their leashes and went rummaging behind his counter, pulling out a plastic box marked First Aid that looked like it had been used far too often.

Sam must have seen the look I gave it, because he shrugged and said, "I get a lot of college kids working here in a hurry with hot coffee and knives. Don't worry. We keep it all clean." He took out a tube of something and a bandage that looked like it could cover a cut the size of the Grand Canyon.

"Great," I answered. "Now I have to think about all those scalded, lacerated college students. I'll never be able to buy coffee here without weeping."

He ignored my remark, which was probably wise. "Let's get you cleaned up first. This might sting a little."

"That's what they always say in the movies before the tough guy hero starts breaking down and calling for his mommy."

"This won't be that bad. Probably." The dogs were making themselves at home. Bruno was walking the perimeter, no doubt on the lookout for any intruders who might come by and try to breach our fortifications, while Steve crawled up next to the heating duct and lay down. Eydie, nose held high, was trying to figure out what those strange aromas were, and whether there was anything she could demand until we gave it to her. She walked toward the back of the room, where the refrigerated counter bins were, but they were closed and, you know, refrigerated, so there wasn't much to smell. Quite the mystery for Eydie.

Sam dabbed at my arm with a cotton ball soaked in something, and it did sting a little, but it wasn't really all that bad. He had a light touch and I'm a tough Jersey girl who actually grew up onstage in the Catskills and the Poconos. I didn't cry or anything.

Then he came at me with that bandage and I held up my left hand. "Hold it," I told Sam. "I just scraped my arm a little. That makes it look like I almost cut it off."

"It's not a deep scrape, but it covers a good amount of your arm," Sam argued. "What do you want me to do, put on seventeen Band-Aids you'll have to rip off individually later?"

"You've got to have something smaller. You could sell advertising space on that thing."

Once again he completely disregarded what I'd said and started taping the bandage to my forearm. "Hey, if you don't like the medical attention you get here, you can take your business to another coffee shop."

"My parents are going to think I got hit by a bus."

He reached into the kit and took out an Ace bandage. "I'll wrap this around. You can tell them you strained yourself mildly while trying to refine your golf swing."

"With three dogs?"

"Yeah, since when do you have three dogs? Where'd your new friend come from?" He tucked in the end of the stretchable bandage and patted my arm, declaring it done.

I told him about Trent, or Moshe, or whomever, and what had happened today, which seemed like it should have taken at least the better part of a week. Sam listened well, not interrupting unless he didn't understand and, unlike most guys, not trying to inject himself into the conversation. He'd probably never had an experience where a customer of the coffee shop had been stabbed and then fell into a dog's water bowl.

"You're in an interesting business," he said when I'd finished relating the tale.

"That's it? What do you think I should do?"

Sam started putting the first-aid kit back together, but I saw his wry grin. "Why are you asking me? You've already decided what you're going to do."

"Oh, have I? I must have neglected to write down the plan. Tell me, Oh smug one, what is it I've decided?"

He slipped the first-aid kit back under the counter. "You're going to do what the cop asked you to do and talk to the people at the theater and you're going to tell her everything they say. You've decided you don't like this Louise person and that she's probably not worthy of the fine dog she has, so you're not going to bring Bruno back and you'll probably end up adopting him.

That's especially true if it turns out Louise killed her husband, because then Bruno will definitely need a new home. How am I doing so far?"

"You're completely wrong about Bruno; he goes back tomorrow."

"Uh-huh."

"Uh-huh yourself. As for the theater, well, I have to be there anyway because I'm in charge of Bruno's rehearsal time now. And everybody will be talking about what happened to Trent, even though almost none of them has ever met him, because there's nothing show people like better than gossip. And if they say something that can help in the solving of a very serious crime, well, I'd be a bad citizen if I withheld that information from the police."

Sam clapped his hands a few times. "Very nice. An almost flawless rationalization." It was good he wasn't going to ask me out again, because he wasn't doing himself any favors with this self-satisfied attitude.

"Rationalization for what?" I asked. "Do you think I should refuse to help Rodriguez?"

"No, I think you're absolutely doing the right thing. But let's be honest. You're not going to snoop around because of what they taught you in seventh-grade civics class and you're not doing it because you've been cornered and trapped by your parents and the detective." Sam sat on the counter and looked down at me. His wiseguy smirk had given way to a concerned gaze.

"No? Then why am I doing it?" I asked.

"Because you're a show person too, and there's nothing you like better than gossip. You're nosy and you want to know who killed this Trent guy. And you want to know it before everybody else so that you can tell everybody else. Deny that."

"I don't have to take this abuse," I said, standing. "I can go home and take other kinds of abuse."

"You hate it when I'm right, don't you?" he said.

I picked up the leashes from the counter and examined the billboard-sized bandage on my arm. "I'm not a showbiz person, Sam. I got out of that a long time ago because I didn't like the life. I'm a lawyer and an agent and a business owner. That's what I am."

I got the leashes on Steve and Eydie, who had walked over as soon as they saw I'd picked them up. Bruno was being more reticent only because he didn't know the routine here. In fact, he didn't know "here" at all.

"Now, if you don't mind," I continued, "I have to get this dog ready for rehearsals of his musical tomorrow."

"Of course. It's been a pleasure. Feel free to fall down outside my store anytime." Sam was back to the wiseguy smirk, and I think I liked him better that way.

"I'm not showbiz, Sam," I reiterated.

"Did I say something?"

I had to think about that conversation all the way back to the house. I had turned my back on the whole stage life when I told Mom and Dad I wanted to go to veterinary school. I didn't like the fake façade, the idea that I had to pretend to be happy when I really wasn't, the ritual of putting on a show every night and making it seem like I'd never done it before. I felt embarrassed in front of a crowd. I didn't want anyone to notice me.

If my face didn't resemble both of my parents, I would have

thought I was adopted from a well-meaning family of introverts who couldn't afford to put me through the quietest school in the country for fear that I'd in some way attract attention.

Why did I care what Sam thought about me anyway? I'd known him for years and he'd been a decent friend, certainly not the first person I'd call when I'd had a hard day or just couldn't see how I was going to make this business work.

That would have been my father. Followed by my mother.

And anyway, just because I was an agent, it didn't mean I was a real showbiz person. I was performing a function that required knowledge of legal and technical issues and a good understanding of human nature at every turn. And it helped that I generally liked animals better than people. I could communicate in ways that some of the "professionals" who handled the non-human actors hadn't thought of yet. I was using the skills I had been given and I was doing pretty well for myself, thank you.

Who was I mad at, again? Right. Sam.

Okay, so I would admit that I do enjoy the odd piece of gossip, but who doesn't, really? And I did feel at home in a theater, but come on. I actually did grow up in one (it was in a resort hotel, but let's not split hairs, shall we?).

The heck with Sam, I told myself. I was right to turn him down when he asked me out that time. He'd probably just needle me until I had to think about what he'd said all the way home with three dogs, two of whom were actually mine.

And that was why I wasn't thinking about what was actually going on around me when I arrived home, brought the dogs in through the back door, and gave them each a treat. I was consumed with my identity crisis, and that's the excuse I'm going to use from now until the rest of my life.

Because once I made my way into the living room while considering pouring myself a fairly stiff drink, I saw a young woman sitting in the armchair looking at my parents, who were on the sofa looking slightly uncomfortable, although I'm sure the young woman didn't see that. Mom and Dad were pros at making the audience feel welcome and giving off the aura of absolute joy at having people in to see them.

When I say "young woman," I mean one in her late twenties who had been given gifts of genetics and didn't mind showing them off. She was wearing, if that's the word, a pretty low-cut shirt and jeans that might very well have been sprayed on. And that was her idea of casual, clearly.

I didn't hear what they were talking about before I walked in, but the guest's presence had thrown me a bit. She certainly wasn't one of the potential acts for the senior-center show, and she wasn't anyone who would have been there to visit me, so I was hoping she was there to offer my parents a lucrative booking, perhaps in a country other than the one I live in. Just for a few months.

"Sorry, am I intruding?" I said. All three heads turned in my direction.

"Oh, there you are!" Mom looked at me, then at the bandage on my arm. "What happened?"

"It's nothing. I couldn't find a smaller bandage. What's going on?" I walked a little farther into the room to get a better look at our guest.

She was young but not naïve, sexy without being beautiful, blond but not really. She smiled at me with a look less practiced than the one my parents had been giving her, but not nearly as professionally authentic. She wasn't a great actress, and she wasn't that happy to be in my house.

She stood up and extended her hand. "You must be Kay," she said. "I'm Taylor Cassidy." Then she looked at me, waiting for a reaction, as if the name should have meant something to me.

"Hi," I said, trying not to make it sound like a question.

"Taylor has been telling us about her job with Trent and Louise Barclay," Dad said, not overplaying his role for once. "She came all the way from the city."

"That's a long ride," I said. "Why haven't my parents given you a cold drink?" The idea of a nice shot of . . . anything had not yet left my mind.

"I didn't need anything, really," Taylor said. "I'm just here to pick up Bruno and bring him home."

It shouldn't have alarmed me; I knew Bruno wasn't my dog.

"You work for Louise?" I said. Proof of employment would be necessary before I gave up the dog to anyone.

"Yes," Taylor Cassidy said. "I'm their dog walker."

CHAPTER EIGHT

Okay, *that* was awkward.

Les McMaster had said he'd heard—from Louise—that Trent/ Moshe had been having an affair with the woman they'd hired to walk Bruno, presumably when both he and Louise were out doing . . . something. And now here she was in my living room, asking for Bruno's leash. And I'll admit to some hesitation in giving it to her.

To be clear, the leash itself I wouldn't have minded handing over, but Bruno? The dog sitter had taken a long drive to retrieve him.

If, of course, she really *was* the dog walker.

"Do you have some identification?" I asked "Taylor."

She nodded, smiling. "Of course. I wouldn't just let a dog I was watching walk out the door without some assurance either." She reached into her purse, which had been sitting on the floor next to the easy chair, and produced a valid New York state driver's license with her picture and the name "Taylor Cassidy" quite clearly printed on it.

"I have a problem," I told her, even as my father was eyeing the young woman warily. Dad has good instincts about people, and if he was worried about Taylor for any reason, that was good enough for me.

Besides, Bruno was getting along so well with Steve. The two of them were back on Steve's dog bed, lying peacefully, tails occasionally wagging. It would be a shame to break them up.

Taylor looked at me, seemingly confused. "What? That's me." She pointed at the license and I handed it back.

"Oh, I'm sure it is, but how do I know you're Bruno's walker? He didn't come over to you and greet you like I would expect he would if you were such a good friend, someone he sees every day. In an unfamiliar setting like this, he should be thrilled to see you, but he didn't move a muscle." He was, in point of fact, snoring at the moment, but I didn't see how that was relevant. Bruno had adapted easily to my house and seemed not to have any separation anxiety when I'd taken him from Louise, but his lack of response when we'd come back from our walk and discovered Taylor in the room was curious.

"Well, he doesn't know me that well. I only walk him occasionally, when both Louise and Trent are out of the apartment, and that's only been once or twice a week." A likely excuse. I'd met Bruno all of four times in my life and he'd come home with me like I was a . . . kindhearted woman and he was a drunken sailor on shore leave. "You can call Louise and ask if she wanted me to come get him," Taylor added.

Louise, who had tried to get me arrested this very afternoon and who had been ignoring my calls all day, would very likely reject the number again if I called her. "Do me a favor," I said to Taylor, "and give her a call. I'm not sure I have the right number for her cell." I started to say I'd always dealt with Trent, which was mostly true (I still had Louise's number, obviously) but then something struck me as odd.

Taylor had referred to Trent in the present tense.

"Of course," she said, pulling her phone out of her pocket. "Happy to do it." She pushed a button on the phone—she apparently had Louise on speed dial—and waited a few seconds. "Louise?" she said casually. "It's Taylor."

I gestured to her to hand me the phone, and she did so without saying a word about the change of conversation partner. "Louise? It's Kay. Did you send your dog walker to my house in New Jersey to pick up Bruno?"

The person on the other end of the phone hung up.

I considered that for a moment. Then I said, "No, she isn't a small redhead. She's tall and blond. Do you know her? I can take a picture and send it to you if you like. Let me get my own phone and send it to your number."

Taylor grabbed the phone out of my hand. "She hung up on you," she said, a real edge to her voice now.

Mom put her hand to her mouth. "That's so rude," she said.

"Yes, she did," I said to the blonde. "How did you know?"

"I could hear it."

"No you couldn't," Dad answered before I could say it myself. "Not from that distance."

I took a step closer to the younger woman. "You want to tell me what's really going on?" I asked.

Taylor's mouth became a horizontal line so straight you could use it to level a bookshelf you were hanging. "I told you," she said. "I'm here to take Bruno home because Louise asked me to come get him."

"Why didn't Louise call me to tell me you were coming? Why did she just hang up on me now?"

She sneered a little. "She doesn't like you. She says you're bossy and you think Bruno is your own dog, but he's not. Trent thinks the same thing."

There it was again.

"Trent?" Mom asked. "Isn't that the man who—"

"Yes," I cut her off. "The man who is trying to get Bruno a part in *Annie*. That's Trent." For some reason this woman didn't know Trent was dead. And since this appeared to be an adversarial relationship now, I felt any information I had that she didn't was definitely an advantage.

"He's going to fire you," Taylor snarled.

"I sincerely doubt it. Now, who are you really and why do you want to take Bruno away?"

Taylor could have reacted with anger, which was what I expected. She could have scoffed and told me I had no idea what I was talking about, which was an option. She might have laughed with an evil edge, twirled her mustache, and kicked one of the dogs while demanding I submit to her every whim, which would have been appropriate only if she were a character in an eighteenth-century melodrama. All those were choices.

Instead, she started to cry.

"I'm sorry," she gasped out between sobs. "I was supposed to come and get the dog and that was going to be it. I just had to bring him back to Manhattan and feed him, I swear. Nothing bad's going to happen to the dog, honest."

I sat down. Maybe I was stunned by this odd change in the room's mood. I was simply lost for a reaction to her outburst, had dozens of questions, and didn't know which one to ask first, or whether I'd be able to trust the response to any of them.

Luckily my father stepped in. He dropped his voice down to a kindly murmur and looked Taylor in the eyes. I could see him consider taking her hands in his, then deciding against it, thinking it too much for the character he was playing.

"It's okay, honey. Now, you just sit down here and tell us the whole story from the beginning." I think he was channeling the character he played in our longtime first-act closer, *Nudnik,* which consisted of Dad pretending to be a milquetoast who was always acceding to his shrewish wife and bratty daughter (you can imagine the casting). Got lots of laughs with that one.

Taylor sat and Mom handed her a tissue from a box on the table next to the piano, no doubt used for those auditioners who might care to clear the sinuses before belting out yet another rendition of "New York, New York" as it might have been sung by Ernest Borgnine. She nodded a few times, as if agreeing with something someone was saying to her that only she could hear.

It took a few moments, but she got control of herself and her nose (after two more tissues), and Dad again suggested she start at the beginning.

"It wasn't anything bad, I promise," Taylor said. "Louise called me about four this afternoon. She said Bruno didn't need to get walked because he was here in New Jersey." (People from New York think New Jersey is all one place, like once you cross the

Hudson River it couldn't matter less if you're in Short Hills or Camden. After a while you just let it pass.) "So I was making plans to go out to a bar with a couple of my friends and I got a text on my phone."

I get texts all the time, but Taylor made that one sound like it had death in it. She shuddered a little. "Who sent the text?" Dad asked. He was still in his *Nudnik* role but much more subdued than onstage, where everything had to be played broadly. This was just a gentle old—um, middle-aged—gentleman asking her questions because he wanted to help.

The man was a master.

Taylor shook her head. "I don't know," she said. "The number was blocked, and normally I'd just delete something like that. But the first words were, 'If you value your life,' and that got me so scared. I read the whole thing."

"What did it say?" Mom asked. She was definitely not playing her *Nudnik* role of the overbearing wife. Mom isn't as natural an actress as Dad is an actor; she tends to fall back on actually being herself, which is a welcome change of pace in my family.

Taylor looked at her, as if just being reminded there was anyone in the room except herself and Dad. "It said that they knew where I lived and they could get to me, and if I didn't come here—whoever it was had the address—and bring Bruno back to the city, they'd know how to find me. I can show you the text."

She punched the screen on her phone a few times, and showed it to Dad. He took the phone from Taylor—and I cringed at the thought of fingerprints, but Dad held it gingerly by the edges—and turned the screen toward me.

Sure enough, the text message, which did not show a sender's address or phone, read, *If you value your life, bring Louise Barclay's dog Bruno to the address being sent in a separate text.* It then gave my address as the place to find Bruno. *The dog will not be harmed, but must be brought here. You are being watched. If you don't follow our instructions exactly, we will know how to find you and you won't know when it's coming.*

"You see?" Taylor said, the quiver coming back into her voice. "I had to do it or they were gonna kill me!"

"Why didn't you call the police?" I asked. I'd found my voice somewhere around the time Taylor had dropped her second used tissue on my side table. I must not have sounded as comforting as Mom and Dad had, because Taylor looked like I'd slapped her.

"They always say not to call the police or something bad will happen, don't they?" she said. How stupid I must have been to think otherwise!

"I think maybe it's best to ignore that advice," Mom said, her voice soothing over my thoughtless impertinence. "Call the police. If you have the address where you were supposed to take Bruno, they'll be able to find the people who sent you that text, won't they?"

"They're *watching me!*" Taylor groaned, and Bruno looked up at her. He couldn't smell her from that far away—probably—but he still didn't seem to recognize the woman making those odd noises. "They're probably out there *right now!*"

Well, that wasn't a fun thought. I looked at Dad. "You think?" I asked.

He made a face like something smelled bad. "I really doubt it. But I still think we should call the cops. If someone *is* out there, we can end this right now and probably catch the person who killed Moshe Berkowitz." Then, in as theatrical and phony a gesture as I have ever seen from a seasoned pro, my father put his fingers to his lips as if he hadn't just meant to let that information out.

I looked at Taylor. Her eyes crinkled up and her nose got four creases in it. "Who's Moshe Berkowitz?" she asked. "Is that, like, a code or something?"

Dad was an actor, but I was an agent. I knew how to negotiate terms and how to hold back and share information when necessary, for strategic purposes. So I said to Taylor, "Moshe Berkowitz was Trent Barclay's real name."

I saw Mom turn to watch Taylor's reaction as well.

It was pretty spectacular. Her eyes grew to the size of Eisenhower silver dollars (pretty big) and her lips retracted into her mouth. She made a few noises I'd never even heard one of my clients make, and then she took some deep breaths. "Trent's *dead*?" she croaked.

I nodded. "Somebody stabbed him in the back last night in his apartment. I'm sorry I had to be the one to tell you." I wasn't that sorry. Taylor had tried to dognap Bruno and had dropped used tissues on my side table. There are some things that simply can't be forgiven.

"The police," Mom reminded. "We should be calling the police."

"No!" Taylor insisted. "Listen. Here's what we'll do. These people have killed Trent, and that means they're not kidding. If they're watching us, the only thing for us to do is let me take Bruno outside, make it look like I'm going to drive him away. I'll put him in my car, drive around the block once, and then come back after I think they've left. Okay? I'll bring him right back."

Having had more time than Taylor to get used to the idea of Trent being dead, I wasn't buying the "we'll-be-watching-you" act her blackmailers had offered. "No chance," I said. "You're hysterical. You're scared. You'll take Bruno exactly where they want you to take him. I'm not going to let that happen. As his agent, it's my job to give him the best advice possible, and tonight that advice is to stay right where he is and be cozy with Steve."

Steve, indeed, had his right forepaw on Bruno's shoulder. Steve was also snoring so loudly that Eydie grunted in disgust. From the kitchen.

"No, really," Taylor attempted. "I promise. He'll be back here in five minutes. Just don't make me walk out that door alone." She looked at my front door as if it led directly to the guillotine. Which was silly. We had the guillotine removed from the front yard years ago.

"You won't have to," Dad told her. "I'll go with you."

"Jay!" my mother said.

My "Dad" was a little less urgent, but it carried the same message.

He looked at us as if we were mental patients off our meds. "Just to the car," he said. "There's no one out there, so there won't be any danger."

"I'm not going without the dog," Taylor tried to demand. But her voice just couldn't carry it off.

"Okay, suppose I were stupid enough to let you put a leash on Bruno and take him out the door," I said. "And let's say— although I think it very unlikely—that you're telling the truth and you'll bring Bruno right back here in a few minutes. How does that help you?"

"They won't shoot me on my way to the car," Taylor offered in a "well, duh" inflection.

"But you won't bring Bruno to the designated spot," I reminded her. "So you haven't bought yourself more than an hour or so."

Taylor's mouth made some very interesting movements. Her lips moved back and forth, horizontally, at the same time they were going into, then out of, her mouth. She looked like she was chewing on her own lips and trying to decide if they needed more salt.

"After I drop him off, I can leave the state," she said. "I have family in Ithaca."

"Why do they want Bruno?" Mom asked.

Everybody turned in her direction. "What?" I said.

"Why are these mysterious people so dead set on getting Bruno?" Mom answered. "Is he filled with diamonds or something? He's a sweet dog, but they could probably find another one at a decent shelter. Why do they need Bruno?"

It was a good question.

"How am I supposed to know?" Taylor whined, as if we'd expected an answer out of her. "They're gonna kill me and all you care about is that dog."

"That *dog* is my client," I told her. "It's my job to see that nothing bad happens to him at all. I'm the only one looking out for him right now, so I'm going to make the decisions in matters of his welfare. And that means right now, I'm going to call Detective Rodriguez and tell her exactly what's been going on. Give me your phone. It's evidence." That sounded professional.

"No!" Taylor turned and ran out the front door before any of us could even comprehend what it was she was doing. I heard her footsteps, running, on the gravel in front of my house, then her car start up and drive away, the engine noise fading into the distance.

I heard absolutely no gunfire at all.

We stood there for a long moment. Then Dad let out a long breath and sat down on the sofa next to Mom. "What did it for you?" he asked.

"The bit about driving to Ithaca," Mom answered without hesitation. "It was just too rehearsed. Who thinks of Ithaca that spontaneously?"

He nodded. "For me it was the reaction when she heard her boss had been murdered. She didn't ask any questions. She just spent all her energy being shocked."

Mom nodded. "I saw that too," she said.

Dad looked at me. "How about you?"

"The way Bruno didn't care if she was here or not. Even if she really is his regular dog walker, he doesn't like her as much as he likes me, and he's known me less than a week."

Dad digested that. He patted Mom on the shoulder and leaned back on the sofa. "I suppose we really should call Detective Rodriguez on this one," he said. "But one thing's for sure."

Mom, after decades of feeding him straight lines, knew how to play the scene. "What's that, Jay?" she asked.

"That was one of the worst acting performances I've ever seen."

CHAPTER NINE

Rodriguez took the information I had for her over the phone, saying it was late and she didn't see any reason to drive out to what she called "the boonies" to take a statement she could hear just as well from her home in Astoria, Queens. New Yorkers call the police their "finest," but don't pay them nearly enough to live in Manhattan.

"What do you think it all means?" I asked her when she was finished taking down the whole bizarre Taylor incident.

She sighed. "That I'm going to be working late tonight, and probably tomorrow. You going to the theater tomorrow?"

"Yeah, I'll be there at noon."

"Noon? They don't get started until noon?" Rodriguez seemed appalled at the slavish nature of theater folk.

"Yeah, and they work only until about one in the morning. It's a damned soft life," I more or less snarled. I won't identify with theater people, but they are my family. You make a wiseass crack about them and I'm going to get testy.

"Okay, okay," the detective answered. "Nobody's trying to say anything bad about your pals. Just ask around and let me know what you hear." Then we said our goodbyes and I disconnected the call.

Mom and Dad had finally gone to bed, Dad still insisting that it would be helpful for him, at least, to come with Bruno and me to rehearsal the next day. I saw this as a thinly veiled attempt to go meet Les McMaster, but I didn't say that to my father because the man could argue Eva Braun into attending a bat mitzvah. I saw no point. If I left early enough in the morning, Dad simply wouldn't be awake in time.

I made sure all the water bowls were full and put the food bowls up on the counter for the night. Dogs need a routine, and eating late at night, especially in (for Bruno) an unfamiliar house would not be helpful to the dogs or my rugs. They probably wouldn't get up to eat during the night anyway.

I sat down at the kitchen table after pouring myself a bowl of Cap'n Crunch. Hey, you can eat kale at midnight if you want to, but sugary cereals are my snack of choice when I need to think. And I needed to think.

All I'd wanted to do was help Bruno get a role in *Annie,* one that didn't actually have all that much stage time and was probably sort of underutilizing his talents. Strategically, it would be great for him, giving him exposure and getting that first big role under his (metaphorical) belt. It might lead to some TV or film work or possibly some advertising, which could be very lucrative.

But in my attempts to ingratiate the dog to a Broadway director, somehow I'd ended up boarding Bruno, hiding from Louise, dropping a dime on Taylor, snooping for Rodriguez, and wondering two things: who had killed Trent, and why I'd never known his real name was Moshe Berkowitz.

Perhaps the first question was more pressing than the second.

One thing about Cap'n Crunch cereal is that it lives up to its name. I could hear nothing but the crunching in my head, and that's part of the appeal. There were no distractions from anywhere to take me away from my ruminations.

The trouble was, my ruminations weren't getting me anywhere.

It wasn't my business to solve Trent's murder; that was Rodriguez's problem. All I had to do was get a few juicy tidbits to her and let her do the rest. My job was getting Bruno through the process of learning to be adorable on cue, something he could pretty much do in his sleep.

But I couldn't help trying to put the puzzle pieces together. There had been no signs of forced entry at Trent and Louise's apartment, Dad had noticed. So whoever killed him either had access to a key or lived there, because the police found the door locked after Louise's 911 call.

The dog walker might have a key to the apartment. If she *was* the dog walker. Neither Trent nor Louise had ever mentioned a dog walker to me, and I was fairly well involved with the care of their dog.

But it was certain that Louise had a key to the apartment, she admitted to being in the bedroom at the time, and she apparently knew that Trent was having an affair with someone. Les had told me he'd heard the fling was with their dog walker.

Taylor was becoming a central figure no matter how you sized up this crime. But what motive would she have to kill Trent, leave Bruno in the apartment, and then come to my house in New Jersey the next night to try to dognap him? Why not just take him after Trent lay facedown in the water bowl, if it were that important?

I had a lot of questions, almost none of which were my direct responsibility, and yet I didn't think I'd be able to sleep. The cereal wasn't helping, which was unusual. I don't get a "sugar rush," and think such a thing is a myth, but normally just sitting quietly and crunching along would relax me to the point that I could sleep. Not tonight.

There was only one thing to do: Internet research. That'll put me to sleep faster than a glass of warm milk while reading spreadsheets and listening to a politician's oration.

I figured if I could purge the subjects currently monopolizing my mind, I might be able to move past them and get to sleep before the sun rose in my bedroom window. That was a good few hours off, but I was already preparing for a losing battle. I'm a glass-half-never-filled kind of girl.

The name Moshe Berkowitz, unsurprisingly, got 122,000 Google results. Everything gets at least 122,000 Google results. You'd have to be a silent monk in the Himalayas to get less than 122,000 Google results.

I'm saying Google tends to overrepresent.

I sorted through the listings, many of which were about one particular man who had never turned into Trent Barclay and was therefore not relevant to the research I was doing, which at the moment had no focus whatsoever. Once those were out of the way, there were the usual LinkedIn listings, Facebook pages, a couple

Twitter feeds, four news items about Moshe Berkowitzes who had ended up in jail (two items each for two Moshes), and several listings for attorneys with that name.

The one that attracted my attention at about two in the morning (so much for getting enough sleep tonight) was one that on the surface didn't seem to pertain to my Moshe/Trent. And it didn't appear to have much relevance to his murder. At first.

It was a graduation notice, some twenty years old, from a Yeshiva in New Rochelle, New York, whose graduates included one Moshe Berkowitz. That didn't seem to have much to do with anything, and I was about to leave the web page, until my eye happened to stop on one of the other names in the graduating class.

Akra Levy.

Okay, of course this couldn't be the same Akra who was Les McMaster's assistant. Could it? I mean, how many Akras do you run into during the average day? But her having the same name as one of Trent Barclay's old Hebrew school classmates was just a little suspicious, wasn't it?

Would it explain, for example, why the Barclays—when there were still two of them—had gotten the call for Bruno's second audition instead of his agent (that's me)? You thought I forgot about that? I had not forgotten about that.

Would it explain why Les had heard about Trent having an affair with his dog walker, presumably Taylor? Suddenly the connections between Les and the Barclays seemed easier to explain, yet considerably shadier.

It took another half hour or so to track down Akra Levy.

She was widowed, her husband having died—of cancer, not murder—at a very young age, which was tragic.

And according to her Brandeis University alumni magazine, she was now "working as an executive assistant to a major Broadway director."

This was not helping me get any sleepier.

I resolved to call Rodriguez in the morning—okay, later in the morning—with the connection I'd uncovered. I'd done enough staring at a screen for one night, and besides it wasn't having the desired effect, which was to render me unconscious.

I shut down the computer and dragged my weary butt into my bedroom, where an honest-to-goodness book lay on the night table. I turned on the light over the bed, turned off the overhead fixture, got under my comforter after kicking off my slippers, and settled back to relax and read. That for sure would relax me, especially at this time of night. It started working immediately, as within half a page I felt my eyelids gaining weight faster than Steve when there was leftover chicken for dinner.

And that's why I came close to having a major heart attack when my cell phone buzzed.

Who could be calling me at this hour? That's not ever a good thing. Luckily Mom and Dad are my only family, and they certainly weren't calling from the other room, so the disaster being communicated couldn't have been too horrible. I caught my breath and grabbed for the phone, which luckily was not far away. It almost immediately stopped buzzing, which indicated the contact had not been a phone call, but a text message. That didn't make its timing any less alarming.

I hit the button for the text and looked for the indication of its source. There was no number or name, just the words "Caller Unknown," which is about as helpful as someone telling you there's a foolproof way to assure you'll win the Powerball lottery, but they've forgotten what it might be. I clicked through to the message, hoping it was simply a misbegotten advertisement or an overzealous client's owner wanting to know why her pet hamster was not yet a household name. That would be okay, because I wouldn't have to deal with it until at least daylight.

Instead, the text I opened began with the words, "If you value your life . . ."

CHAPTER TEN

"I don't think it means much of anything," Det. Alana Rodriguez told me.

I was sitting in her "office," which was essentially a small cubicle without walls (a desk) in the Sixth Precinct of the New York Police Department, having gotten a grand total of no sleep and shown up here at seven in the morning. I'd waited forty-five minutes for Rodriguez to arrive, bagel and coffee in hand. And she had the nerve to look annoyed that I'd interrupted her morning routine.

"I got a text message that said I should essentially abandon a dog I'm watching, who's a client of mine, to some fate I can't be sure of or my life will be in danger, and you don't think it means much of anything?" I gave Rodriguez my best skeptical look. "I feel so much better." I looked around. "Is there a tip jar? I'd really like to thank you for your efforts."

She sat down and moaned a little at my amateur emotionality. "I'm not saying I don't care. I'm saying I think this is an empty threat. You got the same message you said that dog walker got yesterday, and as far as my morning bulletins can tell, she didn't end up facedown in the Hudson River just yet. Someone's trying to scare you."

"They're doing a really effective job."

Rodriguez took a sip of her coffee, which was not from a fancy chain and I would bet money was hot and black. "What's interesting is that somebody really wants that dog of yours." She looked down at Bruno, who was sitting attentively but calmly next to my chair. "Can you guess why that might be?"

I scratched my client behind his ears. "He's very good at whining and looking worried," I said. "That's a marketable skill. Do you think maybe he saw the murder and someone is afraid he can point to them?"

Rodriguez's forehead wrinkled. "That happens in the movies," she said. "Unless the dog is going to stand up, point at a suspect, and shout, 'That's him, Officer! Get out your zip strips!,' I think his value as a witness is fairly limited."

I flattened out my lips. Okay, I pouted. I don't do it as winningly as Bruno, but it felt right at the time. "It doesn't make sense that this whole melodrama with Bruno isn't connected to Trent's murder," I mused, really saying aloud what I'd been kicking around since the text arrived early—and I mean early—this morning. "I can't believe whoever's behind this is suddenly convinced he's worth millions and is trying to blackmail first Taylor and now me into turning him over. It's got to be something else."

"I have a few leads," the detective said, reminding me that she

was part of the conversation. "Now, get out of here. I'm conduct-
ing some interviews with a few of the theater people, and it won't
do to have them see you here talking to me if you're going to be
my CI."

Um . . . okay. "What's a CI?"

She actually rolled her eyes, which I think took a considerable
amount of nerve. If she hadn't understood a term I used, like
"callback," for example, would I have made a show of how un-
informed she was? (Yeah, I probably would.) "Confidential in-
formant," she said slowly, as if I might not understand the words
because they weren't being spoken in my native Latvian.

"Swell. I'll add that to my CV," I said, hoping she would ask
what those initials meant. She didn't. I stood up, took Bruno's
leash from the floor, and led him out of the room and the precinct house.

"Frankly, I don't think she's giving this the attention it deserves," I told Bruno once we hit Christopher Street. I hailed a
cab at the corner—the MTA isn't crazy about dogs in the subway if you don't have a carrier, and I didn't, especially not one
that would fit Bruno—and headed to my office because it was a
few hours early for Bruno's rehearsal.

Bruno did not answer, perhaps pondering whether he believed
Rodriguez was as concerned with his welfare as she should be.
He was a very sensitive dog and might have taken some offense at
her callous treatment. Or perhaps I was projecting.

Consuelo was already at the office—naturally—when we got
there, and Maisie, upon seeing Bruno enter, squawked up a storm
to the point that we put the cover over her cage to get her to shut
up. You'd think the bird would have gotten used to having other

animals in the room, but she was a diva and, Consuelo would say, a brat.

"I'm taking on the Siamese today," Consuelo told me. "It's not a real audition, just posing for head shots, so I figured it would be okay with you. You did ask to clear off time so you could take Bruno to rehearsals."

"You know I'm fine with it." Consuelo truly believes I see her as competition. I'd love for her to be an agent in my agency. I'd get part of her commissions. Oh, and she's great and I love her.

She set up in front of my desk. "Let's get the picture." She got her phone out of her purse and aimed it at my desk.

We take a picture whenever a client visits our office, which we then post (okay, Consuelo posts) on the company's website, in the somewhat silly hope that someone with the next Grumpy Cat will see it, think we're nice people because we're smiling with the nice kitty (or in this case, dog), and immediately call up demanding our services. It hasn't actually translated into any clients yet, but as Consuelo says, it's free and you never know. Consuelo should have worked for the New York State Gaming Commission.

I couldn't lift Bruno up onto the desk as I had with some feline clients and Maisie, but he was happy to jump up on my office chair and I threw a convivial arm around him to show how friendly I am. Consuelo demanded we smile and I did my part. Bruno was on his own.

"Got it!" she said. "The first one worked like crazy this time." She showed me the picture on her phone as if the tiny image was in fact visible and I nodded my approval. Consuelo seemed pleased and put her phone away.

I sat down behind my desk and let Bruno reacquaint himself with the room. He'd done what he had to do before we left Scarborough and then again on the way back from the cab, so I wasn't worried about my office. "If it works out with the Siamese and the owner likes you, maybe you'd like to see if you can find another cat you can represent yourself," I told Consuelo.

She smiled. Consuelo has not been shy about her desire to be an agent, and I have tried not to pigeonhole her into the role of assistant with no chance of advancement. A second agent in the business would be much more valuable than an office manager, even one as efficient as Consuelo. "Thanks," she said, looking determined.

"Anything going on I need to know about?"

Consuelo looked over her clipboard, where she kept most of the paper messages. She's okay with the computer, but doesn't trust servers or the cloud. If you can't see it, she believes, there's no way of knowing it exists.

"Just one thing," she said. "There was a message left with the service before I got here." I'm the last business in New York City to keep an account with an answering service. Most people rely on voicemail and cell phones, but I still get enough calls during off-hours to merit the expense, and it looks good on my taxes.

Besides, it keeps me from having to talk to certifiably crazy client owners at ridiculous hours of the night if I choose not to.

"What's the message?" I asked. I looked through the few pieces of actual physical mail that Consuelo had put on my desk. Three were for credit card applications I didn't want (one for a client, a chimp who probably didn't need a Visa card); one was the office's utility bill (despite the fact that I'd signed up for e-billing); and one was a manila envelope with an eight-by-ten picture of a goat in it. I put that one in the "Follow Up" file on my desk, which I almost never look at.

"Well, it was weird," Consuelo answered. "Whoever it was didn't leave a name or contact information, but said that they were glad to see you last night and to remember to take care of Bruno. That was it." She spread her hands in a gesture of puzzlement.

Uh-oh. So the mysterious texter knew my office phone number too. Why did that somehow seem more imposing than the fact that he could find me on my cell phone at any moment?

I must have registered the concern on my face because Consuelo's eyes narrowed. "What is it?" she said. Consuelo thinks she's my surrogate mom when my actual mom isn't around. The fact that she's probably fifteen years younger than my mother didn't really seem to factor into the calculation here.

"It's nothing. I just don't understand it." I tried to sound nonchalant, but my tone was as chalant as they come, and I could tell I wasn't fooling Consuelo.

"You're lying," she said. "Your nose has that look."

My nose? My nose looked like it was lying? "Okay, I'm lying," I answered her. "It's bothering me, but I really don't want to have to tell you about it right now. Okay?" With Consuelo, honesty is always the best approach. Because she'll find out what she wants to know anyway, so I might just as well streamline the process.

"Okay," she answered, and went back to her desk. She sat down, very proper, and pretended to be completely engrossed in her computer screen. She didn't so much as steal a glance in my direction.

It was excruciating. Could I somehow make an excuse to go to Bruno's rehearsal two and a half hours early?

I decided that two could play at this game. I went through my emails—which had no threatening messages, thank goodness—and checked on a couple of sites I always scan in the morning. Then I read the headlines from the newspaper I'd brought with me (my eyes had been too bleary to read when I'd not awakened from not sleeping), considered and decided against the crossword puzzle in this condition, and checked my calendar despite knowing that there was nothing pressing on it.

Phone calls! That was it! I could make some follow-up phone calls on clients who had been on auditions in the past week or so. That would kill some time. I opened the address book application on my computer. All I had to do was not look in the direction of the other desk . . .

"Fine!" I shouted at Consuelo, who didn't even have the decency to look surprised. "I got a threatening text and now I'm getting vaguely threatening phone messages and I didn't want to tell you because I don't want you hovering over me like a mother bear worried about her cub. Okay?"

Consuelo smiled pleasantly and looked over at me. "Now, was that so hard?" she asked.

She made me tell her everything about the evening and night before, leading up to the text threatening either my life or Bruno's and how I hadn't slept at all because it had unnerved me. She didn't lord it over me that her sheer force of will had forced me to tell her what she wanted to know, and I in turn didn't mention that she would make an excellent interrogator for any shady intelligence organization that might care to recruit her. It's a mutual admiration thing.

But Consuelo couldn't offer much more than sympathy after I'd told her the story; she didn't know who had left the message, although she said she would immediately check with the answering service to see if the number could be traced. She didn't know how to track down a text that the police wouldn't bother tracing back to its sender (assuming it was sent from a burner phone anyway), and she couldn't decipher the rather cryptic language being used especially in the telephone message. It was all just a little eerie, and a knot was starting to form in my stomach that I knew would only be relieved by significant quantities of ice cream.

"The only thing to do is go through your day like it's normal," she said finally. "I mean, it was already not normal because Trent is dead and you seem to have inherited Bruno. But don't let the messages get you crazy. They're out of your control, and the detective is probably right—they're just supposed to scare you."

"You don't think they're going to come after me?" I don't know why Consuelo's tone was more comforting than Rodriguez's, but I wanted to snuggle up next to her and let her pat me on the head. It was like being Bruno.

"If they were going to hurt you, you'd be hurt already," she answered. "That's the way it works in my neighborhood."

In the end, there was nothing left to do but go to Bruno's rehearsal, but by the time we'd cleared the air and Consuelo had helped me with advice and Dunkin Donuts coffee, it was actually the right time to leave for that anyway.

I arrived at the theater twenty minutes early, which is when I'd usually arrive even if nobody was sending me messages designed to scare me to death, if the senders didn't take care of that detail first. I brought Bruno inside and he, having been backstage twice before today, knew the routine. He was such a pro that I expected him to call the stagehand at the door "Pops" just out of nostalgia.

Les, of course, wasn't in the house yet, which was just as well since I wanted to do some snooping for Rodriguez before Bruno had to get to work. Oddly, though, the first person I ran into backstage was Akra, who was usually attached at the hip to the director.

"I'm paving the way for Les this morning," she said before I could ask her why she was soloing for the first time in my presence. "He's in talks for a straight play, at the meeting right now, and he says there's no time to waste once he gets here. So I have to make sure everything is lined up for him."

I normally open with "How are you?" but everyone has a unique style. "What are you lining up?" I asked. Icebreaker. Don't ever say I'm not subtle. Bruno and I had to keep up at Akra's pace, which was quick, as we made our way around the back to the dressing rooms, where there should not have been anyone at this time of day. There was no matinée scheduled; the evening performance didn't begin until seven; and only Bruno and Annie's stand-in, Olive Ramson, would be working the rehearsal. The current Sandy, a Labradoodle called Horatio (I'm not making a word of this up), would be at the rehearsal too, presumably with his trainer, to show Bruno—literally—how it was done.

"The two dogs should be acquainted with each other before Les arrives," Akra said. "He doesn't want there to be a delay as they decide which one is the alpha animal."

I figured Bruno could get along with pretty much anybody, but Les's provision did make a certain amount of sense. Of course, it was designed specifically to be convenient to Les and no one else, but that was to be expected.

Akra was hurtling around the dressing-room corridor like she had to evacuate before a grenade went off in the building, which after all that had gone on didn't seem all that implausible today. Bruno did not pant—he loved the quick movement—but my exercise regimen had been somewhat lax (or nonexistent) for a while, and I was breathing harder than I normally would. Note to self: Look into the possibility of an elliptical trainer to put in the basement, if Bruno's employment lasted longer than just today.

"So when does Horatio get here?" I asked between gulps of air.

"That's the thing," Akra answered. "He should be here already. I'm checking to make sure they didn't come in through the wrong door." That seemed unlikely, as Horatio had been working in this theater for months and must have known the routine. His trainer, whom I assumed was human, probably knew it even better.

"Why is Horatio leaving the show?" I asked.

Akra didn't break stride. "Les fired him," she said. "He's been forgetting his lines."

Uh-huh. "I've read the script," I said gently, respectful of those with mental illness. "Sandy doesn't have any lines."

"He has to bark on cue," Akra said, a slight edge of impatience in her otherwise professional voice. "Horatio has missed his signal four times in the past two weeks."

She opened each dressing-room door as we passed without

regard for anyone who might have been, you know, dressing in there, but there really were no actors present in the theater yet.

"He just forgot when to bark all of a sudden?" I said. Bruno, unworried by the talk of consequences, trotted happily along at my side.

"He's thirteen years old," Akra said. "It happens."

"How's he taking the news?" I asked, just to see how far this could go.

"Horatio is fine with it, but his trainer, Gwen Harper, is not being totally professional about the severance." Akra was about as funny as a Clint Eastwood film festival.

We reached the last door, which Akra opened. Again the room was empty, so she shut the door. I breathed a sigh of actual physical relief, but my respite was brief. Akra was off like a shot again, so Bruno and I had little choice but to keep up her racing pace.

I was just hoping this was a sprint, and not a marathon. My lungs weren't built for this sort of casual stroll.

"Is anybody else in the house?" I asked. Maybe I could find someone to gossip with who was standing still or, better, sitting. Maybe lying down.

"Some technical staff," she said. "A publicist. Probably someone in the box office." It was her warm and personal approach that endeared Akra to all of us. Whoever we were.

We made our way out to the stage, which Bruno crossed like the pro that he was, not caring about all those empty seats in front of him. Akra was headed to the other side of the wings, presumably in pursuit of Gwen Harper and Horatio, whom she no doubt believed were avoiding her on purpose. My guess was they were stuck in Midtown traffic.

But a voice from behind me demanded my attention before we got there. A familiar voice. One that had an angry tone I'd heard only yesterday.

Louise Barclay's voice. I turned toward her even as Akra's mission went on its course at warp speed. Louise was wearing a black suit, very tasteful but not exactly as mournful as you might think, as the skirt ended an inch or so above the knee. It was like she was ready to go speed dating straight from the cemetery.

"So there you are," she said, voice dripping malice. "You and the dog you abducted."

I stopped. So, I was amazed to see, did Akra. I didn't think anything smaller than a Humvee could have interrupted her mission. "Abducted?" she said. It was Akra's job to smooth things out for Les before he got here, and now she was hearing that I'd dognapped Bruno, which was about as bumpy an allegation as could have been dropped.

"I didn't *abduct* Bruno," I said so both women could hear me. Maybe this was good—if Akra had been Trent's classmate, maybe she knew Louise just a little better than she'd been letting on. This would be good information to pass on to Rodriguez. "You asked me to take care of him and bring him to the callback. I did. Then you didn't answer my calls to return him. Then you came to my home and left without him."

She tried to answer, but I cut her off, mostly for Akra's benefit. "I understand you're emotionally wrecked with your husband murdered, but there is no reason to accuse me of something you know didn't happen. Why aren't you at Trent's funeral anyway?"

Then I got what I thought I'd been seeking: I saw Louise and Akra share a look with each other. But it confused me.

Louise's eyes registered confusion, even worry. She appeared to be looking to Akra for guidance.

Akra, however, was looking at Louise with something that very clearly approached hate.

Whatever they were communicating to each other, I clearly wasn't on the same frequency, because I didn't expect that Louise would suddenly turn to me and smile.

"You're right," she said. "I'm emotionally shattered by what happened to Trent. I'm so sorry that I said those things just now."

"How about yesterday in front of the police?" I suggested.

She went on as if I hadn't spoken. "I'm glad you brought Bruno here for rehearsal. And I do have to attend Trent's service in two hours. If I give you a key to my apartment, would you bring him back there after his work is done?" She started fishing around in her black purse.

"I can certainly do that," I said, oozing professionalism. "But will you be back in time to take care of him later?" This was my real concern about my client, not so much what was convenient for Louise.

She handed me the key and then waved her hand in a gesture of indifference. "I can call the dog walker," she said. "Don't worry."

That led to an interesting question. "You mean Taylor Cassidy?" I asked. But I was looking at Akra.

To my sincere disappointment, she showed no reaction at all and continued to try to stare through Louise's skull, as if there were something really interesting behind it if she could only see.

Louise looked up at me—I am a few inches taller than her—and looked slightly startled. "You know Taylor?" she asked.

She seemed to be completely in earnest, no hidden agenda, so I answered, "We've met." Because we had.

"Good. Would you rather call her to walk Bruno tonight?"

I had to think fast. I put my hands in my pants pockets. I didn't want Taylor anywhere near Bruno, especially tonight. After the way she'd acted at my house the night before, I couldn't trust that she wouldn't do exactly what Louise had been accusing me of doing just a couple of minutes earlier.

"Sure," I said, having no intention of calling Taylor Cassidy. "But let's be clear." I wanted to be sure Akra heard this part, so I looked at her. She had put her hand to her earpiece, indicating that she was getting a message from someone else in the theater company. That had seemingly broken her concentration, so she'd given up staring malevolently at Louise and was looking at us dispassionately, which was almost as scary. Then she looked almost alarmed, which must have meant we were in the midst of a nuclear war. I chose to spend my waning moments clarifying my status with Louise. "If I can't get Taylor tonight, I'm going to take Bruno back to my house. He was having such a good time playing with my dogs, and I don't mind while you're dealing with all this. You're okay with that?"

I forced eye contact with Akra, whose face had reverted to impassive, and she nodded. Yes, she understood that she was my witness. "Of course," Louise said. "But do call Taylor first. It's easiest if Bruno is at home."

"I'll do my best," I said. I didn't tell her my best consisted of not trying to find Taylor except as a witness and definitely taking Bruno home with me that night. Why spoil the day of her husband's funeral with such small matters?

"Thank you," Louise said. "You're invaluable, really." She patted my hand. This after she had practically tried to have me arrested less than ten minutes ago, and had actually made that effort formally the day before. With real cops.

I looked over at Akra. "Have Horatio and Gwen Harper arrived?" I was taking a guess that was the message she'd just received.

"As a matter of fact, yes," Akra answered. "And Les is on his way. Let's go." She was back into her manic phase, hitting the left lane of life with intentions of passing everyone else. She turned and headed toward the dressing rooms again, expecting me to follow. So I did, but not before turning to Louise.

"My respects to Trent," I said. "Be strong today."

I left before the level of crap could rise any higher.

Akra led me through the maze of corridors and staircases that make up a theater's backstage. I wasn't especially well acquainted with the Palace, so her lead was welcome. But her pace was still at Grand Prix level, so Bruno and I had to stay alert and moving. Luckily, Bruno was in fine shape.

We won't discuss what kind of shape I was in. Suffice it to say the sound of panting wasn't from the dog.

In a dressing room without a name on the door—which was unusual but not unheard-of—were a woman of about fifty in sweats and sneakers, and a brown dog of about forty pounds, not terribly well groomed, with fuzzy, as opposed to curly, fur. The dog looked friendly enough, and neither he nor Bruno growled when we entered the room.

"Is that the new dog?" the woman said to Akra. "He doesn't look like Horatio."

I decided to step in and see if we could start things off on the right foot. Paw. Whatever. "This is Bruno," I told her. "It's nice to meet the two of you."

"That's it?" the woman—I presumed Gwen—said, again to Akra.

"This is the new Sandy, yes," Akra told her. "His real name is Bruno."

"He doesn't look a thing like Horatio," the woman repeated.

"Les decided he wanted to go in a different direction," Akra explained. She gestured toward me. "And this is Kay, who's Bruno's agent." She turned toward me. "This is Gwen Harper, and Horatio."

"His agent?" The woman sniffed. "Horatio doesn't have an agent. I do this all by myself."

"Different strokes," Akra said, and I wasn't sure it was appropriate. "Now, would the two of you like to get acquainted?" Now she was talking to the dogs. I looked over at the dressing-room mirror to confirm for myself that I was still in the room.

"I thought you were going to take the other dog," Gwen said, seemingly not pleased with the choice Les had made. "Now, that dog looked like Horatio." I'm not usually huge on subtlety, but I was picking up the idea that she wanted the new dog in the role to look like her own. I'm not sure why that was important, but it clearly was high on Gwen's priority list.

"Well, Bruno is very smart and very sweet," Akra told her, kneeling down to give Bruno a nice pat. I considered sneaking out of the dressing room and letting Gwen and Akra finish this scene on their own, since I didn't seem essential to the conversation. But Bruno needed to be here, and I needed to be near Bruno.

"I'm sure once Horatio gets to know him, they'll be the best of friends."

Gwen regarded her with a look of pity and impatience. "It doesn't matter if Horatio likes him," she said slowly. "It matters if *I* like him."

Akra stood up and Bruno's face followed her as she did. Why would someone ever stop petting him? It was a wonderment. "Of course," Akra said. "Well, I'll leave you to it. Les is ten minutes out and I need to get everything ready." Without elaborating on what "everything" might be and before I could ask, Akra was out the door.

That left me, Bruno, and Horatio alone with Gwen Harper. I considered calling out for reinforcements.

She stood from the sofa—old and rumpled, as in most theater dressing rooms—to better look down her nose at Bruno and me. She sized him up as if deciding how much he was worth per pound.

"He's not much," she said finally.

There was no point in engaging on that, so I picked the script pages we'd need out of my purse. "Why don't we let the guys get to know each other before we start work?" I said. And without waiting for her answer, I removed Bruno's lead from his collar, giving him the run of the dressing room. Being Bruno, he just sat there and looked at me, but it was the principle of the thing that mattered.

Gwen looked, sniffed again, and gave Horatio, who had never been on a leash to begin with but had seemed totally disinterested with the whole proceedings, a push on his backside, indicating he should stand up. He did.

He walked over to Bruno, who stood up and did what dogs do by way of acquaintance for a moment. Having satisfied themselves that, yes, that other animal was indeed another dog, each one took a moment to reflect on that information.

Then out of nowhere Bruno began to howl.

He was wailing like I'd never heard him before. It was as if he'd discovered some horrible secret about Horatio and was trying to warn me, everyone in the theater, and most of West Forty-Seventh Street about it before it was too late.

I knelt down next to him and stroked his neck and back to try to get him to calm down. "Easy, Bruno," I crooned. "It's okay. Horatio just wants to be friends, that's all."

For his part, Horatio was doing the "what's-that-crazy-mutt-howling-about" thing, like a little kid who's figured out the weak link in the kindergarten class and has just begun blaming his own misdeeds on the poor sap.

"Horatio is being a gentleman," Gwen suggested. "What is wrong with your dog?" She had an odd smile on her face, one that made me want to punch her even more than I had a moment before.

I had an urge to explain again that Bruno wasn't my dog, but it wasn't going to do him any good to be abandoned by his only ally in the room. "Nothing's wrong with him," I said. "Something about Horatio has gotten him upset. What do you think it could be?" When in doubt, throw the ball into the other person's court.

Gwen shook her head. "It's nothing. There's nothing wrong with *Horatio*. You'd better get that animal out of here."

That was the first thing Gwen had said that I agreed with, so

I reached over to put Bruno's leash back on his collar. His howling had not stopped and he was actually backing up toward the door, always keeping his eyes directly on Horatio. He wasn't aware of me, so he turned his head quickly and sort of snapped at me when I managed to attach the leash. He didn't bite me, exactly, because he pulled back at the last second, but he was clearly very badly shaken.

"He did the very same thing when that man brought him here the other day," Gwen said. "That is a very unstable dog. I can't imagine why they would want to hire him. He should be muzzled."

That was way too much information to process right away. "What man?" I said as I opened the door. Bruno was already bolting out. "What man brought Bruno here before?"

I had to follow the dog out of the room, but as I did, I heard Gwen Harper behind me answering the question. "Whoever that guy was. Brent, or something? The dog wailed like a banshee then too." By then Bruno and I were halfway down the hall with no sign of stopping soon.

But I wanted to call out to Gwen now. She'd met Bruno before? And he was with the man I can only assume was Trent? Why hadn't anyone mentioned this to me before? Just how mad was Gwen that Horatio was getting nudged out of his role in *Annie*?

Mad enough to kill?

CHAPTER ELEVEN

"Yes, Trent brought Bruno here once, after you were here, the night he died." Les McMaster sat on the apron of the stage, looking up at me, his face the very picture of innocence, although puffier than when I'd seen him before. He was, as had become something of a custom with us, explaining why he'd gone behind my back professionally and then neglected to inform me he'd done so. "He felt bad about the way the audition had gone and he wanted to make it up."

"This is even worse than the story you told about how Louise called you up to set up the callback and you didn't tell me," I informed him. Bruno, eager to get to work, was stage left, panting, but there was no one to give him his cue just yet. Gwen and Horatio had left the building. "At least that time you could try to pretend it was an oversight and blame it on Akra."

Les did a "sue me" face. "Look, the guy showed up here an

hour and a half after he'd stormed out. He didn't tell me he was coming; I probably wouldn't have spoken to him if he had. We passed Gwen and Horatio but didn't speak. Is it my responsibility to keep track of your clients for you?"

"Ooh, better. This time it's going to be *my* fault." There was a chair at stage center, so I made use of it. Bruno walked over to me because he was confused, so I petted his head a few times to reassure him that he, among all of us, had surely done nothing wrong. "The best defense is a good offense, isn't it, Les?"

He shrugged. "I have already spent about four more hours on the casting of a dog for a bit part than any other director on Broadway," he said. "I'm tired of justifying every decision I make and every decision everyone around me makes. Kay, does Bruno want the part or not?"

The one thing we could agree upon was that Bruno wanted the part, so I caved in on Louise's behalf, which was the core principle of my job description. My needs were less important than the dog's, and even those of his owner, which didn't seem right. But fifteen percent was fifteen percent.

I decided, in the interest of being Rodriguez's eyes and ears in the production, to try to make up with Les. "I'm sorry Bruno and Horatio didn't get along," I said.

It had been decided that there was no point in the two dogs trying to rehearse together when Bruno had been unable to actually stay in the same room with Horatio without shouting to the clear blue skies the imminent danger to society he clearly believed the Labradoodle to be. Gwen, in something even more than her usual huff, packed up Horatio's things and threatened, momentarily, not to bring him back for the evening performance.

Les had said something about breach of contract and mentioned that there was in fact an understudy if Horatio couldn't go on, whose salary the company would surely expect Gwen to cover if her dog didn't make his entrance on time. Gwen grumbled, but gave in even more completely than I had.

"Horatio has been the terror of the company from the first day he set paws on the stage," Les answered. "It's one of the reasons we fired him."

From Gwen's attitude alone I had gathered that Horatio had been released unwillingly from the part of Sandy. The role in the musical is elastic—that is, each director decides what to do with Sandy pretty much for every production because there isn't that much in the script—but Les had given the dog more to do than most, and had gotten great reviews for it.

"He chased everybody around backstage and actually bit one of the dancers," Les said. "And I'd had to cut back on his work because he wasn't wagging his tail enough. The little old ladies and the kids love it when Sandy wags his tail."

"Did you call me back specifically because you knew about Bruno?" I asked. Bruno raised his head hopefully at the mention of his name. I knew Les was sizing him up and deciding what to teach him first, but so far there was nothing for the dog to do. He wasn't sad, but he was puzzled.

Les looked surprised. "No," he said. "How would I have known about Bruno?" Again, the dog turned to the person speaking his name and got the same result. "We called because Akra said you specialized in animals for plays, and you suggested Bruno to me." His eyes narrowed, wondering if I was crazy. "You do remember that, don't you?"

You have to carefully place your gossip time bomb to get the maximum effect, and I believed I had done so expertly. "Well," I said, "I thought Akra might have recommended Bruno because she and Trent had gone to school together a long time ago."

Les was a wonderful stage director, but he was a lousy actor. He tried to stifle his surprise, but his eyes bulged a little and his eyebrows very nearly hit the ceiling of the theater some thirty feet above our heads. He coughed.

"They did?" he said, his voice trying for calm and managing slightly agitated. "I . . . wasn't aware of that." Score one for my side.

"Yeah, they went to the same Yeshiva in New Rochelle when Trent Barclay was still Moshe Berkowitz and Akra was, actually, still Akra. I figured that was the connection." I stopped and looked away, as if struck by a thought. "You don't think she was involved in what happened to Trent, do you?" Beat, two, three . . .

This time Les reacted as if I'd thrown a bucket of cold water on top of him. He straightened as if he'd been electrocuted and stared at me in amazement. "*Akra?*" he demanded.

Sure enough, her voice came from the wings. "You need me, Les?"

That gave Les the moment he needed to compose himself. "No. Not now, Akra. Do me a favor and go to the office. Check on the house seats for Sarah Jessica, would you?"

Akra's voice, still coming from the dark offstage, sounded a little puzzled. "Um . . . sure. I'll get right on it." I heard her footsteps bustling away.

Les turned back to face me. "You can't possibly think that Akra had something to do with Trent's murder," he said.

"I have no idea," I told him. "I can't begin to imagine what happened. I was just speculating, you know, like playing a game of Clue."

"This is no game." Les seemed personally offended, as if Akra were his daughter, which wasn't chronologically possible. "You can't start throwing people's names around and causing suspicion. Suppose the cops had heard that."

"Sorry." I petted Bruno's smooth head fur some more, then tried to lighten the tone. "Do we want to try something with Bruno now?" I asked Les.

But he didn't seem to want to let go of his thought, no matter how irrelevant it might be. "I mean, you go around accusing people," he said.

"I didn't accuse anyone. I asked you what you thought. What *do* you think? Who do you think killed Trent?" I knew what he'd say, but I was trying to move the conversation away from the area that seemed so distressful to Les.

"You know what I think," he said, an indication that my strategy was beginning to work. "Louise had the motive if she knew Trent was fooling around on her. She lives in his apartment and could have stabbed him in the middle of the night. And besides, I don't like her." Sound reasoning, especially that last part.

I made a show of stroking my chin "in thought." That didn't take immediately, so I moved my lips back and forth as if I'd sucked on something itchy. That did it. Les squinted a little, and he wasn't looking into any of the few lights that were turned on. "What?" he asked.

"It's too typical," I suggested. "It fits the pattern of too many murders in movies and on TV. The jealous wife offs the cheating husband. It's a cliché."

This time Les grinned and snorted a small laugh. "You're basing your argument on the fact that the murder isn't original enough?" he asked.

"Well, how about this: Why did she wait until the middle of the night? You're right. Louise lives in Trent's apartment. She lives with Trent. If she finds out he's having a fling with . . . someone . . . why wait? If it's a crime of passion, why did she put it off until three o'clock in the morning?" *Also, why did she then send Taylor to kidnap her own dog and send me threatening texts for the same purpose?* I didn't mention that to Les because I wasn't sure he didn't kill Trent, and there was a certain necessity to keep the threats to my own safety quiet. Maybe the killer would forget about them if they didn't come up often in conversation. Hey, it was a plan. I didn't say it was a *good* plan.

"Well, why not?" Les answered, engaged in the guessing game now that Akra's connection wasn't being discussed. "Maybe that's when she found out about Trent and the dog walker. Maybe once Bruno was getting the job, he was more valuable than before and she didn't want to have to share him with her husband. Maybe she'd always wanted to put a knife in his back and that was the moment she finally couldn't stop herself any longer." Les had a really interesting view of marriage; I'd looked up his page on the Internet Broadway Database (ibdb.com) and sure enough, he was divorced. Twice.

"Are you going to be paying Bruno *that* much? Because the contract I saw didn't include enough money to kill somebody."

Bruno, bored enough, got up and started to walk around the stage. I took a squishy toy out of my bag, one shaped like a hamburger, and threw it over his head. He happily chased it and then brought it back and lay down in front of me, chewing blissfully away at it.

I'm not an animal agent for nothing, you know.

Les conceded the point, nodding in a knowing fashion. "Okay, you're right. Bruno's not commanding Brad Pitt money just yet. But I still don't see a reason for anybody other than Louise to kill Trent." He stood and started pacing the stage, but I could tell he was figuring on blocking for the scene Bruno would be playing, looking at one side of the stage, which was set for Oliver Warbucks's mansion, then at Bruno, then at the fake door, then at the fake staircase, then at Bruno again. He started to hum "Shut Up and Dance" absently.

"Maybe the dog walker killed him because he wasn't going to leave Louise for her," I suggested. I knew Les could think on two planes at the same time. He'd told me it helped him think about the scene "organically" instead of "intellectually." I figured however the guy directing the show wanted to think was his business as long as I got Bruno's commission.

But Les's voice was less focused when he answered because he was in full director mode now. "How'd the dog walker get into the apartment?" he asked.

"She probably has a key; most of them do. If Trent or Louise was home to let her in, they could walk Bruno themselves."

"No, it was Louise." That settled it for Les; he gestured to Bruno. "Come here, boy."

Bruno wanted to keep chewing on his cloth hamburger. You

could see it. But man, he was a pro. He dropped the toy and walked over to Les as if it had been his idea. "Sit, Bruno," Les said. Bruno sat, probably wondering why he'd gotten up from his chewing just to do that. "Good boy."

"Why not just divorce Trent if she was that mad?" I asked. "Why bother putting a knife in his back? Frankly, I don't think Louise has the upper-body strength to do it." I had no clue about Louise's pectoral power, but I felt like Les was deciding too easily, and I didn't want to see anybody get railroaded. (Not that Les had even spoken to the police as far as I knew. But the whole Akra thing was too big a coincidence, and now I couldn't bring it up or he'd fly off the handle again.)

"What am I, Sherlock Holmes?" Les said absently. He lifted his hand, saw Bruno follow it with his eyes, and smiled. "Sorry. I didn't mean to snap at you." It was the least combative thing he'd said to me in the last five minutes and he was apologizing. "I got some bad news about a job and I'm cranky." He went back to looking down. "Okay, Bruno. Walk to here." Les, hand still in the air, took six steps backward to a pristine-looking sofa that was probably all plywood. He knew exactly where it was on the stage, and didn't have to look to stop in exactly the right spot.

Bruno, following the hand, got up (now no doubt thinking the man was crazy—sit down, stand up, sit down, stand up . . .) and walked over to the spot to which Les had led him. He did not sit down when he got there. "Wow, you're smart," Les told him. Personally, I didn't think Bruno had shown a fraction of his brainpower yet, but if the director wanted to be impressed, I certainly wasn't going to argue. I guessed that bad news about a job was something about the straight play he'd been meeting about. It's rough when directors (or actors, or writers, or anyone in showbiz) tries to break out of the mold and do something different.

Without so much as breaking his gaze with Bruno, Les said to me, "Look. I think Louise killed her husband because he was screwing some other woman. If you want to think something else, go ahead. It's a free country. Why do you care so much?"

Why did I care so much? A man was dead. Shouldn't I care? I'll grant you, he was a man I didn't like much, but that's not really a reason to applaud his murderer. "I care because I knew Trent and somebody killed him," I said. "Isn't that enough?"

"Not for you to be playing Nancy Drew. Get up on the sofa, Bruno." He patted a sofa cushion and Bruno obligingly leapt up onto it. He sat, the very picture of a . . . whatever breed he was . . . and even opened his mouth in a small grin at his precociousness. He knew dogs weren't allowed up on such fancy furniture. If it was real.

But I was still ruminating on Les's suggestion that I was investigating Trent's murder. Was that what I was doing? Wasn't it just collecting information for Detective Rodriguez? Wasn't I more of a spy (of the dirty, rotten variety) than a sleuth?

"I'm not playing Nancy Drew," I said, believing it in my heart of hearts (which is just your heart, when you think about it). "I'm being a hopeless theater gossip, like you."

"The audience is going to love that entrance," Les said, looking at Bruno. "Audacious without being obnoxious." He turned toward me. "Has he ever worked in front of an audience before?"

Probably something he should have asked sooner, but then, it was probably something I should have told him already, so let's call it a draw.

"Not one this big," I said. It wasn't technically a lie; it was more of a dodge. Certainly Bruno had never done Broadway before.

"Well, he's going to get applause and he's going to get laughs," Les said. "He'd better get used to the sounds."

"Maybe we should have him here in the auditorium during a performance," I suggested. "Somewhere he won't be conspicuous, but where he'd be close enough to see and hear the audience. See how he reacts."

"That's an excellent idea," Les said. "Can he make the show tonight?"

While Louise was dealing with Trent's funeral and had asked me to take care of the dog? Yeah, I thought I could manage that, but I'd have to ask Mom and Dad to walk Steve and Eydie. Consuelo was handling the office, so that wouldn't be a problem.

"I don't see why not. Where's a good place for him to stay?" I looked around the theater. "We don't want it to be backstage; that wouldn't be like a real audience experience."

Les broke his concentration with Bruno and took a quick look into the auditorium. "There's a box upstairs that only gets used when we have a total sellout," he said. "Bruno would be in the audience, but not in the orchestra or the balcony. He can be in the room but not cause a distraction."

We agreed that sounded like a good idea and Les snapped his fingers or rubbed a lamp or whatever it is he does and Akra appeared, to be given instructions on how Mr. Bruno would be accommodated at the theater this evening. After that Les walked

Bruno through some simple moves on the stage, shouting out the lines of dialogue that would cue those moves so Bruno could get used to hearing them. After about a half hour, he proclaimed Bruno sufficiently rehearsed for his first day and released us back into what is laughingly referred to as "the real world." Then he muttered something about "trying to save my career" and summoned Akra, who already had six phone messages for him.

I didn't know how much reconnaissance I'd managed for Rodriguez, but as soon as we were back on the street I called the number she had given me and told her about Les's theories, Akra's odd attitude toward Louise, and Gwen Harper's probably meaningless acrimony toward Trent, or as she called him, "Brent."

The detective listened—although I thought it was possible I heard her stifle a yawn—and asked what I thought it all meant. "Isn't that sort of your job?" I asked.

"You're my eyes and ears in the theater. What's your take on what you heard?"

I stuck my hand out to hail a cab. Try doing that sometime in Manhattan on a weekday when you're traveling with what appears to be a walking area rug. This was going to take a while. "I don't think anybody knows anything, but if one of them does, it's Akra," I said finally. Three cabs with their signs lit up passed me in hopes of finding a fare that wouldn't make the cab smell like a dog, or worse.

"I haven't spoken to her yet." Rodriguez sighed. "Les McMaster thought he was such a big deal discussing a man he met once that he took up all my time."

"He met Trent twice," I reminded her. "Trent apparently came to the theater behind my back."

"It's all about you, isn't it?"

I considered ordering a ride from Uber when an actual taxicab slowed to a halt and let Bruno and me into the backseat. I gave the driver the address for Louise's apartment. I figured if Louise was back, we could pay our respects and tell her about Bruno's appointment at the theater tonight. If she wasn't, I now had a key and could both let Bruno relax in his familiar home and maybe snoop around a little for Rodriguez, although her lack of enthusiasm was sort of deflating that idea.

"Akra's still my best bet for knowing something," I said. No sense getting into a war of nerves with Rodriguez. She didn't have any nerves.

"Maybe I'll pay Ms. Akra a call before the show tonight. If you think she's involved in the murder . . ."

"That's not what I said," I warned. "I said I didn't think anyone at the theater knew anything, but she was the closest you'd get."

"Noted. I'll be at the theater by six." She hung up before I could explain that two hours before curtain was absolutely the worst time to disturb a theater company. She'd probably ignore that anyway, because, you know, she was the police and they were just silly actors.

When we got downtown to Louise's apartment, Bruno actually showed some signs of wariness on approaching the building's entrance. His tail went down, although not between his legs, and his ears were not at full height. He'd seen something bad there, all right, and he wasn't happy about it. Dogs have memories, despite the fact that they'll act like you've been gone for weeks when all you did was take out the garbage. They're not great with how much time has passed, but they do remember what happened.

He didn't resist when I led him into the building, which I thought might be a possibility. He got into the elevator after only a second of hesitation, and he did not whimper. Bruno was a brave dog.

I rang the bell a couple of times and knocked on the door, which made Bruno bark. I'm not sure he knew which side of the door we were on, and he was probably used to alerting the humans when he heard that noise. It didn't much matter, as there was no sound in the hallway and Louise did not answer the door. I used the key to let us in.

I let Bruno off his leash. He wasn't as hesitant as he'd been the first time he'd walked into my house, but he also didn't get excited and scamper about the room the way you might expect a dog who hadn't been home for most of two days to do. He walked around, tail back up but not wagging, looked in each room, then took careful note of where I was—in the little office area off the kitchen—and lay down right where he could see me.

Let me say right off that I am a fervent advocate of privacy and do not believe in looking into someone else's private files. But since I believed myself to be a duly deputized agent of the New York Police Department, and having been given a key to the apartment by its owner, I thought it was necessary to see if I could uncover any evidence that would exonerate Louise in Trent's murder.

Hey. I had to look on her computer and I needed a way to justify it. Think what you want; I sleep fine at night.

I didn't know how much time I'd have. In theory, I could stay here enjoying Louise's unintentional hospitality for at least three hours. But I don't like being in someone else's house when they're not there, so I wanted to make this quick. Besides, Louise could also come through the door at any moment and wonder what the hell I was doing looking through her personal files.

The question was: What should I be looking for? I wasn't a trained (or any other kind of) investigator. If there was a file on Louise's hard drive called Stuff About Trent's Murder, that would be helpful, but it was fairly unlikely. I turned the computer on and waited for it to boot up.

While it did, I looked over at Bruno, who had fallen asleep, and wondered what kind of life he'd had here if he was so unimpressed at being back in the place you'd think he'd call home. Trent had told me he and Louise had owned Bruno for six months after adopting him from a shelter, but had only recently decided he'd make a great theater dog. Before that, he'd been a full-time pet. He seemed now like he loved the showbiz life, so maybe his previous time here had not been that exciting. Some dogs need the action.

The screen came to life. I opened the hard drive and started scanning folders. There were files clearly marked for projects from Trent's software business, with names like Bugger Off and Twinker that turned out to be a security program and a fledgling social network based on junk food. I was hoping these were not projects Trent had left unfinished, because they weren't going anyplace now.

There was also a folder for something called Landfill, but I couldn't figure out what it was because the spreadsheet inside was unmarked, just showing potential profit projections and expenditures in the hundreds of thousands of dollars, which I'd doubt Trent could have dreamed of providing.

Aside from that, the folders were pretty standard. There were sample contracts, calendars, invoices, income records, and other by-the-book business files, as well as personal files, including Trent's checkbook, which I did not open. Even when I'm sneaking through someone's hard drive, I have my standards.

But then it became necessary. I noticed that every receipt Trent had received in the past three years, every oil change (for a man who lived in Manhattan?), every pair of socks, every restaurant bill, was scanned and stored in a file marked, oddly, Kittens. I supposed that was Trent trying to be cagey. Or funny.

So I had a good look at all the purchases he'd made, and his incredibly thorough recordkeeping made it possible to pretty much trace the man's life in detail. On October 14, for example, he had purchased a dozen doughnuts (with a debit card), then had lunch at John's Pizza in the Times Square area, then taken a cab to his home, then ordered Thai food from Suit and Thai, which must have seemed witty at the time, and capped off the evening buying three songs (Taylor Swift, Kanye West, and ELO?) from iTunes. That was not an atypical day.

But with all the detailed records and the almost insane attention to chronicling all that was Trent Barclay's financial life, there was not so much as one record showing the date, place, or price paid for Bruno's adoption. There was no license recorded. There was nothing indicating a veterinarian appointment. There were receipts for dog food and supplies, but that was it.

For six months.

That went beyond odd. Bruno's life with Trent and Louise was practically undocumented in his files. For a man who had actually kept receipts from Dunkin Donuts for single iced coffee purchases, it was a huge warning sign. The only problem was, I didn't know what it warned.

Bruno, the object of my consternation, snored a little at my feet. I'd have to think of feeding and walking him before the show tonight, and had no idea where Louise kept the dog food. I had his leash and always carried bags (for the walk) in my pocket, but a quick search of the place was definitely called for pretty soon.

Maybe I should check on Louise's computer first, though, I thought. If Bruno's records were there, it would answer a number of questions.

The thing was, Louise operated off a laptop, I'd noticed the last time I was here. And it was not anywhere in sight at the moment.

I stood up, which sort of woke Bruno. He opened his eyes, raised his head, saw I was still there, and decided nothing alarming was going on so it made the most sense to just go back to sleep. Bruno was a very logical dog.

He didn't stir even as I stepped over him to walk into the kitchen. I had, I'll admit, been avoiding this room, but the crime-scene tape was now gone and I was careful not to look too hard at the floor, where Trent's body had fallen. Now I was on a mission to find Bruno's food, mostly because I had no idea where to look for Louise's laptop. For all I knew, she'd taken it with her to keep up on Twitter during Trent's funeral. Maybe she didn't have a smartphone.

I figured Bruno's food would be in the small closet to the left of the refrigerator. I had no idea if it would be in cans or bags, but the cabinets over the sink and under the sink would probably be devoted to dishware and cleaning supplies. So I opened the closet door and looked inside.

And that's when the apartment door opened and Louise walked in.

"What are you doing here?" she asked, annoyed.

She walked in, followed by two people I hadn't met before. All three were dressed in black: Louise in the somewhat va-va-voom suit she'd had on when I saw her at the theater; the woman behind her, older and smaller, in a black dress and hat; and a man, in his forties, tall, slim, and not looking that mournful, in a black suit with a really blue tie.

Bruno got up, indifferent, and walked over in the hope someone would pet him. Nobody else made a move, so I stroked his head. *I'm your friend, Bruno.*

"I'm looking for food to give Bruno," I told her. "I figured I'd give him a break for an hour or so." I told her that Bruno was expected back at the theater by six, which was probably early. I just wanted to see the reception Rodriguez got from the company when she got there.

The older woman looked me up and down and clearly found me wanting. "Who brings a dog to a shiva?" she asked Louise. She thought Bruno was my dog. Apparently she didn't visit much.

"No, Mama, she's not here for that." Sometimes it's nice to hear how people refer to you when you're not there. I clearly wasn't here now, but this was not one of those times. "She's here to take care of the dog."

The older woman seemed confused. "Whose dog is it?"

"Mine," Louise said.

"You and Moshe have a dog?" She said "dog" like it was "nuclear waste material."

I held out my hand in an attempt to prove I was still in the room. "I'm Kay Powell," I told the woman. "I help negotiate Bruno's contracts."

The woman took my hand, but clearly would have preferred I put on a pair of gloves first. No, mittens. "I'm Moshe's mother," she said. "We just came from my son's funeral."

The tall man, smiling in a way that was both ingratiating and creepy (which is not easy to do), took my hand willingly after the older woman let go, as soon as she possibly could. "Mike Goldberg," he said. "Family friend. Glad to meet you."

"Mike came all the way from New Rochelle," Louise said, her voice vague and unfocused. She was still on sedatives, I'd bet.

"I wish it could be under happier circumstances," I told Mike. That's what you say.

"The food's under the sink," Louise said. "Yellow bag." She made no move to get it, as that was clearly my cue to earn the fifteen percent I had probably already spent from Bruno's commission.

"Thanks," I said, and went to get Bruno his early dinner. I found the bag, poured some of the kibble into the bowl, and put it next to Bruno's water dish, which I fervently hoped had been washed since it had become Trent's nose's final resting place.

Now, one of the things you don't want to say is, "How was the funeral?" First of all, that's a stupid question. Are there good funerals? But it would be odd to say nothing, so my mind was racing in search of the proper sentiment, and I settled on, "How are you holding up, Louise?" That seemed to at least acknowledge the awful turn her life had taken while showing some concern for her own welfare. Often at a funeral the attention is so heavily focused on the person in the room least likely to appreciate it that the survivors, whose futures have just been massively uprooted, are lost in the shuffle. So I thought I'd done fairly well.

Not so Louise. "My husband was just knifed to death," she informed me as I poured some food into her dog's dish. Bruno walked over to eat and gave me a glance as he did, apparently thankful for my effort even if it was the same old kibble. "How do you think I'm holding up?"

"I'm sure it's extremely difficult," I said. You have to remind yourself sometimes that even though the animal is the client, the money comes from the people. It hardly seems fair, but the financial system is fixed in the favor of humans.

Mike sat down on the living-area sofa as if it were his own. He loosened his neon-blue tie and crossed his legs. If there had been a coffee table, he might well have taken off his shoes and rested his feet on it. I was glad there was no room for one. But at least he tried to bail me out of Louise's (you should pardon the expression) doghouse.

"The service was very touching," he said with almost no inflection in his voice at all, as if he were reporting on pig-belly futures. "The rabbi did a very nice job."

"The man didn't know Moshe at all." Trent's mother, who had not even told me her name, said with a sniff. "He was practically reading off cards." She turned toward Louise. "Since when do you have a dog?"

"You know about it, Mama," Louise said. "You've known for months."

"No I didn't," Trent's mother said.

Mike Goldberg smiled sadly and shook his head a little. Apparently Mrs. Berkowitz had some memory issues.

Bruno, unperturbed that his adopted grandmother didn't know him, ate each piece of food separately and looked up with each bite to make sure someone was watching him. A born performer, he clearly felt that everything he did would be of the utmost fascination to the humans in the room. I made sure to maintain eye contact with him whenever he looked up. Nobody else was paying him any attention.

"That rabbi didn't know Moshe," the older woman said again. Apparently she was falling back on her greatest hits.

"Trent wasn't very religious," Louise said to her mother-in-law. "Rabbi Engler didn't really have time to get to know him. He did the best he could."

"It wasn't good enough for Moshe." That settled it.

"We should be expecting people to start showing up soon," Mike told me. "We're sitting shiva here for three days."

We?

I looked over at Louise. "Would it be better for you if I took Bruno home with me until you're not expecting more people?" I asked. "I don't want you to have to worry about him during this difficult time." I was stressing the difficulty just in case Louise thought I was trivializing her burden.

She stared at me. "Why do you keep trying to get Bruno away from me?" she demanded. "You wanted to take him home tonight and now you want to keep him for three days. What's your angle?"

My *angle*? Who was I, Edward G. Robinson? "I have no angle," I protested. "I'm trying to make things easier for you and keep Bruno on his schedule for work. If you prefer I don't, I'll be happy to let you take him to the theater tonight. But I know you're expecting people, it's bound to be very late when it's time to come home, and you've had a long day."

"You're plotting something," Louise said, "and it won't work."

Again, Mike tried to come to my defense. "Lighten up on her, Lou," he said. "She's just trying to help."

Oddly, Louise changed her whole bearing as soon as he spoke. "Of course," she said, her facial muscles pulling into a smile she clearly hadn't planned on her own. "My apologies, Kay. But I prefer you bring Bruno back to the apartment tonight, okay?"

"Sure." Bruno had finished eating, lapped up some water, and was now walking around in an attempt to be noticed and petted. Trent's mother literally turned up her nose at him. Louise didn't actually notice Bruno at all. Mike patted him twice on the head awkwardly like someone who was once bitten by a dog and is pretending he's not afraid. Bruno didn't really react to any of them because he was coming over to me.

I scratched him behind the ears and Bruno sat without being told to do so. "I'll be happy to deliver him home as soon as I can tonight," I said to Louise. I reached over for Bruno's leash, which I'd left on the kitchen counter. "But now I think it's time for him to go out and then over to the theater." Bruno did need a walk, and frankly I wanted out of this apartment as soon as I could find the door.

Mike stood up and extended his hand again, careful not to get it too close to any part of Bruno. "So nice to meet you, Kay," he said. The real pros have all sorts of memory devices to speak back the name of a new acquaintance and make her feel special. It wasn't really working in this case, but that was largely because I was trying to understand the mysterious hold Mike seemed to have over Louise.

Trent's mother did not turn her head or look at Bruno and me as we headed for the door. I was the help, he was the inconvenient pet, and the whole thing was just too hard for her because nobody was watching her suffer properly.

"Try to be quiet when you bring him back," Louise said at the door. I assured her I would and then hightailed it out of that building as fast as I could.

CHAPTER TWELVE

"They're all busy," Det. Alana Rodriguez said. "Everybody's getting ready for the show. But you probably knew that would be the case, didn't you?"

I held Bruno's leash tightly, although he had shown no signs of anxiety since we'd come back to the Palace. I was more anxious about this evening than I'd anticipated, and I couldn't figure out why. All I had to do, after all, was sit with a dog and watch a musical.

"Well, I tried to say something, but you hung up on me," I protested, but even I wasn't buying it. I was trying very hard not to grin at the detective, who was standing in the wings, stage right, watching pieces of scenery moved into place and seeing actors in varying states of undress flitting about in an incongruously casual fashion. Most of them, after all, had been doing this every day for months. There were no opening-night jitters in this crowd and hadn't been for quite a while. "Still, you are the police. Wouldn't they talk to you when you flashed your badge or something?"

One of the dancers, stretching hamstrings, wandered a little bit too close to us, so Rodriguez said, "Ms. Powell, I'm just trying to find out what happened the day before Trent Barclay was murdered. Don't you think you could be a little more cooperative?"

She was covering for me, making sure nobody would find out I was her theater snitch. And she seemed just a little irritated when I stifled a laugh at her attempt.

"These are performers," I told Rodriguez. "They're thinking so hard about themselves now, concentrating on the show and wondering when they'll get a call from their agents telling them they have a shot at a featured role that will get them out of the ensemble, that you could scream confidential information into the rafters and nobody would hear it."

But Rodriguez was not breaking character. I guess cops can be Method too. "This is not my idea of cooperation, Ms. Powell," she said. "Do I have to run you in on a charge of obstruction?" Classy.

I made my face serious again by focusing on my own anxiety. Maybe it was being so close to a show about to start, I thought. The old instincts were kicking in and I was getting butterflies vicariously. I didn't have to go on tonight, but my digestive system didn't know that.

"Okay," I said quietly as the dancer stretched herself away from us. "Sorry to spoil your mood. What can I do tonight? I'm just sitting up in a mezzanine box with Bruno."

"There isn't much," Rodriguez admitted. "I spoke to your Akra, and got the same story you did, just from her mouth. She went to school with Barclay back when he was Berkowitz, hadn't seen him in years until he showed up with the dog the other day." She pointed at Bruno, in case I didn't know which dog she might have meant.

"Do you think that's likely? She just runs into this old school chum and he gets a knife in his back that very night?"

Rodriguez shrugged. "There are coincidences in the world. I can't say I think that's what happened, but until I have evidence to the contrary . . . look, if you think you can stonewall me, I can show you what the NYPD does when it gets serious." From the direction in which her eyes were looking I could tell there was someone from the company behind me, and a little over my head. Someone tall.

Les McMaster said from the very area in which Rodriguez was looking, "Don't be too hard on her, Detective. The woman is here at my invitation." Les, like most showbiz people who have achieved any success, can't conceive of a set of circumstances that are not truly about him.

"I understand, Les," Rodriguez answered. *Les?* "I'm afraid I showed up at an inconvenient time for your cast and crew."

I turned to look at Les; he shrugged. "We're a busy company," he said. "But the morning no one's here, and after the show everyone's exhausted. There's no such thing as a good time to ask us about a knife murder, I'm afraid. Feel free to bother people until twenty minutes before curtain, all right?"

"Sure, Les." Rodriguez had clearly been told—probably by Akra—that the police department gets the rare privilege of addressing the famous director by his first name. I'm sure also that she was sufficiently awed by her good fortune.

Les walked away after giving Bruno a head pat. "So you heard the man," I said. "I'm sorry—you heard *Les*. Go bother his crew. You're not going to find out anything more from me." I said that last part a little more loudly than the rest in case Rodriguez wanted to maintain this bad drama that she was intimidating me into giving up the dark secrets I harbored about Trent's murder.

"If that's the way it's gonna be." Rodriguez was an amateur and had to have the exit line.

I gave a yank on the leash. "Come on, Bruno. Let's go find our comps." I wanted it to sound like I was dissing Rodriguez with the information that Bruno and I weren't paying for our seats. Childish? Of course. This is the theater, darling.

Bruno got up and followed good-naturedly. It didn't hurt that I had some liver treats in my pocket and he knew it. He'd pretty much follow me anywhere anyway, but with all the chaos around us I wanted to make sure he was focused on me and didn't walk into a stray piece of scenery or into an open trapdoor. I hadn't seen this production before; for all I knew Les had set entire scenes in quicksand and needed ways to drop actors through the stage. While singing upbeat songs, of course.

As we headed toward a door with an Exit sign that I knew led to a stairway, we had the great good fortune (I have learned the ways of sarcasm while living in New Jersey) to run into Gwen Harper, who thankfully did not have Horatio with her at the moment. No doubt he was backstage getting his nails done.

"What are you doing here?" she demanded. Always tactful, that Gwen. "Horatio's going on tonight."

"I know," I assured her. "Bruno's just here to get a feel for the place with an audience in it."

"Huh. They didn't do that for Horatio."

Just pretend she's not a shrew. "I guess he just had more stage experience, huh?" I said. See, there are ways to sound like you're being sweet when in fact you're sticking in the knife, and I was certain Gwen would notice it.

"Yeah, but they're still firing him. I've got him locked up in a dressing room so he won't take out his frustration on somebody, you know?" Gwen looked like she wanted to take out her own frustration on somebody, and I was climbing the list rapidly. Time to head upstairs, I thought. But just one thing.

"Did you know Trent Barclay?" I asked Gwen out of the blue. You can get an honest response from people when you catch them off guard.

"Who's that?" she asked. And I believed in her performance.

"Forget it," I said. "Which way is the mezzanine?"

Gwen pursed her lips at my ignorance of the theater. She pointed in the direction I'd already been walking. "*That* way." I'd given her that opportunity to feel put upon and superior at the same time, and I'd done it for free. Never say I'm not a kind person.

I wasn't really familiar with the guts of the theater, but finding our way upstairs to the mezzanine wasn't really difficult at all. There are only so many stairways going up that are situated toward the front of the house, after all, and besides, Akra was leading the way because she just seemed to always show up whenever anyone needed anything. Perhaps Akra was some sort of clairvoyant/empath who could sense what you needed and provide it, all while being my favorite current suspect in a rather grisly murder.

People are such interesting contradictions, don't you think?

"These are the house seats," she said, pointing to two in the "box" on the side of the mezzanine, the seats people always think are for when counts and duchesses show up. They're actually house seats, those given to insignificant types like the playwright, because they usually offer a partial view of the stage and are therefore less marketable than something all the way in the back row of the balcony. "I hope you enjoy the show." Akra in a crime of passion? Wouldn't I have to prove she had a pulse first?

She walked away with another thousand or so things to do, so Bruno and I settled in to our seats. Yes, Bruno took a seat. Why should he have to watch my feet while I saw a professional Broadway musical? Besides, I wanted him as much in the action of the show as possible so I could see how he reacted.

But the curtain wouldn't be raised for another half hour. No actual paying customers had been allowed into the auditorium yet, although they would be any minute now. I settled back in my chair—Bruno simply sat up in his and looked around, tongue hanging out of his mouth. It had occurred to me to bring treats in case he got antsy, but I hadn't thought about a water dish. I looked down toward the stage to see if I could attract someone's attention.

There were a few company members ambling around the stage, warming up and socializing with one another. The curtain would be lowered in a minute or two and they would no longer be visible, but right now I could see down well enough.

Les McMaster was standing in the wings looking like Steve Jobs about to introduce the iPhone. He was in a dark turtleneck and jeans and had his hand up to his chin with the other across his chest, supporting the right elbow. He was the very picture of concentration. Which was weird.

The director of a successful musical hit normally wouldn't even be in the theater on a weeknight seven months into the run. He'd be off directing his next successful musical hit in another theater, one designed specifically to siphon off ticket sales from this one because that's the kind of business the theater is, and if anyone tries to tell you it's a family and a great big support group, I would urge you to suppress your laughter until you are out of their earshot.

Why was Les this active in a show that had been running all this time? Why was he in the wings before an average performance, clearly showing off how hard he was thinking about the show? Because he had to replace a *dog* who was in the show for only a small percentage of the stage time? There had to be something else.

Les had apparently lost his chance to direct a serious straight play, and he was consoling himself by watching his hit musical fire on all cylinders. That was my guess anyway.

But that wasn't my immediate concern; finding a water dish for Bruno was. I could search for Akra, who seemed to handle every situation that came up in the company, but she was no doubt rewriting Act Two while replacing some lightbulbs in the marquee and making sure the bartenders' bow ties were all straight. Which the bartenders themselves probably weren't, but that's a whole other story.

Anyway, it wasn't Akra who caught my eye from the mezzanine; it was Louise Barclay. She was walking down the aisle toward the stage, trailed by Mike Goldberg, still dressed as they had been at her apartment. What the heck were they doing here on the day of Trent's funeral (when they supposedly had guests coming to Louise's apartment), and how had they gotten seats for tonight? More important, why again had I not been told? What was the strange hold that Louise held with this company that she could pretty much do as she pleased and everyone felt it necessary to keep her whims quiet? Or was I projecting?

Bruno looked down at Louise and I heard him whimper a little. That was the first time I'd heard him make that sound except when he was called upon to act, so it took me by surprise. I'd seen Bruno in Louise's presence a number of times and he had never so much as taken notice of her, let alone been worried about her presence. What had he seen in her apartment two nights before?

Louise and Mike ambled their way down to the apron of the stage, where I expected her to try to engage with Les, probably about Bruno's demand to have all the small Milk Bones taken out of the candy dish in the dressing room he wasn't going to have. Instead, Louise beckoned toward the opposite wing, and Akra appeared, clipboard in hand, headset on, to have a quick conversation with Bruno's owner—and the wife of the man she'd known in school so many years before. For someone who hadn't been in touch with Trent, Akra seemed to know his wife fairly well.

I stood up, intending to grab Bruno's leash and try to make it downstairs in time to find a water dish of some sort before the audience was given access to the house. But once I was on my feet, I stopped and stared down into the orchestra pit.

Just inside, talking to the conductor, was Taylor Cassidy. She was dressed in a low-cut top that was drawing a decent amount of attention from the man with the baton, and a pair of capris that she must have been born in because that was the only way they'd made it onto her that tightly. And she didn't even have the decency to look uncomfortable.

As soon as I noticed Taylor, she nodded to the conductor, climbed the steps out of the pit, and walked onto the stage as if she held the lease to the Palace herself, which I thought was just a little cheeky for the replacement mutt's dog walker. But I didn't get to see where she went or who she was talking to because the curtain was lowered at that moment. They were about to let the paying customers in.

What the heck was going on here? Of all the people I'd seen milling about the stage before a routine performance for tourists and suburban families, the only one who had any real business being in the building was Akra, and even her presence was questionable. She was supposed to be Les's assistant, but I couldn't figure out why Les was necessary to tonight's show, so why should he need someone to assist him?

My first thought was to send a text to Rodriguez. But as I was mentally composing the message, I realized that all I'd be telling the detective was how people she could see for herself were in the theater. She probably hadn't met Taylor or Mike before (well, Mike anyway—she'd seemed to know about Taylor when I'd mentioned the name), but she knew Louise, Les, Gwen, and Akra from previous interviews. What would I be alerting her to that she didn't already know?

I could take Bruno down with me to the stage to ask around, but the idea was supposed to be that he get a view of the experience from the auditorium to see his reaction. He couldn't be on the stage, which would be the closest experience to his actual performance, and it was now too close to curtain for me to let him wander about, even on a leash. Especially if Horatio had come out of his dressing room (was he changing his fur?) and would be in Bruno's line of sight.

Hey, I was just Rodriguez's snitch. She was in the building. I could relax and let her annoy people professionally. I sat back and stroked Bruno a few times. And then I remembered I still hadn't found a water dish for him, and his tongue seemed to be getting longer as I watched.

Taking him to stage level was not an option, and taking him to the ladies' room was probably a health-code violation. Besides, I didn't have anything out of which he could drink, so the water there would be fairly useless.

All I needed, I decided, was one of the cups in which they served severely overpriced drinks at the bar. That was on this level and wouldn't be at all a long walk. If I asked the bartender nicely, he might even just put water in it himself.

I looked over at Bruno, who was sitting as quietly as a lightly panting dog could on his theater seat. The ushers hadn't taken their stations yet, so there wasn't anyone scowling at his sitting there and leaving dog hair behind.

"Just stay right here," I said. "I'll be right back, Bruno. I'll bring you some water."

He looked grateful for that, so I got up and climbed up the stairs—that's how these boxes work—to the corridor, making it to the bar in about thirty seconds. The guy behind the bar, who didn't have any customers yet, looked bored.

"Can I get some water in the widest cup you have?" I asked. Nicely.

"Sure," he said. "But they're all the same size."

"Not a problem."

He turned to the task, which wasn't much. "Ice?" he asked.

It would take up too much room, although melting would be good for later. "No, thanks," I said. Then it occurred to me that theater staff see and hear everything. "Did you hear about the guy who got killed night before last?" I asked him.

He turned back toward me holding a cup of water. With ice in it. "What guy?" he asked.

"There's this guy who owns the dog who's going to be the new Sandy in the show," I said. "And he got a knife in his back just two nights ago. The police are trying to figure it out."

The bartender shook his head at what a crazy world this is. "All that because he owns some dog," he said.

Okay, so the bartender didn't have any juicy info. "Yeah," I said. "What can I tell you?"

Real paying patrons started finding their way from the stairwell to the bar, so I nodded my thanks to the young man and walked, gingerly carrying the water cup which he had filled just a little too high to the brim, back toward the box where Bruno and I were seated.

"See?" I said as soon as I got through. I watched the level of water on the cup carefully, not wanting to spill anything on the rug. Wouldn't want anyone to think that was Bruno and not some nice harmless water. Dogs have somewhat unwarranted reputations. "I wasn't gone that long."

The steps going down to our seats were tricky, but I had almost navigated them when my father's voice came back to me. "I wasn't that worried," he said.

It caught me by surprise. I looked up from the water and started to ask, "What are you doing . . ." But I stopped short.

Dad, looking down at my feet, also seemed stunned. "Kay," he said.

We asked the same question in unison.

"Where's Bruno?"

CHAPTER THIRTEEN

"The dog is missing?" Detective Rodriguez wasn't asking so much about the fact as she was questioning the judgment of a woman who would leave a dog alone in a Broadway theater seat. "Nobody saw where he went?"

"I had to go get him some water," I said. Again. "I knew I shouldn't leave him there but he was really thirsty."

"You realize I'm going to have to inform the dog's owner that he is missing, right?" Rodriguez added. "I believe she's here tonight."

We were standing backstage as the performance was about two minutes from beginning. The mikes were getting turned on, so our voices were lowered. The last thing either Rodriguez or I needed was the audience at a family musical finding out that the upcoming dog performer everyone was going to love had left the premises without warning.

"Everybody's here tonight," I told the detective. "I swear, it's like they're having a reunion of everyone who might have killed Trent Barclay. Have you seen them all?"

"Bruno," my father reminded me. He stood to my right and touched my arm gently. "That's what we're talking about right now."

He was right, and I was mortified. How could I have been so stupid? Knowing someone was probably trying to dognap Bruno for some purpose I couldn't begin to imagine, I'd left him sitting unattended in a public place while all the shady characters involved in Trent's murder were in the same building. I should be drummed out of the animal agenting business.

"Please, Detective," I said. "There's got to be something you can do."

She raised an eyebrow. "You want me to put out a BOLO on a dog who's been missing for ten minutes? Be On the Lookout for a big hairy walking leg rest? Look around the theater. He's got to be here somewhere."

"You don't understand," I pleaded. "I think Bruno's been abducted."

Rodriguez closed her eyes tightly as if trying to squeeze out what had just happened. "What?"

"There have been threats. I told you. Where's Taylor Cassidy? She was the one so hot to get Bruno yesterday. I'll bet she took him. Do you know where she is?"

Rodriguez looked at my father. "Has she always been like this?" she asked.

Dad regarded her carefully. "Reasonable?" he said.

Her eyes narrowed. "Why are you here, again?"

"My daughter had comp seats to a hit Broadway musical. Her

mother wanted some alone time, so I showed up here. What's your excuse?"

The detective coughed by way of an answer. "Ms. Cassidy," she said, ignoring Dad and looking at me, "is in a seat in the third row center of the orchestra." She pointed.

Sure enough, Taylor and her cleavage were taking up a prominent seat, which I was willing to bet had also been comped by management. I wondered what connection she'd used to get that.

"Why is she even here?" I said. "Did you ask?"

"She's here as a guest of Akra Levy," Rodriguez said. "Apparently she knew Ms. Levy based on her friendship with the deceased Mr. Barclay."

"And you don't find that suspicious?" Dad wanted to know.

"I find the whole thing suspicious," the detective shot back. "But that doesn't make her a killer and it doesn't make her a dognapper. See? There she is. There's no dog. I'm telling you, he's running around this theater somewhere and you're wasting time talking to me."

The house lights dimmed and the audience settled down. In a few seconds the orchestra would begin playing the overture and then the performance would begin.

I had to get the hell out of here.

"Come on, Dad," I whispered. "We can find him on our own."

Dad nodded and we left through the wings, dodging actors and dancers getting in place. We did our best to be unobtrusive, and finally took an emergency exit (which was thankfully not connected to an alarm) out onto the street.

"We'll swing around to the front of the theater and go back

in through the lobby," I told Dad. "Maybe we can find Bruno upstairs somewhere if he really did run off."

"He didn't, and you know it," my father told me. "There's no point in searching the theater."

And that's when it all came crashing down on my head. The one thing I absolutely had to do was protect my client, poor Bruno, who wouldn't hurt a fly in his angriest moment, and I'd left him to some evil person who wanted him for unknown reasons that I couldn't convince myself would be pleasant. I'd be out of business once word of this got around, and I wouldn't be able to blame the people who fired me or talked about me behind my back.

I sat down, leaning on the wall of the theater. I didn't cry. I wanted to, but I didn't. The more I thought about that friendly, innocent dog being taken away, the more it ate at my insides, but . . .

"It's okay, sweetie," my father said.

And for some reason that set me off. I mean, you always have a short fuse with your parents even after you're sixteen years old, because you know they have to love you no matter how idiotically you treat them. But for Dad to look at me now, knowing what all this meant and how I loved animals, and say that, was just too much.

"It's *not* okay!" I yelled at him. "I had responsibility for Bruno and he got taken. He's probably scared and worried and sad and that's all my fault, don't you understand? This isn't a show, Dad. It's not something you can fix up in a rewrite. I don't know if I'll ever be able to find Bruno again and that's going to bother me for the rest of my life. So don't tell me it's okay. It's *not* okay. Okay?" Strong emotion doesn't bring out my most eloquent side.

Dad squatted down next to me; sitting on the pavement in Manhattan was something he would never do. He spoke gently, just like he did when I used to skin my knee or get upset because I'd gone up on my lines onstage. "It *is* okay, honey. I promise you. Everything is absolutely fine."

Mentally I rolled my eyes. He just wasn't getting this. "Really? Everything's fine?" I asked. "Do you know where Bruno is?"

Dad smiled just a little. "As a matter of fact, I do," he said.

"I don't believe it," I said. And that was only because I really didn't believe it.

"Believe it," Dad said.

We were standing in a parking garage on West Forty-Sixth Street just off Seventh Avenue. Parked in a space thankfully not by one of the concrete pillars that held the building up was my parents' ancient Oldsmobile Toronado, a car so large you could land aircraft on its hood. Sitting in the passenger seat with the window open was my mother. In the backseat were Steve and Eydie.

And Bruno.

"*You* dognapped Bruno," I said incredulously.

"We most certainly did not," Mom protested. "We protected him. We saved him from being dognapped, if anything." She got out of the car and stood next to it, checking on the dogs but then folding her arms and looking up at me with an expression that would be kindly on other women but on my mother was defiant.

"He was with me," I said. "Did you think I was going to abduct Bruno?"

"Of course not, sweetie." My father put his hand on my shoulder and squeezed a little. "But we got a fax in your home office about three hours ago threatening the dog. I figured the best thing to do was get him out of there fast."

"You could have texted me," I said. "You could have called. You just stole him when I was away for one minute." My parents are lovely people, but they tend—okay, *Dad* tends—to act impulsively and worry about the toll it takes on other people . . . later.

"The idea was to convince the person or people threatening Bruno that someone else had taken him," Dad said. "That might force a move that brings them out into the open, and either way, it gets Bruno out of the line of fire."

"How did you . . . how did . . . how?" I was relieved that Bruno was safe, yes, but I was upset and angry and drained and confused and probably a couple of other things I hadn't really isolated and cataloged just yet. So my power of speech was just a teeny bit impaired.

"I waited outside the theater," Mom said. "Dad went up and got Bruno when you were away and brought him down to me. I took him to the car. It's really very simple, dear."

Simple? My parents' best plan was to steal one of my clients and make me think that I'd been responsible for his abduction, and she thought that was simple?

"It's not simple, Mom," I said. I looked into the backseat of the ocean liner my father insisted on driving because it "holds both of us and some trunks, and we're not on top of each other." "It's far from simple."

Bruno, for all his trauma, was lying on the backseat, probably asleep. Steve sat up next to him, watching his pal and occasionally scratching behind his left ear. Eydie, in her usual state of disapproval, lay on the floor behind the console, appalled at her drop in status. Imagine, having to lie on the floor of an Oldsmobile.

"Why didn't you tell me?" I said without looking at Dad. "Why did you let me think something horrible had happened and it was my fault?"

"Aw, Kay." Dad sounded positively mournful. "I didn't want to hurt you, baby. Never. And—you're a terrific performer onstage. You can make an audience laugh and you can make them love you. But let's face it: You're not that great an actress."

Not that I didn't know that already, but on top of everything else that had gone on tonight, the last thing I needed was to be told that I was the third best at the family business in a three-person family. "Dad," I said. I wanted to say more, but nothing came out.

"I needed to convince Detective Rodriguez that Bruno had been taken," Dad went on. He didn't say anything about the words he knew must have hurt me, but his voice conveyed his regret and having had to say them. "If you believed it, you'd sell it to her. And I was going to tell you. I figured when I got to the theater, you'd be there sitting next to Bruno and we'd work it out. When you weren't there, I figured I had an opportunity."

Dad always could improvise.

So I decided I'd let him keep improvising. "So what's the plan?" I asked.

I knew there was no chance he'd say he didn't know. "We go home," he said. "Nobody is looking for Bruno there because you were the one who was distraught about him being missing. We can relax a little and plot our next move."

"Besides, you're tired," Mom piped up. "It's been a really tough couple of days for you. Let's go home and you can put your feet up."

"What do I do about Bruno's rehearsals?" I asked Dad. "He's supposed to start as Sandy a week from Tuesday."

"Tell the director he's still missing," Dad suggested. "He'll understand."

"He *won't* understand," I said. "He's already cranky about losing a straight play he wanted to direct. He'll recast the part and Bruno will lose his chance. My reputation will be destroyed and I'll have to do real-estate closings to make the mortgage payments. I don't know anything about real estate, Dad. I can't tell Les I don't know where Bruno is when I clearly do."

Dad reached into his jacket pocket and presented me with a piece of paper he found there. "Open it."

I unfolded the paper, which showed the fax that had come through to my home machine sending my parents on this bizarre errand. It read: *We know you have the dog. We will be coming for him. Offer no resistance and there will be no trouble.*

That sent a shiver up my spine, all right. But it did something the senders probably didn't want to accomplish—it brought out my vindictive side.

"How do we find these people?" I said, thinking out loud.

Dad actually hesitated, not having thought that element through. But he was lucky because that was the moment my cell phone chose to ring, and the incoming caller was shown to be Louise Barclay.

"What happened to Bruno?" she wailed before I could so much as say hello. "I left you in charge of my dog for how long? And now he's missing!"

It wasn't like I hadn't been playing this very scenario in my head continuously since I'd walked back from the theater bar, but now I knew precisely where Bruno was and that there was absolutely no danger to him whatsoever. Dad was right; I was no Meryl Streep. But I was a good agent, and that meant I knew how to tell the truth in a noncommittal, not necessarily informational way.

"I'm so sorry," I told Louise. "I came back from getting Bruno some water to drink, and he was gone." So far, no variation from the facts at all.

"I don't care if you're *sorry*," my client's owner responded. "I want that dog back, you understand?" I'm used to people being mad at me, but I'm not crazy about it. Louise had gone through an extremely difficult time and was still in the thick of it. I had to overlook the fact that I didn't like her very much to understand exactly how much pressure there was on her. After all, the cops very likely thought she had killed her husband.

"I just don't see what I can do about getting Bruno back to you right now, Louise." Actually, I could see what was possible; I could just have driven Bruno back to his home with Louise and gone off to be his agent, but somehow that didn't seem like the best plan of action just at the moment.

"Did you look through the theater?" Louise wasn't immediately signing on to the idea that Bruno had been abducted. She was operating on the assumption that I, incompetent dog sitter that I was, had simply let him run off. I could use that.

"I didn't find him in the theater," I told Louise. No, I'd found him in my parents' aircraft carrier in a parking garage, but that part wasn't necessary information just at this moment. Maybe it would be tomorrow, after I'd figured out some way to discover who was threatening Bruno and forced Rodriguez, against her will, to arrest them.

"So what are you going to do?" Louise was challenging me.

"I'm going to go home," I said. Because I was. I just couldn't get into the car yet because then she might hear the "missing" dog snoring in the backseat, where I would be stationed. If you ever want to feel like an eleven-year-old again, take a ride in your parents' car with them.

"Home?" Louise was appalled. "You're not going to do anything else about this?"

"I can't think of anything else to do, or I'd be doing it." That was one hundred percent true.

"I'm going to sue you," Louise Barclay told me. "I'm going to take you to court and get you to pay for every dime that dog would have been worth. You'd better get the deed to your house, lady, because you'll be signing it over to me real soon." Then she hung up.

I put the phone away and got into the backseat of the Toronado with the rest of the children. Bruno, startled, looked up, saw it was me, and put his head back down on Steve's leg. Eydie gave up being appalled at everyone's behavior and lay on her side, letting out a long sigh.

"Let's get out of here," I told my parents when they got into the front seats. "It's been a hell of a long day."

CHAPTER FOURTEEN

I did not tell Les McMaster that Bruno was still missing. I didn't tell Les McMaster anything at all, but that was only because Les never called me to ask anything. Les, I learned from Akra, had left the theater ten minutes into the performance the night before without telling her—Akra—where he was going or when he would be back.

"That's just weird," Akra informed me. It was roughly the seventeenth weirdest thing I'd heard in the past three days, so I didn't really react much.

"I was surprised Les was there at all," I answered. "Why was he there for a weeknight performance?"

"He's considering changing some of the blocking," Akra said. "He doesn't like the way 'Hard Knock Life' is playing and he has to replace some of the child actors who are getting too . . .

mature. But the fact that he left without telling *me*—that's weird."
Apparently Akra thought Les's behavior was weird.

I was sitting in my kitchen, having walked Steve and Eydie.
Mom and Dad (well, Dad) had warned me against walking
Bruno just yet because Taylor had been at the house looking for
him the night before he was threatened again by people who
claimed to know where he was all the time. "No sense being reckless," he said. I believe that there is indeed no sense in being
reckless, almost by definition, so I'd let Bruno out in the backyard
with the two other dogs for a while and then walked my own
pets and left Bruno to explore the place on his own.

I'd avoided Sam's coffee shop on the walk, in fact staying away
from the center of Scarborough and heading more in the direction of the woods. It was easier to think, but I still hadn't come
up with much.

Louise had called three more times, which I had ignored. I'd
called Detective Rodriguez, which she had ignored, probably
because she didn't want anyone to know she was associating with
a known dog loser. It was possible I was projecting.

"Well, I can't tell you much," I told Akra now. I was watching
the dogs interact. Eydie had suddenly taken up an if-you-can't-
beat-them-join-them attitude and was playing with the two males,
who seemed a little confused by her abrupt change of mood.
"Les didn't say much of anything to me."

Akra had called out of the blue and I was trying my best to
hustle her off because I didn't want her asking about Bruno. If
she'd heard he was missing, he could lose his gig, which would be
bad for my business. If she expected Bruno at rehearsal that day,

I could get killed taking him there, which would be bad for me all around.

Or Bruno could get abducted, which I was especially anxious to avoid. The tag-team wrestling match that had been going on in my stomach when I'd thought he was missing hadn't completely subsided yet. I couldn't risk going through *that* again.

"I thought maybe he'd asked you about today," Akra suggested. "I haven't heard from him at all and I need to know his schedule. I mean, I know it, but he's always changing it. He usually tells me so I can keep him going, but he's just been, well, gone since the beginning of Act One last night, and that's just . . ."

"Weird," I said. It was a reflex. I was tired. I had not mainlined nearly enough coffee yet this morning.

"I *know*," Akra agreed. "So, did he?"

I knew I was supposed to have kept up with this conversation, but Steve and Bruno were now playing tug-of-war over a knotted chew toy and Eydie was standing between them, looking like a referee. I almost laughed, but that would have been misconstrued by Akra, and I didn't want to be rude.

"Did he what?" I asked.

"Ask you about today," she answered with a slight edge of incredulity at what a complete idiot I had turned out to be.

Oh. That. "No," I answered honestly. If I said no more, maybe the subject of today and rehearsal and Bruno could be avoided.

Bruno let go of his end of the chew toy and Steve recoiled a bit, taken by surprise. I thought Eydie was going to bust out laughing, but she was way too classy a dame to let that happen. She lay down on the floor and contemplated life, womanhood, and a really old piece of rawhide. She decided to do nothing about any of them.

"Nothing?" Akra was surprised, after a moment. She'd probably expected me to say more. "He told me that he was pushing rehearsal because he had an appointment that conflicted."

Better yet. Now I could buy a day for Bruno and me and it wouldn't even be my fault. "I didn't know about that, but it's fine with me," I told Akra.

"Good. So instead of coming at noon, please be here at three, okay?"

Dammit!

My mind raced. I really didn't want to take Bruno out of the house, let alone into Manhattan, today. The threatened danger to him and, by extension, me, was not theoretical—Trent was dead and Taylor had clearly been terrified when she'd shown up here two nights ago. (Of course, last night at the show, she'd seemed anything but terrified, dressed to kill and . . . well, maybe that was a poor choice of words.)

But I couldn't deny Bruno his shot at Broadway stardom and, after all, technically Louise was still calling the shots for him. The fact that she believed Bruno to be missing at this moment didn't really change that; she had definitely wanted him to be in *Annie*. I had to respect the wishes of the woman who legally owned my client. But maybe I could buy myself some more time to iron all this out. Sure, it would take an iron the size of Utah, but nothing is impossible, right?

"Can we make it four?" I asked Akra. "I'd thought Bruno would be done before three, so I made him an appointment for a grooming." Or I would now anyway.

"Les has a dinner at nine," she said. "He's got a photo shoot at seven and a meeting with a producer at six. Four might be pushing it." The big ones never give so much as an inch.

Those who are simply agents to the paws, however, are push-overs. "Three it is," I said. I hung up before she could ask anything else.

"That doesn't leave us much time, Bruno," I said, and he looked up at the mention of his name. He dutifully walked over and sat next to me, as if he were expecting me to explain the whole situation to him. But since I didn't understand it, that seemed like a pointless exercise. "Let's make a plan."

Bruno seemed up to it, so I got a pad and pen—you can't really make a plan on a computer—and sat down at the kitchen table.

"Here's what we need to figure out," I told Bruno. "First, why someone is after you to the point that they might want to take you away from Louise or from me." Luckily, Bruno's knowledge of English was limited, or this idea might have upset him. Instead, he lay down and his lips vibrated as he made a deflating sound. "That's the most important thing right now, and Detective Rodriguez doesn't seem nearly as interested in finding out. She thinks who killed Trent is more important, despite the fact that Trent will still be dead after she finds out. Once we figure out who's after you, on the other hand, you will be much safer." That part was for me, not Bruno, who was watching a little dust tumbleweed roll across the floor. My housekeeping skills could be more developed. I grew up in hotels. Other people clean up in hotels.

"So let's think about this," I went on, after having put the heading BRUNO on the paper in front of me. "Let's face it, pal.

You're a dog." Bruno wagged his tail. Steve looked over, because I'm pretty sure he thinks his name is "Dog." "You're a good dog, yes you are, and you're a smart dog, but I don't really see why this person or these people are so desperate to get their hands on you. Did you see what happened to Trent?" Bruno watched the dust bunny a little more and closed his eyes. "Well, if you can't tell me, you can't snitch to somebody else. So it's not like you're the dog who knew too much, is it?"

I got up. Despite my affection for written lists, I actually think better on my feet, pacing. There's not a ton of pacing room in my kitchen, but I did what I could, careful not to step on any tails. I was waving my pen in my hand as I paced.

"The thing is, I don't think anybody is trying to get hold of you because you're such a brilliant actor." I looked over at Bruno, who did not seem at all insulted. "You are, of course; you're a star, believe me. But there still isn't a great fortune in dog roles in show business. You can trust me on that. Rin Tin Tin ended up in the Actor's Fund Home in Englewood, New Jersey, you know." That last part wasn't true, but it could have been.

"So if they don't want you because of your acting and they don't want you because you saw who killed Trent, why do they want you? That's the question, isn't it?" There had to be some other way in which Bruno was valuable or in some way important that I wasn't seeing. "This is a job for the Internet, I fear."

My laptop was on the kitchen counter, so I retrieved it and booted up at the table. Eydie had decided to follow the sun to another spot nearer the back door, but Steve stayed on the dog pillow, which was his favorite place in the world besides under my bed. Steve would pretty much live under my bed if he could.

So he was considerably more familiar with the dust bunnies than Bruno, and paid them no mind.

I tried running searches on every possible scenario making Bruno an irreplaceable dog. I'd had him long enough to know by now that he could not have been carrying large amounts of drugs in his intestines, the way some cartels transport their wares across borders. And he was not the long-lost pet of a king, prince, or princess as far as I could tell.

Then it occurred to me that Trent Barclay had no record of Bruno's adoption on his hard drive, and how curious that seemed. I hadn't been able to access Louise's computer, but Trent had appeared to be the one who kept all the records, and the ones that indicated how they'd added a member to their family were nowhere to be found. Why would Trent omit or delete those records?

He wouldn't. The man had kept records dating back to the manufacturer of his dental retainer from when he was sixteen. If he had records about Bruno's adoption, they would have been visible on his computer.

That train of thought led to only one station: Trent and Louise had not adopted Bruno the way they'd told me they had. I made a note to call Consuelo and ask her to organize a better system for vetting the owners of our clients before we get them to sign the contracts.

So if the Barclays had in fact not gotten Bruno through conventional pet adoption services, where had they managed to find the big hairy mutt? (And I mean that with the greatest affection.)

There were a number of possibilities. Trent or Louise could have had a friend whose dog gave birth to puppies, and they adopted Bruno. They might have just found him wandering alone on the streets of Manhattan with no identification and taken him in. They might have gotten him from a shelter out of state, or from a pet store (don't buy your pets at stores!).

Any of those methods would have been legal. Any of them was plausible. But the problem was that Trent had told me he and his wife had adopted Bruno through a New York City–based shelter and that they'd "overpaid" for him. And that clearly had not happened. Trent hadn't kept the records.

So I started to form an opinion, and no matter how insane it seemed at the beginning, I had to admit to myself that it fit all the facts as I knew them. From what I could piece together, it seemed that Trent and Louise Barclay had not adopted Bruno at all.

They had stolen him.

CHAPTER FIFTEEN

"Stolen?" Dad asked. "Where are you getting stolen from?"

I'd spent much of the morning on the phone, talking to Rodriguez again, then to some friends I had in pet shelters around the tri-state area. My friend Betty Vassar at a shelter on Long Island had promised to nose around even more, but hadn't called back yet. Nobody had any records of Trent or Louise Barclay adopting a dog, one named Bruno or anything else. Unless they'd flown him in from Utah, it was very unlikely that the Barclays had gotten Bruno through the usual—legal—channels.

Dad had gotten up around eleven, an early morning for him. He had senior-show auditions scheduled beginning at two and was then going to make up the list for callbacks and start getting in touch with the lucky finalists late in the afternoon. But now, in his pajamas and bathrobe (after all, it was only noon), he sat across from me at the kitchen table and frowned.

"Stolen?" he said again.

"It fits what I know," I said. "There are no records of the Barclays adopting Bruno. There are no indications they got him from a friend, and if they'd bought him at one of those hideous puppy mills, for one thing he'd be a lot younger than he is and for another, there would be some sales records. Rodriguez made a few calls and couldn't find any."

Dad kept his voice low because Mom was still sleeping, even if she was two rooms away. "They could have found him. They could have brought him in from another state. A lot of dogs come up from the Carolinas these days; you told me that yourself."

"But Trent didn't keep any records, and he kept records of everything," I countered. "Come on, let's take the dogs outside." Without waiting for an answer, I got up and opened the back door. Bruno, Steve, and Eydie all stood up and walked out, down the stairs to the fenced-in yard, and started sniffing around. It wasn't like they hadn't been here before, but the smells were just too interesting to ignore.

"So there's nothing on his computer," Dad said once we were outside in the sun. He could increase his volume to normal conversational levels now. "You don't know that Louise didn't keep the records, because you haven't asked her."

"What am I supposed to do, call her up and say, 'Hey lady, can you prove you didn't steal your dog?' That's a little on the nose, don't you think?"

"I'm just saying, it sounds to me like you're making a jump," Dad said. He was watching the dogs, who had traversed the perimeter of the yard, making sure there were no threats. I picked up a tennis ball from a small basket I have on the deck and threw it where there were no dogs at the moment. They all ran to chase it. "I'm thinking you need more to go on before you go accusing your employer."

"I'm not accusing anybody of anything," I told him. Usually Dad is more supportive of any nutso idea I have, so his reluctance to hop on the stolen-dog bandwagon was confusing. "I just think it's strange and I'm making some inquiries. If Bruno was stolen, and I think it's likely, I'm going to have to find his real owners and bring him back to them."

"Maybe it's his real owners who are looking for him," Dad suggested. Now, that was more like it. He was starting to see things my way, or at least acknowledge that it was possible.

"And they're using blackmail and threats to find him?" Eydie came up with the ball and started to do a victory lap around the yard. The two males followed her, caught up in the moment.

"They don't know you're not the person who stole their dog," Dad suggested. "They're mad."

"They know enough to send Taylor. What did you make of Taylor, besides her being a bad actress?"

Dad thought. "She wants everybody to see her chest," he noted.

He's not one to make random statements like that, and he's not a lecher. "What does that tell you?" I asked.

"She doesn't think she can get by on anything else. Believes she doesn't have any talent. Insecure." If the stage hadn't called, my father could have been an excellent psychologist. Or a great phony psychic.

"I think we have to find her," I said. Eydie brought the ball over to me, presenting her prize, and I took it from her mouth.

It was considerably less dry than before. Another couple of tosses and it would be unusable. I decided to give them one more round, but to favor Bruno with the direction of my throw. He was the guest, after all.

"Taylor? She was at the show last night, so she clearly hasn't skipped town in terror like she wanted us to believe she would." Dad twitched his mouth, a habit when he's thinking hard. "What *was* she doing at the theater anyway? How does she score house seats in the orchestra?"

"Very good questions. How do you propose we find her?"

"Call her," Dad said simply. "She wanted you to get in touch about Bruno. Tell her he's missing and you're worried. Ask where the supposed shady characters who were threatening her life wanted him dropped off. Get her to meet you there."

"So you believe that Bruno was stolen now?" I said as Bruno, as planned, corralled the ball just a stride ahead of Eydie, who was faster but farther away. She wasn't pleased.

"I never doubted you, sweetie," my father said. "But this is one crazy show you've got yourself involved with."

Taylor answered on the second ring; she'd seen my name in her caller ID. And despite what Dad thought about my acting, I was able to convince her—while staring at Bruno, who was lying in the sun and getting Mom to rub his belly—that I was at my wit's end worrying about the dog's welfare.

"Where did they want you to take him?" I said, voice quivering just enough that it wasn't overacting, but with sufficient force that it would be audible. "Tell me where, and I'll go there to look." I figured it was better to make it Taylor's own idea that she should accompany me. Dad, standing to the side in the living room and taking the occasional glance out the window for auditioners who wouldn't show up for another ninety minutes, scowled a bit. He's not huge on subtlety. It's not that he can't play it; he just chooses to do things more broadly because it pleases the audience faster.

But Taylor was a little slyer than I'd anticipated. "I don't think that's the way to go," she said. "They gave me the address; that would be the first place we'd look."

Fifteen years of ad libbing onstage had given me the ability to think on my feet. "But don't you see," I said, "they won't know that we're working together. They think they sent you here and I refused to help you." Get the adversary to consider herself an ally. Because for all you know, she is.

"Well, they *did* send me there and you *did* refuse to help me," Taylor answered. I felt it was wrong of her to dredge up the past, but I kept my mind on the objective.

I cried.

"I know, and I've been miserable about it," I said. "If we'd worked together then, Bruno wouldn't be in such an awful situation now." Bruno, at the mention of his name, looked up and appeared about to bark. I hit the Mute button on my phone, but he just yawned, rolled over, and let Mom rub his belly again. It was becoming her hobby.

"What's that?" Taylor asked. "Are you on mute?"

I pushed the button again. "I didn't want you to hear me crying," I said. Now, tell me I wouldn't have killed at Second City.

Taylor sighed with a hint of exasperation. "Okay," she said. "I'll give you the address, but you shouldn't go there alone."

Give her just enough line, and then reel her in. "Maybe I can get my mother to come with me," I suggested. Even Mom looked amused at the thought.

"Your mother?" Taylor sounded less amused and more thunderstruck. What kind of a complete idiot was she talking to? "Look. Just get in your car. I'll meet you there in an hour."

Bingo.

The drive to the Lower East Side took forty-seven minutes, according to my portable GPS device. It had felt like it took that long to convince Dad he shouldn't cancel his auditions and come with me "for muscle," but Mom and I had managed. I did call Rodriguez and tell her where I was going and what I was doing. I'm not stupid.

No matter what Rodriguez thought.

"Are you out of your mind?" she asked the Bluetooth device installed on my sun visor. "You've convinced yourself that dog you're looking for was stolen by his owners before they owned him and now you're going to meet the people who want you to bring him back?"

Oh, yeah. "I'm not searching for Bruno anymore," I told the detective. "I know where he is, and he's safe."

There was a long silence, to the point that I wondered if my Bluetooth had run out of battery life or something. But finally, Rodriguez said, "You know where the dog is. Do you have the dog?"

Bruno was not in the car with me; that seemed far too

dangerous a thing to try to pull off. Mom had promised to meet me at the theater with him in time for rehearsal, which was going to be tricky considering that I wanted to wrap this whole thing up before he went out in public again.

"No, I don't have Bruno with me," I told Rodriguez. Well, it was true. "But I'm telling you, I know where he is. What's important right now is finding out who wants him and why."

You could hear Rodriguez's eyebrows furrow. "What exactly does this have to do with the murder I'm investigating?" she asked.

"If I knew that, I wouldn't have to drive to a bagel factory to do some snooping."

Her voice dropped an octave. "A bagel factory?" Rodriguez would have made some lucky comedian a great straight man.

"The address Taylor gave me—the one the supposed dog-nappers gave her—is the headquarters of a bagel bakery that went out of business two months ago," I told her, and gave her the Houston Street (in New York, that's pronounced HOW-ston Street) address. "I just want you to know where I'm headed in case, you know, something happens."

"Like they're out of marble rye?" More proof that Rodriguez would make a terrific straight man—she was no comedian.

"It's abandoned, I told you. Look, I don't know who I'm going to be meeting in fifteen minutes. If I don't call you back in an hour, I'd appreciate it if you could send someone to that address to pick up my body. Is that really too much to ask?"

"Show people." Rodriguez sighed and hung up. I took that for an indication that she'd do as I'd asked. Taking it any other way wasn't going to get me anywhere.

I circled the block five times before someone left a parking space open and I grabbed it. This wasn't really my area of town, so I didn't want to have to wait for a parking attendant to get my car if I needed to make a quick getaway.

Besides, the meters are a lot cheaper.

The Lower East Side is not exactly ritzy, but it isn't a scary part of town. But when you're uncertain about your facts, alone on the street, on the way to meet people who probably threatened your life in a text message, nothing is exactly a safe, comforting walk. Everything hits me in the stomach, so I had butterflies, much like I used to get before a performance.

I didn't see Taylor outside the Mitzvah Bagel Factory, a store-front that had clearly been abandoned for greener pastures—probably in Brooklyn, where the bagels could be considered "artisanal"—a while ago. I doubted my journey from Scarborough had been shorter than hers from another area of Manhattan, so that wasn't really a great sign. I approached carefully, head in a constant state of swivel to search for danger.

You know what would have been really helpful in these circumstances? A dog. Alas, I didn't have one with me.

When I had almost reached the narrow storefront, a figure turned the corner of an alley two doors down to the south. Taylor, dressed—I swear—in a trench coat with the collar turned up and boots almost to her knees, should have been smoking a cigarette and wearing a wide-brimmed fedora, but whomever it was from Central Casting who had dressed her had neglected those details. I never worked a really classy venue, but even a performer of my experience has some disdain for those who embrace the cliché without even considering doing something more imaginative.

It was her wardrobe choice now, I will tell you, that alerted me to the fact that Taylor was full of crap and badly playing a role. It doesn't take Meryl Streep to recognize a lousy actor when you see one.

Oddly, that realization made me relax a little, making me feel that I knew who I couldn't trust at this rendezvous. It would have been worse if I'd gone in thinking Taylor was entirely on my side here; I would have expected her to have my back. Now I knew she would only be trying to find the soft spot in it to slip the knife in if she could get close enough.

"Taylor," I said with the requisite tone of affected urgency and quiet. "I'm over here." Anyone that devoted to the mundane and predictable would expect me to act like I was also in a cheap melodrama. It made the illusion work better. For Taylor. She slunk over to me. I half expected her to puff on a cigarette and stand with one leg up on the base of a streetlamp, but she somehow managed to resist the urge.

"Do you think you were followed?" she asked as soon as I was within stage whispering range.

Followed? From Scarborough, New Jersey, to Houston Street? "No, I'm sure I wasn't," I answered. I would definitely have to be on my toes once we got inside. This was a setup if I'd ever seen one, and I'd seen one. In the movies, to be sure, but I had seen it.

"Good. Come around back. I can get us inside." She turned and walked back toward the alley.

I wasn't crazy about following, and was careful to check the alley for anyone who might be lying in wait, but there was no one. Some of what I saw wasn't exactly pretty, but it wasn't threatening either.

"Do you think Bruno's inside?" I asked Taylor as I followed her through the alley to the back of the building.

"Probably not." That was encouraging; at least she wasn't trying to put that one over on me. "I doubt there's anyone inside at all." Nonsense. A flirt like Taylor didn't get this dressed up unless she was *certain* someone other than me was going to see her. She was the most photogenic liar I had seen in quite a while, and I work in show business.

"Then what do you think we'll find?" I asked.

She turned and looked at me disdainfully. "An empty bagel factory. You were the one who called me with this crazy idea. If they took Bruno here, they're long gone by now." Damn! That was what she'd say if she was on the level. Still, the collar on her trench coat couldn't lie—Taylor was in on the plot somehow.

I reached into my pocket and fingered my cell phone. Dad had insisted I write a text message saying "Emergency," address it to him, and then only hit the Send button if I needed help in a hurry. Since I had no idea what I was about to walk into, it was better to be safe than stupid.

We reached the end of the alley and Taylor turned right, so I followed her. There was a back door to Mitzvah's, and it was closed with a padlock that was hanging loose, inviting the foolish inside. Taylor, apparently, was foolish, so she climbed the two stairs to the padlocked door, removed the lock, and made a show of "quietly" opening the screen door, then the business door, and looking around for danger before she walked inside.

I steadied myself at the back door, looked through the small window in the door to make sure no one was waiting behind it with a blackjack (we seemed to be in a 1940s Warner Bros. crime movie), and pushed the door open. I went into the building.

The "factory" was about the size of a small luncheonette, which it had probably been before Mr. and Mrs. Mitzvah had taken over the place to spread the sweet message of ethnic carbohydrates throughout the land. There were a couple of wooden tables in the center of the room and large ovens behind them. None of the equipment was being manned, of course, nor was the sales counter at the other end of the room. But there was still the smell of flour and sweat in the former bakery.

"How did you get the lock off?" I asked Taylor.

She didn't turn around. "It was like that," she said.

Sure it was. And you just happened to walk around the back to see it. "That was lucky," I answered.

Taylor turned and regarded me with some disdain. "No, it wasn't. Whoever was here waiting for Bruno must have left it that way. Now, shut up and look around."

Okay, so that made sense, but the Lauren Bacall outfit said otherwise. "What are we looking for?" I asked.

"How would I know? This is your idea." Taylor walked into the front room through a pair of swinging doors. That must have been where the retail part of the business had operated.

It was fairly obvious there was no one else in the room; there just weren't many places to hide. So scoping out the possible danger didn't take very long. The mission as I'd described it to Taylor was to search for Bruno, who was supposed to be missing. I knew better, so I spent remarkably little time on that task and tried to discern exactly why this would be the location the killers/aspiring dognappers would choose as a safe haven.

Mitzvah was out of the way, certainly. This section of Houston Street wasn't exactly bustling, even now in the afternoon. And the building was definitely abandoned; there would be little need for anyone to come by and witness . . . what?

"There's nobody in here," I called to Taylor. "How about in there?"

She didn't answer, and that's when I became concerned.

I walked quickly to the swinging doors and pushed one open. The front room had been the retail area; there was a counter and the dust was slightly less thick where a cash register had no doubt once stood. But there was no Taylor. The front door was ajar. It had never occurred to me to check when Taylor had said to come around the back to get in. I went to the front door, looked out and up the street. There was no sign of her.

Confusion is not my best friend; I tend to stop and think when I should act. What would be the motivation, I wondered, to lure me to this building when it was clear I wasn't bringing Bruno (because they thought I didn't know where he was)? What was the point of Taylor making me come in through the back door when the front one was unlocked? It wasn't like there was a huge crowd outside that would have seen me enter, and why would that have been a problem anyway?

And once inside, why would Taylor walk through the back straight through to the front door and bolt?

The clear reason was that whoever had set up this hilarious prank wanted me to be alone in the back room. So the next question had to have something to do with why that would be a desirable goal.

I walked back into the bakery, where the ovens still stood, cold, and looked around again. What would be the advantage for some nefarious people to have me back here, or for that matter anywhere in this building, without Bruno?

There wasn't much to look at back here. The tables, the dust, the floor, the ceiling . . .

The ovens.

Sitting there, the two large industrial ovens, stainless steel with treadmill-like conveyor belts that would take the dough through the very hot interior to bake them, then drop them off the end into baskets left beneath the open doors. There were no baskets now, the doors were not open, and the ovens weren't the least bit warm.

Or were they? I walked over gingerly, expecting the level of heat in the air to increase as I approached, but it didn't. Very quickly and lightly I touched the steel door. It was perfectly cool. Okay, the ovens were definitely turned off.

The only thing left to do was open the door, but that seemed pointless. Still, one must explore every possibility. So I gripped the handle and lifted up.

And there was something in the oven. It was small and square and made of metal. And it was ticking, which seemed strange.

I remembered, in that nanosecond, an article I'd read somewhere. See, the thing about bombs is that unless you're sitting on one, it's not generally the explosion that kills you any more than it's the gunpowder that kills shooting victims. Some devices are packed with nails, metal objects, and other debris that can embed in a body, and others rely simply on the environment around them to propel things into the air that can find their way into you and cause great damage. It was an interesting thing to know.

The smart thing to do would have been to run out the front door right after Taylor, who was clearly protecting herself from the blast she'd known would be coming. If I survived, I would definitely have to look into the possibility of revenge on that little bitch.

Instead, all I had left to do was to dive directly onto the dusty, grimy floor. Uncomfortable? Yes. Humiliating? Yet to be seen— if this didn't help, embarrassment would be the least of my worries. But out of the line of the oven doors, which were made of heavy metal? Definitely. And I'd left the one open.

The explosion, when it came a second later, was actually something of a disappointment. You see movies and TV and bombs always seem to sound like the end of the world. Flames shoot from them. Cars tend to blow up. People walk away without looking back and light a cigarette.

None of that happened here. Instead there was a pop sounding like the opening gun of a 5K race and then some smoke, followed by a little shaking in the room, and yet more dust falling from the ceiling. It hardly seemed worth having hit the floor. I got up and brushed myself off the best I could.

Oddly, the fact that it wasn't much of a blast was little consolation. Someone had tried to *blow me up,* and that's not the kind of thing that sits well with me. I'm just funny that way. Also, I had enough adrenaline flowing through my system to motivate Trent Barclay through a fifty-yard dash even in his present condition.

But it was the kicker to the blast that really got me mad: The payload for this bomb, rather than being metal shavings, nails, or bolts, was made of paper. Strips of paper almost like the ticker tape that Wall Street used to drop on returning heroes during parades through New York's Financial District. A number of these little strips had fallen at my feet as I lay on the floor. Now I bent down to pick one of them up.

On it were clearly printed the words *This was a warning.*

Now I was pissed off.

CHAPTER SIXTEEN

"A bomb?" Det. Alana Rodriguez, as I'd noticed had become her custom, was acting like a threat to my life was less a danger to me than an annoyance to her. She stood in the back room of the bagel bakery looking at the damage done by the explosion and shook her head. "You got someone to plant a bomb in a bagel bakery?"

"What do you mean, 'I got' them to do it?" I asked. I'd brushed off as much of the dust, soot, paper, sweat, and flour that had collected all over me after I'd dialed 911 and alerted the NYPD to the explosion. "You think this was part of my ingenious plan to get you to pay more attention to me?"

"You know what I mean," Rodriguez answered. I probably *did* know what she meant, but getting blown up had made me cranky. "Why exactly would somebody go to all this trouble?"

"I'm guessing they wanted Bruno and thought I was an obstacle," I told her. "Blowing me up would get me out of the way."

Rodriguez looked over at the bomb tech named Hogan who had come with her. He checked over the remains of the explosive in the oven, glanced at her, and shook his head. "Nobody tried to blow you up," she said.

That was news to me. "How do you figure that? They lured me here and planted a bomb in the bagel oven. You think that was a way to get me to date them?"

"They wanted to scare you," Rodriguez said, taking her arms out of their naturally condescending crossed position and picking up some of the threatening confetti that was currently decorating the room. "If they wanted you dead, they wouldn't have bothered to put snarky notes inside the bomb for a dead person to read. And this device wasn't strong enough to do much more than make the windows rattle anyway."

"Tell that to my molars; I think they're still vibrating," I told her. "All I know is that I walked in here following Taylor Cassidy, and when she snuck out the front door, I found a ticking metal object in the oven which blew up two seconds later."

"Ticking?" Rodriguez said, smiling in a wry, annoying manner. "Bombs haven't ticked in decades. Who has a clock running on gears anymore?"

"That's what's interesting," said Hogan, who walked over with some piece of electronics held with tweezers in his left hand. "This device was rigged to tick like an old clock. It actually was programmed with that sound, so anyone who got close enough to it would hear the thing supposedly ticking when in fact it was running completely digitally and without any moving parts inside. It's an awful lot of trouble for a programmer to go through just to make a retro-sounding bomb."

Rodriguez listened to him carefully, glanced at the mangled processors in his tweezers, and blinked once or twice. This was an indication that she was thinking. "It *is* a lot of trouble," she agreed. "Why would someone bother with all that?"

"I just do the tech stuff," Hogan told her. "You're the detective. Detect something." It was nice to see her get the same treatment she was so quick to give out. But it didn't seem to have an effect on her.

"The only explanation is they wanted the bomb to be found," she said. "Which makes sense when you understand that its only purpose"—and here she turned to look directly at me—"was to scare someone, not to do any real damage."

"Fine," I told her. "I get it. They wanted to scare me, and it worked. So how come you're not out looking for Taylor Cassidy? She clearly worked with the people trying to get Bruno, or she is one of them herself. She brought me here and left before the bomb could go off. She must have known it was going to happen and ran as fast as she could. Why isn't she your number-one suspect right now?"

Rodriguez's arms returned to their customary folded position. "What makes you think she's not?" she said. "Do I go around telling you how to get dogs acting jobs?"

Dogs with acting jobs! "What time is it?" I asked.

"Time for you to tell me why you're so sure this is about the dog," Rodriguez answered, which was about par for her usual level of helpfulness. "Why isn't this actually about you?"

I missed the implications of that remark because I was fixated on the time. I took my phone—which miraculously had survived the terrifying blast intact—out of my pocket and looked at it.

The time was 2:28. I still had thirty-two minutes to get to the Palace Theater and take Bruno's leash from my mother in time for his rehearsal.

"I have to get uptown," I told Rodriguez. "My car's parked outside. I have just enough time."

"Enough time to answer my question," the detective countered. "What's your connection to all this?"

I started toward the door. "As soon as you find out, could you let me know?" I asked. "I thought I was just the dog's agent."

She did nothing to stop me from leaving. I wasn't sure how to take that, but I got my car as quickly as possible and made it to the theater with two minutes to spare. Sure enough, there were Mom and Bruno standing outside the stage door. I thanked Mom for the help.

"Did Dad find a genius to headline your show yet?" I asked. I was being sociable. People like it when you show interest in what they're doing and don't think just of yourself. But while Mom was trying to answer, I took the leash from her hand and knocked on the stage door. I couldn't be late for this rehearsal.

Ronnie, the guy who was watching the door that night, took a look at Bruno and let me in despite my not having an official *Annie* theater pass. Les had in fact hired Bruno and Louise had signed the contract, so that part was done, but we hadn't been properly vetted by theater security yet. I was waiting for Bruno's ID card, which I sincerely hoped would be hilarious.

Mom followed in behind me, and Ronnie, clearly seeing she was with me, made no objection. Mom was saying something about the singing ventriloquist Dad had been auditioning, but I was moving too fast to really hear. Okay, so I didn't really care. I thought Mom probably was just as indifferent. She hates ventriloquists.

Les was, naturally, not onstage yet when we arrived, but Akra, who was probably one of seven hundred Akra clones created to be everywhere Les needed to be all at the same time, was standing, ever-present clipboard in hand, in the stage-right wings, holding a hand to her earpiece.

"He'll be here in ten," she told me, or the person speaking in her ear, when we approached. "Can you get Bruno ready?"

Bruno was a dog who was being asked to perform for treats. "Um, sure," I said. I looked down at Bruno for a moment. "Okay. He's ready."

"That's not funny," came a voice from behind me, and I didn't even have to turn around. "And neither was telling me that my dog was missing."

Louise Barclay, who should have had better things to do the day after her husband's funeral than watch her dog jump up on a sofa professionally, was wearing high heels. I could hear the *clack* of each step as she approached.

My mother, to my right, turned, looked at her, and sighed. *Oh. That woman again.*

"I was protecting Bruno from a dognapping ring who had targeted him," I told Louise, who came up on my left with Mike Goldberg right beside her. What was he, her, . . . well, "lapdog" seemed inappropriate. . . . "I couldn't let anyone know where he really was."

I felt Bruno wedge himself in behind my legs and push against me. He wasn't happy to see Louise. I could relate.

"You were crying and screaming," Louise noted. "You were

pretending you didn't know where he was and putting me through hell and all the time you had him at your house."

"I actually *didn't* know where he was when I came downstairs and told Detective Rodriguez Bruno was missing," I told Louise, and by extension Akra.

"That's true," Mom chimed in. "I had taken the dog away when Kay was at the bar." There are times I really wish Mom wouldn't be quite so helpful.

Louise looked like her eyes might spring out of their sockets, something I definitely wanted to avoid if possible. "What?" she croaked.

"Are you saying you left Bruno alone in the theater and went to get a drink?" Mike was doing his best to sound outraged, but he was so used to playing the role of the relaxed, friendly playboy that it came out seeming vaguely amused. If he'd been holding a martini glass his outrage would have played even worse, but his tone would have been perfect. Bruno pushed harder and growled lightly. Maybe it wasn't Louise he was less than thrilled to see.

"I was getting a drink for *Bruno*," I said, and then realized I hadn't actually helped myself. "Water. A drink of water. That's why I was at the bar."

"That's outrageous." Mike again. Sounding like he was asking if anyone wanted to play a rousing game of squash.

Louise, finally showing some sense, ignored him. But that didn't really help me much, since she snatched Bruno's leash out of my hand. "That's it," she said, apparently believing that despite her husband being the one who was dead, the past few days had actually been an organized series of events designed to make *her* life miserable. She turned toward Akra, who was mumbling into her Bluetooth link in a voice too soft for us to hear. "I want this woman removed." Louise pointed at me.

Huh? "I beg your pardon?" I said.

"You heard her," Mike said. Akra simply looked mildly surprised. "You've done nothing but try to get between Louise and her dog since you signed her as a client. You're fired. Go represent a bat or something."

"I didn't sign Louise as a client," I told him. "I signed Bruno." Mike's brow wrinkled, as if I'd said something confusing.

Akra, clearly trying to see if this was a real thing, hesitated. "This is your business," she said finally. "Not the company's. I guess you'll have to leave, Kay."

Well, that wasn't good. "You're actually listening to this?" I stuttered.

"It's not my call who represents the dog," Akra said. "It's the dog's owner, and she says she wants you gone."

"That's so rude," my mother told the gathering. "But I'm afraid we can't abide by your decision."

You tell 'em, Mom! "That's right," I said. "We can't. I'm staying."

"You don't get to make that choice," Mike told me. His face was now cold and unfeeling. "The terms of your contract are very specific." He had read my contract? Who *was* this guy?

"The terms are very clear," Mom said, cool and collected. "And Bruno's contract with *Annie* plainly stipulates that Kay and only Kay will bring him to rehearsals. It is very specific in stating that the dog's owner would not be allowed to do so."

I'd known I'd gotten the showbiz gene from Dad, but now

the lawyer gene was making itself known, and it was coming from my mother. I stood in awe for a moment.

Akra blinked. "That's in his contract?" she asked.

"Oh, yes," I said, finding my voice just when I'd thought it had taken a flight to Caracas. "Les requested it—insisted on it, really—himself."

That got Akra. "Well, if that's what Les asked for, that's what we'll do." Mike, not Louise, opened his mouth to protest, but Akra cut him off. "Les will be here shortly. Let's make sure you're not in the auditorium, please." She looked at Louise, then at Mike. "Please."

Louise looked as if she'd been slapped in the face, which she had been (metaphorically), and Mike threatened myriad lawsuits, but the fact was, they were no longer in the auditorium when Les McMaster ambled in five minutes later. I stared adoringly at my mother.

"You're amazing," I said.

She waved a hand at me to dismiss the thought. "Don't be silly. You'd have thought of it yourself."

I doubted it, but there was no sense in arguing with her. "Thank you," I said, and she didn't protest that.

Les looked over at Bruno and me—he didn't appear to see Mom—and squinted. "I got a call from Detective Rodriguez this morning asking me about Bruno," he said. "She said he was missing." Clearly, Rodriguez had called before I'd spoken to her, and clearly she was more concerned about Bruno than she'd let on the night before. Maybe there was a human being in there after all. "He doesn't look missing."

"He's not missing now," I said. "There was some confusion."

That wasn't just true; it was the Mount Rushmore of understatements.

"Uh-huh." Les, who is a tall man, looked down at me because he could. "Good." He took a step closer and . . . sniffed. "You smell like fireworks."

Mom looked concerned immediately, because that's something she does incredibly well. I hadn't had the time to mention my exciting day at the bagel factory and all the brouhaha about Bruno (would that make it a Bruno-haha?) had kept her from asking how the rendezvous with Taylor had turned out.

I wondered how Rodriguez and the cops were doing in their search for Taylor. Which made me look nervously around the house. She wasn't there, at least not where she could be seen, but I felt Les's eyes (and Mom's, if the truth be told) watching me with a combination of worry and skepticism.

"I, um, spent the day in an abandoned bagel factory," I told Les. Mom knew that part, but I could see she wasn't buying that excuse. "I guess the stale flour and stuff got on me."

"Uh-huh," Les repeated. Then he snapped his fingers and shook his head vigorously, remembering that the world did indeed revolve around him and he needed to rehearse his new canine actor. "Let's get to work, shall we, Bruno?" I let the dog off his leash and he walked directly over to Les and sat down. "Good."

They ran through Bruno's scene for about an hour, with Mom reading some of the female lines to cue the dog and Les reading those for the male actors. Mom, reflexively, added nuance and emotion to her readings but Les didn't seem to notice because he was concentrating on Bruno.

"He's got it down already," he said finally. "I could put him in tonight." I wasn't sure whether he was talking to me or to himself, so I didn't answer. In showbiz, always assume the director is talking to himself unless he addresses you by name. Les turned toward me, then looked at Mom. "You were very good," he said. "Who are you?"

If it had been Dad, he would have reached into his pocket and pulled out headshots, a résumé, and the business card of his agent, whoever that was these days. Mom being Mom, she told him her name and said she was my mother. Which was also true, but wasn't going to get her hired for anything.

"Mom is a professional stage performer and has been since before I was born," I told Les. I might not be her agent but I could certainly talk up my own mother. "She's a real pro."

"Thank you, honey," my mother said.

Les opened his mouth to answer and that's when all the lights in the house went out at once. Stage, house, everything. It was utter darkness.

My first instinct was to drop down to the stage floor and call to Bruno. Nobody was going to dognap him on *my* watch. Again. I heard his collar jingling and then felt his nice warm fur, and I held him close and attached his leash. Then I asked Mom if she was all right.

"I guess so," she answered. "I'm afraid to move; I don't know how far I am from the edge of the stage." Mom *is* a real pro, but she's always been more interested in character than performance and doesn't always take blocking well. She fell off a stage once when we were playing an unfamiliar hotel and almost broke her leg. Now she's a tad skittish.

"Don't move," I said. "You're still about twenty feet from the edge, but you're better off staying where you are."

I felt something pull at my hands, one holding the leash and the other with my fingers wrapped around Bruno's collar. I couldn't tell if someone was trying to help me or grab Bruno so I held on tighter and said, "Hey!" It was the best I could do under the circumstances; I don't have a go-to response for that situation.

The fingers pulling at me retreated. At least I thought they were fingers. They could have been chopsticks or unsharpened pencils for all I knew. I yelled, "Who is that?" and got no answer. It sounded like footsteps were running from me. But Bruno was still right where he should be. That was what counted. "Coward!" I hollered. No response.

"Akra!" Les's first impulse when anything unexpected happened was to call out to his assistant so that he could blame it on her and she could fix it. It's a system.

But this time Akra didn't answer.

"Akra!" he tried again and got the same response. "Where the hell is Akra?"

"I don't know," I admitted. "She usually just appears even before you call for her. What do you think happened?" Bruno was panting a little bit, but I held his leash tight to make sure he wasn't going anywhere.

Then the lights came back on.

Even though I could feel him the whole time, I checked first to see if Bruno was safe. He licked my hand and seemed completely unperturbed by the experience. Mom, too, was just fine, if a little startled by the whole thing. She looked at me and said, "Thunderstorms so early in the year?"

Les, however, was not quite so unshaken. His head swiveled back and forth as if he were watching the quickest tennis match in history and his mouth dropped open. "AKRA!" he shouted. "Akra, where are you?"

"She must be checking out the cause of the power outage," I said. Why was he so worried?

But Les kept shaking his head to the point I was worried about his neck muscles. "No. She's never not there when I call for her. *Never.* If I call her up at four in the morning, she answers on the first ring." I made a mental note not to ever apply for the job of Les's personal assistant.

He walked from center stage to the stage-left wings and shouted Akra's name three more times. With each yell, he seemed a little more frantic. I would have called for someone else just to quiet him down, but I'd never seen anyone attend to Les other than Akra.

"She's gone," he said finally. He sat down heavily on the sofa that Bruno had been practicing on. Les dropped his head into his hands and actually vibrated a little. "I don't know what to do. She's gone."

How do you tell a major talent—one who could help your career quite a bit—that he's overreacting to the point of insanity? *Jeez, Les, maybe you should go decaf* seemed a little callous and probably ineffective. But watching the man disintegrate before my eyes wasn't really an option.

Luckily my mother, having lived through a teenage daughter, knew how to handle excessive drama. Being married to a stage performer and being one herself probably didn't hurt either. She walked over and put a warm hand on Les's shoulder. "It's all right," Mom said. "I'm sure Akra will be right back."

Les looked up and I swear there were tears on his cheeks. "You think so?" he whimpered.

Mom didn't get the chance to answer, because Les's phone sounded the title song to *Oklahoma!* as a ringtone. He pulled the phone out of his pocket and looked at it, then exhaled . . . well, theatrically, and pushed a button. "Akra is texting." But when he pushed the button, all the tension came back into his face and his neck muscles tightened. Les looked ten years older.

"What?" I asked.

He didn't seem capable of speech; he just extended his hand with the phone in it, so I took the phone from him and looked at it. Sure enough, there was a text message on the screen.

It read *We have your assistant. Bring the dog.*

CHAPTER SEVENTEEN

"I should just put a cot in the back here and move right in." Detective Rodriguez was her usual disgruntled self. I don't think Rodriguez had been gruntled in years. She was standing—never let the witnesses see you sit—on the stage at the Palace, looking at a distraught Les McMaster, a completely passive Bruno, a somewhat nonplussed Mom, and whatever I was, sitting on the scenery for Oliver Warbucks's mansion. If she'd said, *I suppose you're all wondering why I asked you here tonight,* it would have seemed entirely appropriate.

"We can't help it if things keep happening around here," I piped up. "Somebody turned off the lights and took Akra away." Les choked a little behind me. "None of us did it; it was too dark. So don't blame us."

Mom looked a little sharply at me. She doesn't approve of impolite talk, especially when directed at one of New York's finest, who in my opinion hadn't been as fine as she could have been since this affair began. So I ignored the admonishment in my mother's eyes and looked Rodriguez directly in the eye.

"I don't blame you," the detective said without any inflection. "Not yet anyway."

I'd already been blown up and threatened today and someone had tried to take my client away. They probably would have succeeded if they'd had more time and he hadn't been on the leash. So I wasn't in a mood to be docile.

"What is that supposed to mean?" I demanded.

"Akra," Les murmured from the settee. "Akra."

"The text is all you have?" Rodriguez said, completely ignoring my question. "They have the assistant, bring the dog?" She'd already seen and confiscated Les's phone, so she knew that part of the incident for sure.

"That's it," I said. "They don't even say where to bring him. Or which dog, for that matter. What if they actually want Horatio?" Gwen Harper was nowhere in the vicinity; a shame, as it would have been a real treat to see her react to that one.

"I don't think there's much question about which dog they want," Rodriguez answered, as if my suggestion had been serious. "They've already tried to get him from you twice before."

"Have you found Taylor Cassidy?" I asked. "I'll bet she knows all about this." Taylor was my current prime suspect. In two minutes, I'd probably have a different one. I was discovering that I am fickle, suspect-wise.

"We have not been able to locate Ms. Cassidy yet," Rodriguez said, not making eye contact. "She is not at her home or her parents' home and she is not answering her cell phone."

"What about work?" I asked. "She can't make a living walking dogs. What does she do for a living?"

"Apparently her hours are flexible," Rodriguez said. Her lips had gotten thinner. There was something she wasn't saying, but just pestering her wouldn't do any good, I'd learned. Hey, I wasn't trying to solve Trent's murder anyway; that was her job. I was just here watching the director of the show my client was about to begin appearing in have a nervous breakdown. "She appears to be an entrepreneur." *Like Trent.*

Les was breathing heavily, almost to the point of hyperventilating, and had his head between his knees. He was rocking back and forth. I had to wonder exactly what he'd done in his life before he'd met Akra, or whether she had created him completely out of whole cloth for her own amusement.

"What . . . are we going . . . to do about Akra?" he managed between gasps of oxygen. Again, it was a good question.

"We'll wait until there are further instructions about where they want us to bring the dog," Rodriguez said. "Then we'll set up a drop."

I looked up sharply. "A *drop*? You actually want me to bring Bruno to some crazy dog wackos and just leave him there? I'm sorry, Detective, but that's not going to happen. My client doesn't go anywhere he could be in danger." It made me feel so virtuous to say that, until I realized that if Akra was indeed being held, I was doing her no favors with my high-minded words.

"Akra," Les moaned, in case any of us hadn't gotten the point yet.

"I'm not expecting you to do anything of the sort," Rodriguez told me. "I'm saying we'll set up the meeting, make the perps *think* that's what's going to happen, and get them along with Ms. Levy, clean and safe."

That didn't sound the least bit clean or a tiny morsel of safe, but I didn't have a better idea and besides, that was when Les's phone played Rodgers and Hammerstein again. He pulled it from Rodriguez to his face quicker than Wyatt Earp going for his six-gun. "I have a place and time," he croaked after a moment. He handed the phone to Rodriguez.

She read the message and nodded. "Okay," she said, but her jaw was already beginning to clench. "We don't have much time to set up. Let's get going." She took a couple of steps toward stage right and stopped when no one followed her. "Well?"

"Well, what?" I said. "We don't know where you're going or what you want. And I repeat, I'm not taking Bruno anywhere he could be threatened. So what is it you're saying, Detective?"

She was already talking into a cell phone she'd produced from a jacket pocket. "I need snipers and a team at GCT in twenty," she said to the anonymous person on the other end. "So in other words, I need it ten minutes ago. Clear?" She put the phone back in her pocket and looked at Les, then at Mom, then at Bruno, then at me. "We need you to take Bruno to Grand Central Terminal right now," she said. "I promise you he won't be in any danger at any time and you might very well be helping to catch Trent Barclay's murderer and save Ms. Levy's life. Is that good enough for you?"

It wasn't, but what was I going to do? I looked, as I often do, to my mother for an idea. It's what I'd do when Dad had some cockamamie sketch worked out and he'd written a part I knew I couldn't play. Mom would find a way to keep it funny without forcing me to do something uncomfortable, like pretend to be five when I was sixteen and desperate to impress this one busboy who worked weekends.

"Mom?" I said.

"It's showtime," she answered, and stood up, straightened her skirt. She held her head high and led me—and by extension Bruno—toward the wings.

"Akra," Les whispered.

Grand Central Terminal (it's not officially called Grand Central Station, except by everybody) is one of the wonders of New York City. If you ever visit, by all means come and take it in. The architecture is staggering, the ceiling with the painted sky showing the constellations of the zodiac astonishing, and the beauty not at all diminished by time. So definitely put it on your list of places to see.

On this day, however, it was striking me as the least defensible structure on planet Earth, and that was not making me feel better. The fact that it had taken fifteen of the twenty minutes we'd been given just to get to the entrance was not boosting my confidence in the least.

"What's the plan?" I asked Rodriguez. I was holding Bruno's leash so tightly my hand would be cramped all day tomorrow. "How do we find these people and get you to catch them?" Because I'd looked around the crowded, enormous station and seen nothing that convinced me the NYPD's finest, snipers or no, could pick out one particular person in this teeming mass and so much as ask for a driver's license.

"We're not going to be in the main concourse," she said. "We're doing this at the Apple Store on the balcony."

"The Apple Store?" I parroted. "Does the Apple Store allow dogs?" Many welcome dogs, but I wasn't sure about the one in Grand Central.

"It doesn't matter," Rodriguez answered. "We're not going inside. The supposed exchange takes place on the stairway outside the store. The idea is you stand there with Bruno on the leash. Someone comes by with Ms. Levy and once you hand them the leash, they release her."

I didn't stop walking but I slowed down considerably. I didn't care if we were late for this rendezvous. "You realize I'm not doing that, right?" I said to Rodriguez.

She nodded. "I told you. We're going to grab the person with Levy before you can make the switch. And we have snipers at various vantage points around the station. Bruno isn't going anywhere with anybody."

"Snipers?" I said. It seemed I was repeating something Rodriguez said after every time she spoke. It's a hobby. "You weren't kidding about the snipers?"

"Do I ever kid?"

"I thought maybe you just had a really dry sense of humor."

Now I wished Rodriguez had listened to me when I'd offered to wear a wire. Or at least that she'd given me a Bluetooth device so she could talk me through this. But she'd just said there wasn't time and dismissed the whole thing.

We walked upstairs on the Lexington Avenue side toward the terminal balcony and started toward the Apple Store. I wasn't feeling any better about bringing Bruno into this situation, but

I didn't see a way to back out now. And if Les didn't get Akra back soon, we might find a small pool of him back on the stage where we'd left him. That wouldn't be pleasant at all.

"I'm holding Bruno's leash," I told Rodriguez. "There's no chance at all that I'll hand it over to anybody."

She didn't move a facial muscle. "Fine with me," she said. "I'm going to walk away now. Don't follow me. Just wait until you see Levy, walk toward her, and don't get too close to whoever is with her. We need a clear shot."

"Yeah, because that won't cause any commotion at all in the middle of Grand Central," I said, but Rodriguez was already gone. I didn't even see which direction she'd taken away from me. If the cop thing didn't work out for her, she had a real future as a vanishing act. I could probably get her bookings if I represented humans.

"Don't worry, Bruno," I said as we approached the land of Mac. "I'm not letting you go." Bruno trotted along beside me, unaware of the serious drama in which he was playing a leading role. I reached down and patted him on the back. Then we started walking again.

We took a position directly across from the Apple Store, really on a landing of the stairs below the balcony. The store took up the whole balcony and, as usual, it was packed. People were checking out computers and gadgets as if a woman's life and (more significantly to me) a dog's weren't in jeopardy. I leaned on the railing and watched all the retail traffic go by, just casually standing there with "my" dog, but my heart was pounding and my stomach was not pleased with me.

My mother, who had insisted on coming along, was stationed

at a lower landing. I looked down to note her position. She waved at me. Mom is not what you'd call a natural when it comes to police work. I turned back and faced the traffic from Tech Heaven once again.

I knew I would recognize Akra when she came by, but I wondered how I'd know which person was escorting her. If I'd never met the particular dognapper (I guessed now kidnapper would also be true), would s/he be standing close enough to Akra, maybe holding a weapon on her, for me to know? Wouldn't they want to be more discreet than that?

Despite the fiends' insistence that we show up at an exact time, there was no movement aside from the throngs of Steve Jobs acolytes coming up and down the marble steps. After ten minutes had gone by I began to wonder if we'd come to the right Grand Central Station.

Sorry. Grand Central Terminal. Although I wasn't crazy about the sound of that last word.

But then, coming down from the Apple Store with a very severe expression on her face and no headset, which was somehow unnerving, was Akra. She was walking down the steps slowly, in a way I'd never seen her move before, and she looked extremely tense. Normally she just looked extreme, like someone who would never allow anything the least bit inconvenient to happen to Les McMaster, ever. She did keep looking over her left shoulder.

Behind her on that side, one step behind her the whole way, was Louise Barclay.

I had not expected that. Louise trying to abduct her own dog? What sense did that make? She was Bruno's legal owner—or at least she acted like she was; I was still operating under the assumption that Trent had somehow stolen the dog but I had not a single shred of proof. Why would she be involved in this nutty scheme at all?

But there she was, and there was Akra, and here were Bruno and me. There didn't appear to be anything in Louise's hand (like a gun she'd be using to hold Akra). I didn't approach them, but I stood up from my leaning position and waited for them to reach me.

Before I could say anything, Louise got close enough for me to hear in the din. "They've been arrested," she said. "There were three of them, two men and Taylor. The cops cornered them in the ladies' room. It's all over."

I looked up at Akra. "Are you okay? How did they get you?"

Akra shook her head. "I don't know. When the lights went out, suddenly there was duct tape on my mouth and someone was holding my hands behind me. They put a bag over my head and the next thing I knew, I was in the back of a car." She shivered a little.

Louise looked at me and held out her hand. "Let me have Bruno," she said.

What? I'd grasped the leash so tightly in anticipation of someone trying to wrest it from me that I probably had permanent marks on my fingers. "Bruno?" That was the best I could do.

"Yes," Louise answered, looking a little puzzled. "My dog."

Oh, right. Yeah. Louise was Bruno's owner. I loosened my death grip on the leash. But then something hit me. "How did you get here?" I asked Louise. "The last I saw of you was in the theater when you wanted me to go away and I had to invoke Bruno's contract." My head was a little woozy. Things were happening too fast. And, you know, I had been blown up earlier that day.

Louise sniffed at the memory. "I know. That was Mike's doing. He was upset because he thought you got Bruno kidnapped last night."

"What is the deal with Mike?" I asked. I get very direct when I'm wondering who's going to abduct my client and try to kill me next. "What's his connection? He told me he was a family friend, but nobody's really a family friend."

Louise's mouth twitched a little. "Mike was a friend of Trent's in school. They were thick as thieves for a while, Trent told me, and then they had a falling out over a girl or something and Mike didn't get in touch for almost fifteen years. But once he did, he and Trent were right back to being bros. In fact, it was Mike who found Bruno when we wanted to adopt a dog."

Wow—an actual piece of information! I barely knew how to handle it. "How?" I said, casually as if we were at a diner discussing the latest hit musical over coffee. In my head, I was taking copious notes to try and find clues to Trent's murder and all this fuss over Bruno, who was a nice dog but didn't seem worth killing people over. Sorry, Bruno. I hope you're not reading this.

"I don't know. He deals in investments for a regional bank in Connecticut, and somehow he smoked out a kennel that had the right kind of dog, so he called Trent and we had Bruno five days later." She extended her hand for the leash again.

Akra, apparently miffed that her ordeal was no longer the main attraction at this coffee klatch, tapped her foot a little on the marble step. "Are the cops here?" she said. "Did they tell you not to call the cops? I hope you didn't. I could have been killed."

Which brought me back to my main point, sure to annoy Akra since it wasn't about her. I looked back at Louise. "Wait. You didn't tell me how you got involved in getting Akra back. Why are you here?"

"I got a text saying that she'd been taken and that she'd be here," Louise said. "They wanted Bruno, but I couldn't find you at the theater so I got in a cab."

"I was being held in the ladies' room on the main concourse," Akra said, punching the word "held" a little too hard. It's a common amateur mistake when you think the audience isn't getting the point. Audiences are smarter than beginning actors think they are. "Somehow Louise found her way over there, and whoever was holding me told her she should get Bruno for them."

"Whoever it was?" I asked. "Couldn't you see them?"

"I had a black bag over my head," Akra answered, making me wonder how they'd managed to sneak her into Grand Central that way. On the other hand, I've seen people walk through the streets naked and nobody blinked an eye except the tourists. "I heard what was going on, but I couldn't see."

"It was Taylor," Louise told me. "The other two were men, so they couldn't come into the ladies' room. But when I texted back and said I didn't have Bruno but I could get him, they told me to meet them there. They must have been using a throwaway phone, because I already have Taylor in my contacts and it wasn't her number."

You have to love modern criminals. Kidnapping a woman in order to get a dog, putting a dark bag over her head, and forcing her into Grand Central Terminal was okay, but the men couldn't possibly breach the sanctity of a women's public bathroom in a train station.

"Why was Taylor in on this?" I wondered aloud.

"I'm guessing for the money, or the two men have something on her," Louise said. "She seemed nervous, but she was desperate to get Bruno."

"Why? I mean, I love Bruno but what's so special about him? Why are people willing to kill for him?"

"I'm sure I don't know," Louise answered, her tone frosty and formal all of a sudden. "Now, please, just give me my dog so I can go home. I'm expecting people for shiva."

I didn't want to give her the leash. I still had suspicions about how she'd come to own Bruno, although now they were more focused on Mike Goldberg. But the fact was, as far as I knew, Louise was Bruno's legal owner, I was simply the agent who had signed on to get him work, and she was perfectly entitled to take her dog home.

"Of course," I said, and handed her the leash.

Louise took it from me and gripped it the wrong way, like she'd never walked a dog before and couldn't understand how this odd contraption worked. It was not a pistol-grip lead that could conceivably be confusing; it was a straight nylon leash. But she held it like she thought it might bite her. Her voice, on the other hand, tried its very best to sound casual but came out taut and brittle.

"Come on, Bruno," she said. Bruno lay there unmoving for a moment. But he seemed to shrug, accepting the situation, and stood up, walking in the direction in which Louise led him, toward the stairs back down toward the concourse.

Akra looked at me as we watched them walk away. "Are you crying?" she asked.

"No."

"I'm going home now," she said, and headed down the stairs as well.

I didn't. I don't know why. I just stood there, wondering if I'd have been justified at all in not giving control of Bruno back to the woman who, at least as far as I knew, was his legal guardian. I was not crying; get that out of your mind. I'm a professional and Bruno was a client. I wondered if he was still a client. Louise blew hot and cold on the subject, it seemed.

I decided to text my mother because I felt like having her around and I knew she was in the building. I got the phone out of my pocket but before I could even pull up Mom's number (I couldn't see her anymore from my vantage point, meaning she must have moved out of the supposed line of fire), Rodriguez appeared at my left, looking strangely on edge.

"They just walked away," she said. "You let them just walk away."

What was she talking about? "I figured there wasn't any danger," I said. "You arrested Taylor and the two guys in the ladies' room, so I gave Louise back her dog and Akra went home. She must be a wreck."

Rodriguez's eyes widened, then narrowed. I wasn't watching closely enough but I was willing to bet her pupils were dilating. "Arrested who?" she croaked out.

Mom came walking up the stairs with two iced coffees and handed me one. The woman is a saint.

"Taylor Cassidy and whoever she was working with," I told

Rodriguez, reminding her of whom she had in a squad car heading to the precinct. "Louise and Akra said you found them in the concourse ladies' room and arrested the three of them before anything could happen."

"We didn't arrest anybody," Rodriguez told me when she could find speech in her larynx again. "I don't know anything about a women's restroom. I just saw you hand over the dog everybody seems to be looking for and let two of our suspects walk away."

I took a long sip of iced coffee. There was too much sweetener in it, but the caffeine was real. "I told you I should have had an earpiece," I told Rodriguez.

CHAPTER EIGHTEEN

"Have some quesadilla to start," Consuelo said.

She was carrying a platter of them, enough for the 101st Airborne Division in my estimation, and placing it on her dining table in a space that was cramped even with only five people present. And I must say, the quesadillas looked delicious.

Consuelo has made it a habit of inviting me to dinner at her home once a month since I hired her. She says it makes her feel like she's more than an employee, which she is, and I think it's also part of her plot to become a full agent, although I'm doing nothing to stand in her way. Consuelo thinks she's cagey when in fact she's just really good at some things. And cooking is one of them.

When Mom and Dad are in town, they are also invited to dinner and so here they were, having left Steve and Eydie back in Scarborough, freshly walked, watered, and fed. No doubt they were wondering where their pal Bruno had gone, and I couldn't blame them. I was wondering that myself.

"I'm not sure I'll be able to eat much," I said. "I can't believe how stupid I was."

"To give Bruno back to his rightful owner?" Dad interjected. "What choice did you have?"

Diego, Consuelo's twenty-two-year-old son, looked puzzled. "I thought you said you weren't sure this woman really owned Bruno legally. So could you have kept him away from her if you'd realized the drop was shady?" Diego, who prefers to be called "Dee," had just graduated from CCNY, the City College of New York, and was considering his options, which meant he hadn't gotten a job yet. He wanted to go to veterinary school, but had not been able to find one that would admit him (it is incredibly difficult to get into vet school, more so than medical school) and was now considering law school, but had not yet figured out how that would be funded. Having gone to law school myself, I have often suggested that he look into the possibility of owning a Carvel franchise.

"I don't know," I said truthfully. "Detective Rodriguez wasn't clear about that."

The fact was, Rodriguez hadn't been clear about a lot of things. Confronted with the tale I'd told her about Akra being held against her will, Louise just happening to run into her in the ladies' room, and then Taylor and two men—who wouldn't come inside because that was a serious breach of protocol—being arrested while they waited, Rodriguez had looked more pityingly at me with every word. After the first sentence, it was hard to blame her. I'd fallen for an extremely transparent scam because it was being perpetrated by two women I'd mentally identified as victims.

Rodriguez had taken Mom and me back to her precinct, taken our statements, put out a BOLO for Louise and Akra, and then, shaking her head slightly, had sent us on our way, which had in this case been to East Harlem, where Dad was waiting for us at my office. A quick stroll over to Consuelo's apartment, and you're pretty well caught up.

Consuelo retreated back to her kitchen, where she was no doubt preparing way more food than she'd need and it would all be delectable. Consuelo has a sense of proportion that is approximately equal to my cunning ability to see through sob stories.

Diego chewed over what I'd said. "I'm guessing you could have at least held on to him until it was determined if this woman held him legally," he said. Maybe law school was the thing for him after all.

"Detective Rodriguez said she'd be working on that," Mom said, pleased to have some information to impart. I was getting the impression that my mother was finding this whole situation oddly enjoyable, as if she were finally getting a chance to be on the inside of something big that wasn't a three-nighter in the second-best room at a second-rate resort hotel. Mom loved Dad and Dad loved showbiz, so Mom loved showbiz. She didn't so much thrill to the spotlight as she adored watching Dad shine under it from as close to him as she could get. "She said if Bruno was actually not Louise's dog legally, that would open up avenues in the investigation, but she didn't have any evidence of that yet."

In fact, Rodriguez had said, "You don't have anything I can

use, so I'll have to find it myself," and moved on to the next question, which had been about the reason everybody seemed desperate to get their hands on Bruno, and whether that had played some role in Trent's murder, which she was quick to remind me was, "the case that I'm actually working here." As if my exploding bagel bakery and the possible abduction of a big hairy mutt weren't enough.

"Why do you think everybody's after Bruno?" I'd said, stating the obvious in the form of a question that would make Alex Trebek proud. "Do they think he's a witness to the murder?"

Rodriguez rolled her eyes. "I told you. Bruno is not going to point out the killer and explain how it was all done. He's a dog. I think there's some kind of odd custody battle going on over him between Louise and somebody else, and whoever gets the dog has the advantage here. Maybe it's money, maybe it's sex. Maybe it's about just having the upper hand in a relationship or who gets to walk him more often. But the interest in the dog is not about him having seen Trent Barclay get a knife in his back."

"Don't you think it's weird that Louise went through all that cloak and dagger to get her own dog back?" I asked. "If she were the rightful owner, I'd have had to hand over the leash anytime she asked. And she had no reason to think I suspected otherwise."

Rodriguez shrugged. "I have work to do. If I find out something, I'll be sure not to call you. If you find out something, you call me in the next nanosecond. We're clear?"

Mom and I had been on the street in less than a minute.

"It doesn't make sense any other way," Diego was saying now as loud clanking sounds that must have been cooking came from the kitchen. "If she'd had the right to demand Bruno from you, she wouldn't have had to go about creating this big drama. Do you think she really kidnapped the lady from the theater?"

Consuelo burst through the kitchen door carrying a dish I knew from past dinners was her famous chili con carne with rice. And my salivary glands shifted into overdrive. I am a fool for spicy food. Consuelo is a master of preparing spicy food. It was kismet that our paths crossed in the animal-agenting business.

"Stop trying to make Kay feel bad," she said to her son as she placed the large bowl on the table. "And everybody take some, now. This is dinner, not business, Dee."

I didn't mind the question, and told her so. "I don't know whether Akra is part of the plan or whether she really was taken from the theater," I told Diego. "She seemed pretty shook up, for Akra." She hadn't even mentioned the possibility of finding Les to let him know she was safe; I'd made sure to call him and tell him myself. I wasn't sure he'd been crying, but his voice did catch a couple of times. Les was born to be in the theater.

We all dug in and began eating, so aside from compliments to the chef there was little conversation for a while. Consuelo had outdone herself, so my tongue was sending out arson alerts in just a few moments. You're not supposed to drink cold water under such circumstances, so luckily Consuelo had beer.

Once I came up for air, I asked Dee what he thought about the story I'd told him. Diego has an analytical mind and catches things others sometimes miss. He's one of those kids who just knows everything about everything, but he's not arrogant about it and doesn't see it as a big deal. But ask him about astrophysics or the Bolshoi Ballet, and he'll know without consulting Google on his phone. He just absorbs everything.

I trust his judgment and make use of his careful eye. Or in this case, ear.

"I wasn't there," he said after noting his mother's glance and making sure he had fully chewed and swallowed before speaking. "But it sounds to me like they were in on it together. This Akra woman had to know the story about the arrests in the bathroom was a lie and she didn't say that to you. So I'm guessing she didn't get kidnapped at all."

As usual, Dee managed to say something that could make me feel stupid without accomplishing that task. I should have realized that sooner. But then, so should Rodriguez, who was getting paid for this stuff.

"What about Bruno?" I said to the gathered group. "What's so special about Bruno that people are willing to threaten, explode, maybe kidnap, and almost certainly kill to get him?"

"He is a nice dog," Mom said.

Nobody answered that, as it didn't seem all that helpful, but Dad did bail his wife out of the moment by asking, "Is it possible Bruno is like a drug-smuggling dog or something? I read about this. They make the dog swallow drugs in plastic and then take him on a flight or something."

Consuelo frowned. "The cartels do a lot of awful things," she said. "And that is probably one of them. But the only way that dog is that valuable is if he still has the drugs in his body, and he's been around you and Kay for days. I don't think it's possible."

"Well, someone is awfully anxious to get their hands on Bruno—unless they have him now—and I really don't have a clue as to why," I said. "I hate to think of what could be going on." It seemed a little hollow as I reached for another quesadilla. But I was worried about Bruno. It just frustrated me to think about it because I didn't have a clear idea.

"I don't think they'd do anything bad to Bruno," Mom said. She has a way of seeing everything in the best possible light. "They wouldn't harm something they feel is so valuable. It's bad for whatever business they're in." Of course, sometimes she has a point too.

"What kind of a dog is Bruno?" Diego asked.

"He's sweet," I said. "He's fluffy and big but not menacing, and he pretty much goes along with what you want to do most of the time. He didn't like this one dog at the theater, this Horatio, but aside from that he's a real little dear."

There was this pause, which happens when someone in the room isn't getting it, and it's usually me.

"I meant, what breed is he?" Diego said.

"Oh. Well, he's a mix of things, I guess, because I've never seen a dog who looked like him before. He's a big hairy mutt, mostly. Looks like a shag rug that was somehow invested with a brain and the ability to move around."

The young man looked at his mother because he knew she would have better information than I would. "Do you have a picture of Bruno?" he asked.

Of course she did; Consuelo had taken the photograph of Bruno and me at the office on her phone. "*Sí,*" she said. "Hang on a second." She produced the phone from a pocket somewhere and started pushing buttons. "Here."

Consuelo held out the phone for Diego to see. She had enlarged it to the point that I was no longer in the shot, which was fine with me. Mom and Dad, who had actually lived with Bruno for a couple of days, leaned in to get a better look as if they'd never seen him before. Dogs have a funny effect on people, including me. I was gazing fondly at the screen myself.

But Diego's expression was not one of awe or infatuation. He looked extremely serious. "I think I know why everyone is after Bruno," he said.

From a picture? "He's cute, but he's not *that* cute," I said.

Diego was already pushing buttons on *his* phone, which I couldn't see from this angle. "No," he said as he tapped away. "I think Bruno is . . . yes! Here it is. Take a look at this picture."

He turned his phone toward us. There was a very nice photograph of . . .

"That's Bruno," I said. "But his fur's been all puffed up and blow-dried. Where'd you get that?"

"It's *not* Bruno," Diego answered. "It's another dog the same breed as Bruno."

"There's more than one like that?" Dad shook his head. "I never would have believed it."

"Well, you're really going to be blown away in a second," Diego told him. "This dog is a Tibetan mastiff, just like Bruno. And they're very rare."

Consuelo, noting a tone in her son's voice, narrowed her eyes and lowered her voice half an octave. "How rare?" she asked.

"*Very* rare. The one in this picture sold a few months ago to a breeder in China. And he sold for one point five million dollars."

Nobody said anything for a long moment. Then Dad let out his breath.

"Yup," he said. "That's why."

CHAPTER NINETEEN

"Louise Barclay isn't in her apartment," Detective Rodriguez said. "Taylor Cassidy isn't in *her* apartment. Guess where Akra Levy isn't? That's right; her apartment. And you're telling me one of those ladies has a dog worth a million and a half?"

"Probably," I said.

Having had enough of the Sixth Precinct house this afternoon, I'd made sure that we'd finished dinner at Consuelo's (including a lovely flan she'd made from scratch with a real acetylene torch) and then called Rodriguez, insisting that we meet at the fountain in front of Lincoln Center because I didn't want to take the whole subway ride and it was a nice night.

"Probably?" Rodriguez parroted.

"Probably," I repeated. "I can't say for sure that Louise or Akra or Taylor has Bruno with her. Louise *had* him, but she could have passed him off to anybody by now. You don't know where she is; she could have put him on a plane for Zambia by this time."

"These women are suspects in a murder," Rodriguez reminded me. "We've made sure to alert the airports and the train stations."

"It's a big city," my father said. "They could be anywhere without having to leave town." Yes, Dad had come with me, leaving Mom at Consuelo's apartment because she insisted on helping to clean up over Consuelo's protests. I had tried to get my parents to go home, but Dad, who had been telling me about an amazing stand-up comedian he'd "discovered" during his auditions this afternoon, still had a thing about letting me travel around the city by myself at night. It'll only be worse when I'm forty.

Rodriguez didn't answer Dad but she did scowl nicely, so that was something. "If I'd known Louise wasn't just taking her dog home, that the dog was the point, I could have had some officers follow her from Grand Central," she mused. I think to herself.

But that drove me just a little bit nuts. "I was telling you it was about Bruno from the beginning but you didn't want to hear it," I told the detective. "You thought it was about Trent Barclay having an affair with somebody and his wife getting mad at him. Did you manage to track down how Trent and Louise ended up with Bruno?" Betty Vassar from Long Island had called me back before we'd reached Consuelo's. She had nothing.

I sat on the edge of the fountain, which not surprisingly was cold, and folded my arms in what I thought was a defiant gesture. I probably looked like Barbara Eden in *I Dream of Jeannie*. Hey, I get a lot of stations.

"Not yet," Rodriguez said without making eye contact. "But

now that I know he's a valuable dog and a rare one, and with the picture you gave me, I can make some inquiries about kennels that deal in such animals."

There was a long silence. Finally Dad said, "You're welcome." Dad is all about keeping the audience happy, but not when it gets in the way of making sure everyone knows what a genius his little girl (that's me) is.

"Okay, go home," Rodriguez said, once again not responding to my father. "You've done all you can today. Call me if you think of anything else."

"Will you call if anything happens?" I asked.

"No. I'm the cops. I don't have to keep you informed. You don't even live in my city. But I'll tell you what: Since you're my CI, you'll be my first phone call if I need any information on someone in that theater. I still think that Les guy is suspicious." With that, she turned and walked away without so much as a backward glance.

"I'm starting to like her," Dad said.

I stood up. "Well, I guess that's it for tonight," I said. "Let's get back to Mom and I'll drive you guys home. Steve and Eydie need a walk."

"I got Sam to walk them," Dad said. "I think we have somewhere else we need to go."

Despite my not wanting to go all the way downtown again, I am a good daughter and let my father pay for a cab to Louise Barclay's apartment building, where we waited for a resident to exit so we could get in the front door, and then climbed back up the stairs to Louise's apartment door.

The question was, why? And I asked it of my father. "We've been there. I've been there twice," I reminded him. "What is it we're going to accomplish by waking Louise up and annoying her right now?"

"Detective Rodriguez said Louise wasn't in her apartment," Dad said. "That means nobody should be there now. We can have a look around."

"For what? I've been in there, even looked at Trent's hard drive. There's nothing to learn about Bruno there. Besides, how are we going to get inside?" I could have kicked myself for giving back Louise's key, but that would have hurt. I stared at the door, upon which we had knocked just to be sure and whaddaya know, Louise hadn't answered. The door still was locked and looked pretty adamant about not letting us in.

"Watch and learn," Dad said. He reached into his pocket and pulled out a paper clip, which he unfolded and inserted into the lock. After a few moments of jiggling and pulling, during which I stared at my father with a completely different type of respect than I'd ever had before (and worried that a neighbor would pass by and call the cops), something clicked inside that lock and Dad tried the doorknob, being sure to put his sleeve between the knob and his fingers.

The door swung open.

"How did you . . ." I began.

"I worked with an escape artist for a couple of months, back before I met your mother."

We went inside and closed the door behind us. Dad turned on the light in the living room, pointing to the chain on the door. "See? Nobody put that on. That means nobody's home." He walked into the kitchen, where Trent's dog-dish nosedive had taken place, and just stared for a moment. "The problem has been that we've been too focused on Bruno," he said.

"Too focused on Bruno? Bruno's my client. What else should I be focused on?" I walked in behind him and looked where he was looking, but I didn't see anything I hadn't seen before: a refrigerator, some cabinets, a ceramic tile floor in a checkerboard pattern . . .

"This is not just about getting an expensive dog," Dad said, finger pointing upward like the Sherlock Holmes he believed he was all of a sudden. "This is a murder investigation. And there's got to be something here that will help us understand better what happened the night Trent died."

"Isn't that sort of the cops' job?" I asked. Dad was walking, slowly with his director's observant eye focused, around the tiny kitchen floor, not looking down, where Trent fell, but up at eye level, straight on. I had no idea what he was searching for, but then I'm guessing he didn't know either.

"Yeah, how's that been going so far?" he said. His hand went up to his chin in a contemplative pose. Dad wasn't as theatrical as Les, but that was only because he so rarely got to play the main room. "See, sweetie, you're missing the big picture. You're curious about who killed Trent, sure, but you really care about Bruno and making sure he's all right."

"How is that missing the big picture?" I get defensive when

someone suggests to me that humans are more important than my clients. "Trent's dead. He's going to stay dead whether someone figures out who killed him or not. But Bruno . . ."

My father stopped at one side of the kitchen and stared, but not so blankly that he couldn't cut me off. "Bruno's predicament has got to be tied to Trent's murder," he said. "I say you're missing the bigger picture because you don't see that if we can figure out what happened to Trent, we'll have a better idea of how to help Bruno."

His cell phone made a sound like a large man belching after a heavy dinner. He took it out and glanced at it. "Your mother says we should leave soon," he said.

"Is something wrong?"

"No, but she feels like she's imposing on Consuelo and Dee." I knew that wasn't all in a text from Mom. They've been together so long that they can pretty much read each other's minds, which, now that I thought of it, wouldn't be a bad act.

"What are you looking for?" I asked him finally. Mostly because I didn't see anything especially worth looking at, but Dad seemed to think the air in the center of Louise's kitchen was fascinating.

"I'm picturing the scene." He tried to stand on his toes for a second, but didn't seem to find it satisfactory. So he looked around the floor again, found Bruno's large food dish, and picked it up. There was no food in it. Dad turned it over, placed it back on the floor, and stood on it. "That's the right height," he said.

Not if Bruno ever wanted to eat out of that bowl again. "For what?" I asked.

"To see from the killer's perspective. See, Trent was stabbed in the back—no jokes, little girl—and the way he fell onto that water bowl over there, it follows that he went forward rather than to the side. Straight down. That means the person who stabbed him had a downward thrust, not an attack from below or directly. It was a taller person who stabbed Trent." He stepped down off the bowl as if expecting a round of applause.

"Amazing, Holmes!" Okay, so I was being snarky, but you can't let an old ham like Dad go on in his role too long or he starts to believe his own press releases. "We'll arrest LeBron James and be home before tea."

"You're a real wiseass, you know that?"

"I learned from the master."

Dad ignored that remark, which was wise on his part. "If Trent was stabbed by a taller person, even a little taller, that lets Louise out."

"Unless she used the same brilliant bowl-standing technique you just used," I said.

"That seems unlikely. Besides, for someone to knock him down that hard, the killer would have to be pretty strong. Louise is fairly scrawny, especially in the arms and, um, upper body."

"Hey. You're married."

My father gave me a don't-be-ridiculous look. "But Akra is tall, and she looks strong. It could have been her."

"Could have been Les too," I said. "I don't think it was Gwen Harper, mostly because she doesn't really have a motive and couldn't remember who Trent was, but she's not exactly an Amazon either."

"What about this Mike guy?" Dad asked. "I don't really know him at all, but he's not small and he's, you know, a guy."

I thought about it. "He doesn't really seem to have appeared until Trent was already dead, and besides, he was Trent's school chum, not Louise's. But he must have known Akra at some point too."

"Has he got motive?" Dad was playing the inspector now and had to check his natural urge to employ a British accent I knew he could do convincingly.

I shrugged. "How would I know? Nobody seems to have a real motive here, except that Bruno is apparently worth all kinds of money. But killing Trent didn't change anything about that. Bruno is still Louise's dog."

Dad turned to me, a thought clearly having crossed his mind. "Was he always?" he asked.

I'd spent the day trying to figure out this complicated plot, being blown up, handing my client over to his owner while thinking that was a bad thing to do, and then having a delicious authentic Mexican dinner. I was tired to the point that I would do anything to get out of this apartment and back to my nice warm bed. But Dad was on a roll, and I knew the only thing that could possibly placate him was for me to make real progress in what he now saw as his investigation.

"Let's check out Louise's computer," I said, and headed into the living area (it wasn't large enough to be a living room), where I'd seen her laptop on a rather nice side table with two drawers. I picked it up and hit the Power button.

"I thought you did that already," Dad said, following me in.

I shook my head. "I only looked at Trent's. Didn't have time before Louise came back to her own apartment and messed everything up for me." The screen flickered on.

Dad watched over my shoulder as I opened Louise's main drive and looked at the list of folders, which was not especially impressive. She did not keep bank records or any records with Bruno's name listed, a quick search of the system revealed. But with Louise's personality in mind, I figured there had to be one file that would hold some of her personal information, and that might hold a clue. I told that to Dad.

"How do you find something like that?" he asked. "She's not going to have a file marked 'Secret Stuff I Don't Want You to See.'"

"No, but there is one thing I can search for that will lead to at least some of Bruno's records." And I went to the search box and typed in my own name. "She had to get in touch with me once they decided Bruno was a showbiz dog. Why do that with a Tibetan mastiff worth over a million dollars?"

"The only explanation," my father said, "is that Louise and Trent didn't know Bruno was a Tibetan mastiff worth over a million dollars."

"Maybe." I found two mentions of my name. One was in the address book, where my cell number and office number were stored. That was not of much use, seeing as how I already knew my cell and office numbers. "What's this?"

The second mention of Powell and Associates came in a file that had been named, in perfect Louise Barclay fashion, Boring. I'm sure her rationale was that if she labeled it that way, no one other than she would want to open it. I immediately opened it.

"Whoa," Dad said. "The mother lode."

Sure enough, the Boring file Louise had created included every

password and user ID she had on file in case she needed to remind herself. There were (in addition to my and Taylor's contact
numbers) credit card numbers, Social Security numbers for herself and Trent, a mortgage loan on the apartment (who knew it
was a condo?), and information about investment accounts and
bank accounts Trent had conveniently left out of his more straight-
forward and detailed records on his own computer. This was
clearly a family in which delegation of responsibility was more
than a concept; it was a way of life.

"We haven't got anything yet," I reminded Dad. "I'm not
checking Louise's MasterCard balance."

"But her bank account could show you something about when
she adopted Bruno," he noted. "Wasn't it just a few months ago,
according to Trent?"

"Her bank account?" I felt a little queasy. "Isn't that fraud, or
something?"

"It's never fraud if you don't get caught, and you have the access codes." Dad pointed at the spot on the screen as if I hadn't
already noticed Louise's notations about the Wells Fargo Bank
account that was no doubt in her name alone and was therefore the
only one listed just on her computer.

"How about morals?" I said. Was it okay to peer into a woman's
finances if she was possibly holding a large hairy client hostage?

"A man died here a few nights ago," Dad answered. "I think
whoever did that has abandoned the moral high ground."

"We don't know it was Louise," I pointed out. "She's short."

"We don't know it wasn't. Maybe she stood on a box."

"You just said she was scrawny."

"Check." Dad pointed at the screen.

Having broken into her home and opened her confidential files, the fact was I had very little in the way of moral ammunition. I opened Louise's browser, one I would not have ordinarily used because it's so damn slow, and finally got the Wells Fargo website on the screen. I checked back at the Boring document, punched in the ID and password, and voilà, a mere forty seconds later I was staring into Louise Barclay's most recent bank records.

"Is this the kind of daughter you raised?" I asked Dad. "Breaking into a woman's most confidential . . ."

"What does it say?" He cut me off.

"Give me a minute, will you?" The most recent deductions from Louise's checking account were, as one might expect, related to Trent's funeral. There was a fee to a funeral home not far from here, a payment to the rabbi (who apparently had a PayPal account) and the deduction for the slinky little black number she'd been wearing the day of the funeral.

"What are you looking for?" Dad asked.

"I'm not sure. Something about Bruno. Vet bills, a payment to a shelter, a deduction that would indicate they'd paid privately to a breeder or someone less reputable for a dog like that." I scrolled down the page. "But there's nothing here."

"It's been a few months," Dad told me. "Keep going."

I did, but there weren't any suspicious deductions from Louise's account at any time during the past six months. "That's weird," I said. "Even if they got the dog illegally or off the books, you take him to the vet when you adopt a new animal. There's nothing here."

Dad shrugged. "Maybe they're bad pet owners."

"No tags, no license with the city, no records of rabies or any other vaccinations. They're not just bad pet owners, they're nonexistent pet owners."

Dad sat down on the radiator. "So they were doing their best to avoid leaving a paper trail that would attach them to Bruno," he said. "How did they pass your vetting system when they contacted you?"

"I checked with a reference they gave, but . . ." I reached for my phone and dialed Consuelo, who answered on the second ring. "We're fine," I said before she could ask. "Who was the character reference on Bruno?"

"Hang on." Consuelo was no doubt accessing the company's files from her home computer, which took a little time. "They had a license with the city, which I have scanned here. And we talked to a reference, a Ms. Kaly Rave. Remember her? You talked to her on the phone, from the New York Kennel Club."

"Kaly Rave," I said. "Can you spell that?" Consuelo did, and I wrote it on a taxi receipt I had in my pocket. "I'll call her again in the morning." I thanked Consuelo and hung up.

Dad looked at me funny. "No, you won't," he said.

Huh? "No, I won't what?"

"You won't call Kaly Rave in the morning," my father told me.

"Stop being cryptic, Tonto. What do you mean, I won't call Kaly Rave in the morning? She might have some insight into where Louise and Trent got Bruno."

My father squinted at me. Apparently, I was far away, or directly in the sunlight. "You spoke to this woman before. What do you remember about her?"

"Well, we never met. I don't remember her voice especially, but I asked her about Trent and Louise, she said they were okay and they treated Bruno well, and I pretty much left it at that. It wasn't anything special. What am I missing?"

"Just a second," Dad said. "Where did you get Ms. Rave's number?"

"From Trent. I asked for a reference and she's the one he gave me." This was getting a little spooky, just based on the faraway look in Dad's eyes. "You're scaring me. What's going on?"

He snapped out of his reverie and shook his head. "I'm sorry, sweetie; I didn't mean to upset you. But don't you see it? Isn't it obvious?"

"No, it's not obvious, or I wouldn't have to ask you for the seventy-eighth time. What am I missing?"

Dad looked at my note again and nodded. "See, 'Kaly Rave' is an anagram of 'Akra Levy.'"

CHAPTER TWENTY

"An anagram," I said, shaking my head as I walked up to the house in Scarborough. "What is she, Professor Moriarty? What makes a person feel like they should hide themselves, but leave a clue behind? Isn't that counterproductive?"

"These people are criminals," Mom said, a few steps behind me. I could already hear Eydie howling at the sound of the approaching humans, who clearly had forgotten their responsibility to be present when she wanted them. "They're not like you and me."

"They are like you and me," Dad told her. "They're show people. They can't stand to be anonymous." Mom, who probably was thinking they weren't exactly huge stars and was perfectly happy being anonymous, said nothing.

I unlocked the door as Dad brought up the rear. Once I opened it, the two dogs were all over us, lamenting the horrible time they'd spent alone (probably either asleep or walking with Sam) and warning us in their pitiable way never to put them through such an ordeal again.

Calling Rodriguez with an anagram hardly seemed like a good idea. For one thing, Dad and I would have to explain how we'd come about this information, and while I could truthfully say I had gotten the name from my own files, it would have led to questions about why I hadn't noticed the similarity before. Which was a good question.

"Criminals aren't an alien race," Dad told Mom. "They're just people who choose to do something other than what we would do." Dad was clearly trying to internalize the idea of being a criminal in case he ever wrote a part for himself where he had to break the law. Dad isn't exactly a Method actor, but he does like to have a point of reference.

Much like getting in touch with Rodriguez, looking for Akra or Taylor (or Louise for that matter) while the NYPD couldn't locate them also seemed pointless. Besides, I'd already been blown up, lost a client—literally—and committed burglary. That was enough for one day. All I wanted was sleep.

"It's like she wants to get caught." Mom was not letting go. On paper, I didn't blame her—the anagram thing *was* just silly—but in my current state of fatigue the last thing I needed was to prolong this conversation. Mom and Dad, dedicated night owls who had been forced awake earlier than usual the past few days, had to be exhausted too.

"I'm too tired to think about it," I said, locking the front door and turning off the outside light. I let the dogs follow me into the kitchen, where I found treats for both of them and prepared to let them out into the backyard for one last opportunity before I shut the house down for the night. "Just let's sleep on it, okay?"

Mom put her hand on my shoulder as I unlocked the back door to let the dogs out. "Of course, honey," she said. "You've had a rough day."

Dad, on the other hand, had caught his second wind and was about to let the night extend itself. "What I don't get," he said, "is why Trent got killed."

"Dad," I mumbled wearily.

But he went on. "I mean, if the whole thing is about Bruno being worth millions, why kill Trent? He'd be in on the plan; he was the one who'd gotten Bruno in the first place. He had to know the dog was valuable. If we can figure out why he got a knife in his back, we'll know who did it. The person with the motive is the one who does the crime." Dad had once, many years before, played Detective Sergeant Trotter in Agatha Christie's *The Mousetrap*, and he seemed to be reviving the role for a very select audience as my dogs ran out to do what dogs do in the backyard.

"Maybe Trent wasn't in on the plan," I said. "Maybe he wanted a bigger piece of the action. Maybe he just wanted to go to bed and somebody wouldn't let him because they wanted to talk about a murder." Perhaps that was going too far.

Dad smiled crookedly. "I get the message," he said. "Good night, sweetie. I'll let the dogs in." He pointed toward my bedroom door, and I gratefully headed in that direction.

It took me approximately four minutes to get ready for bed because I did the bare minimum, removing my makeup, brushing my teeth, and making a promise to the rest of my body that it would be treated more civilly the following day. As an agent, you learn that sometimes you make promises you can't keep for the client's greater good. You never lie outright—I certainly *hoped* not to get blown up and all that the next day—but you do occasionally deliver the promise as a goal rather than a certainty.

But as exhausted as I was—and I don't think I'd ever been more tired—I didn't fall asleep immediately. The events of the past few days wouldn't stop spinning around in my mind like a jigsaw puzzle whose pieces were subtle variations on the same bland color. You know you can solve this thing if you can just think straight long enough, but you have no idea how to go about doing that.

So when Taylor Cassidy called my phone just after midnight, it came less as a jarring call to awaken than a startling annoyance keeping me from pursuing my ultimate prize, a few hours of turbulent rest punctuated by bouts of frustrating thought about a murder, a dognapping that might or might not have taken place, and my own assumed role in each.

"I'm calling because they're not supposed to have taken Bruno away, and now they are," she said after I registered my surprise at hearing from her.

"What do you mean, taking Bruno away? Who's taking Bruno away?" Even when I'm not actually asleep, it takes me a while to awaken to a state in which I can reliably interact with other humans.

"*They* are," Taylor replied, as if that explained anything. "I didn't sign up for this, and I figured you should know."

That sounded dangerously like a line a bad actress would exit on, so I cut Taylor off as quickly as I could. "Why don't you call Detective Rodriguez and tell her what's going on?" I asked. "What have I got to do with it?"

"I don't talk to the cops," Taylor said. Maybe she was auditioning for a role in the next James Cagney movie. "That's not something a woman in my position can do."

Just when I was about to tell her that the whole speaking cryptically thing was getting old in a serious hurry, Taylor added, "The dog's not going to get hurt. But it's a long trip and it's not right. You should stop them. Remember six fifty-five. Got it? Six fifty-five."

"What's going to happen at six fifty-five?" I said. Now I was annoyed because nobody had told me this problem was going to involve mathematics, and that was always my worst subject at school. When I had school. Sometimes I was tutored, or as they would say now, homeschooled, because my parents (and sometimes I) were appearing onstage in some area where commuting to a classroom would have been a severe disadvantage to my learning process.

It was far, is what I'm saying.

"That's it," Taylor answered.

"Of course. Glad you called, Taylor. Anytime you want to ring up at an ungodly hour and speak in enigmas, you feel free, okay?"

"What?" Taylor said.

Oh my lord. "Taylor," I asked in a soothing voice, "what drugs have you taken?"

"I just smoked a little weed," she answered in a soft, girlish voice, admitting her crime as if I were her parent and she'd been caught with her hand in the cookie jar. "And had a couple of glasses of wine. I didn't do anything bad."

Add drug counselor to my résumé. "You're high as a kite," I told her. "You need to sober up so you can tell me what's really going on with Bruno." Since I had no idea how to sober up from a marijuana-and-alcohol stupor, I refrained from offering specific advice. "You should find someone who can help you. Drink some water." That couldn't hurt.

"That's it," Taylor said again. "Bruno. Six fifty-five. Don't forget, okay?"

It was just before one a.m. now, so I had almost six hours before that time would be rolling around. "Okay, Taylor. Six fifty-five. What's going to happen at six fifty-five?" I pretended I hadn't asked the question before, mostly because I was pretty sure Taylor had no memory of the time, only seconds ago, when I had.

"They're taking Bruno," Taylor said, and hung up.

I tried calling her back three times and got her voicemail three times. I didn't see much point in leaving a message. If Taylor wanted to talk to me, she had proved that she certainly knew how to get in touch.

Meanwhile, it sounded like my client was in some trouble, so like any good agent who wanted to keep earning a steady paycheck, I was obliged to figure out what Taylor had meant, if it had any validity at all considering her inebriated state, and then what action should be taken about it.

This, and I could barely remember waking up this morning. Yesterday morning. Whatever.

Now I'd never be able to sleep, I realized. But since Taylor wasn't answering my calls and it seemed unlikely Louise or Akra would respond well to my name on the Caller ID, I had very little choice. I turned off my light and my phone. Then I lay back down on the bed and, oddly enough, fell into what turned out to be a refreshing sleep that lasted until six the next morning.

I had set the alarm. I was tired, but I wasn't stupid, and Bruno needed me to figure out what the heck Taylor had been talking about and whether it made sense to take her at her strangely delivered words at all.

What was going to happen at six fifty-five? Less than an hour and I had no clue—literally. I could call Taylor back, assuming the number she'd used was her own and not some disposable phone she'd picked up at a 7-Eleven. But I doubted she would be in any shape to tell me anything, and if she were, she would undoubtedly not want to say anything, given that she probably hadn't really meant to tell me anything the night before. It was rationalizing, but it was also probably true.

I could call Rodriguez and tell her . . . what? Something was going to happen in fifty-five or so minutes, and I had no idea what, where, or why, not to mention who might be behind it (although there were logical suspects like my old pal Kaly Rave)? I could wake up my father and consult with him, but he was not great first thing in the morning and was actually an actor on cruise ships and not a detective.

So I took the dogs for a walk.

Here's how I figured it: Walking the dogs helps me clear my head. There was no chance I could get to the city before six fifty-five anyway. So I took my phone with me, and if any brilliant revelations came to me during our tour of Scarborough, I could immediately call the appropriate person.

I suppose you have a better idea. Well, you weren't there.

Eydie was up and ready for a nice brisk stroll this morning, but Steve, perhaps missing his pal Bruno, dragged his tubular body down the sidewalk, looking one way and then the other. He wasn't even sniffing anything, which was extremely unusual for him and every other dog who ever lived.

I started talking to them as we walked, which is what I do when I have a problem. The dogs don't mind, and it helps me air out my brain and arrive at a solution. Onstage I could always remember my line as soon as I heard the other person say his or hers out loud. If I had the first line in a scene, it was something of a crapshoot as to whether I'd get it right. So Dad started writing all our scenes with him or Mom getting the opening line and then I was off book every time.

"So Taylor calls and tells me something is going to happen to Bruno at six fifty-five and she's not happy about it," I started. Wait. No. That wasn't really what she'd said at all.

"Taylor called and said they weren't supposed to move Bruno and now they were," I told Eydie, who had stopped to check out a Carvel cup someone had dropped in the street. I picked up the cup and tossed it into the public trash can that was maybe ten feet from where it had been dropped. People. Deal exclusively with animals, I say. "But she didn't say who and she didn't say where Bruno was being moved."

Steve, dejected, looked up at Bruno's name. I scratched him behind the ears. "I miss him too, pal," I said. "But that wasn't exactly what Taylor said either. She didn't say they were moving Bruno, she said they were taking him away, and that it would be a long trip. Then she made some crazy reference to being a woman in her position, and that meant she couldn't call the cops. What do you think that meant?" Steve didn't know, so we kept walking.

"It meant she couldn't call the cops because she's involved in what's going on with Bruno, right?" Neither dog answered, which was just as well. I was talking in circles. "Unless it didn't."

"Unless it didn't what?" I did not mistake the words for a question from Steve this time; we were standing in front of Cool Beans and it was morning, which meant Sam was going to be very close by. He smiled at me from the doorway to his place, which is one step up from the sidewalk, so he was looking down a little.

"I'm trying to figure something out," I said.

"Fresh coffee helps with that," Sam told me. "Come on in and bring your friends."

"Is that okay with the health inspector?" But I was already leading the dogs into the café.

"The health inspector has three English bulldogs," Sam said. "I've let her bring those in here, so I can't imagine I'll get written up. So what are you trying to figure out?"

I gave Sam the rundown on yesterday, which took all the time he needed to brew a nice strong urn of coffee and pour me a mug, black. I let the steam reach my nose and luxuriated in it a bit. Sam makes really good coffee, which is a plus considering he runs a coffee house.

"So you think somebody is going to take Bruno away in . . ." He looked at the clock over the door. "Twenty-three minutes, and you can't figure out what to do about it?"

"That's it in a nutshell. I'm really worried about my client, but I have no clue what the next step should be." First sip of the morning. A religious experience.

"So you were talking to your dogs about it." He nodded. "Did they have any advice?"

"They're being stubborn," I said. "I think they know exactly what to do and they're holding back."

"I dunno," he said, putting down a bowl of water for Steve and Eydie, who appeared grateful. "I'd think they'd want to help their pal. I think it's you."

Hey! "What's me?" My voice definitely had an edge, and the caffeine hadn't had time to hit my synapses yet.

"You're not hearing the whole message," he said. "Just like I'm guessing you didn't hear the message I left with your service, since you never answered. I mean, I was just trying to be nice."

What message with my . . . oh, for crying out loud. "That was you? The one who was glad to see me and wanted me to take care of Bruno?"

"Yeah. Why? Who else had you seen the night before?"

I thought. That's what it had come to; I had to think about why I'd been feeling threatened *that* time. "Well, I'd been getting these texts . . . never mind. We're off topic. What do you mean, I'm not hearing the whole message?"

"You said it yourself." Sam leaned forward on the counter. Any second now customers desperate for a caffeine fix would start streaming in. "You were so stunned by the phone call and being startled in the middle of the night that you had to think about what Taylor actually said before you got it right. What you thought she said and what she actually said didn't immediately match up."

The coffee was reviving me, and I mentally thanked Sam for that. "But I think I have it all now," I said as Eydie slobbered some water onto the floor by my feet. "It wasn't that she said Bruno was being moved; she said they were taking him away. It wasn't that she said she was afraid to call the police; it was that she said a woman in her position couldn't. And . . ."

Sam grinned. The smug grin of someone who already knows the answer but wants you to come to it yourself so you'll have a sense of accomplishment. Sam is that annoying algebra teacher you had in tenth grade who got you to do work you didn't think you could and whom you didn't actually appreciate until five years after you were out of college. "And . . ." he repeated.

"And she didn't say something was going to happen to Bruno at six fifty-five. She said to remember six fifty-five." That was the piece I'd glossed over in my head, and I knew it had some significance, but at the moment I couldn't quite nail it down.

"That's right," Sam said. "So what does that mean?" *It means x is greater than y minus the sum of x plus y squared, Sam. Feel better?*

"I don't know," I told him. "You tell me. What does it mean?" Clearly he had the answer and was just being insufferable.

Sam shrugged. "How would I know? I wasn't there."

See what I mean? Insufferable.

I put my head down on the counter and was facing the floor, where Steve was looking up at me wondering why nobody was petting him at the moment. People always pet Steve when they see him. They're a little bit more leery of Eydie. "Come on, Sam," I muttered into the counter. "Help me. I don't know what to do."

"Yes, you do." I smelled something nearby and lifted my head. Sure enough, Sam had put a killer blueberry muffin next to my cup. "You just haven't quite put it together yet. So Taylor said to remember six fifty-five. Why would she want you to remember that?"

The muffin was warm. Sam wasn't playing fair. "I don't know. Why do people want you to remember numbers?" I took a bite, and it was better than it had any right to be. I concentrated on the blueberries, which were probably local. There are farms here, people. They don't call it the Garden State because we have a deep sense of irony, although we do.

"Because they think you'll forget them, and the numbers are important." Sam had to walk over to take care of a customer who wanted a double mocha latte at this hour of the morning. He hid his contempt, made the drink, served it, and then was back at my side. "So Taylor accomplished that part of her goal. She wanted you to remember the number and you remember it."

I let one foot rise just a little bit out of the sneaker in the back and Steve licked it. He really wanted some attention, so I reached down and smoothed down his fur, which is ridiculously smooth as it is. Steve is a delight to pet. "But what good is remembering the number if I don't know what the number means?" I asked.

Sam's business was picking up, so he wouldn't have much time to play Yoda for a while. He delivered coffee to three more people who looked undeservedly impatient and then came back, talking faster. "Think about what she said. Someone is taking Bruno away and they're doing it soon, although probably not at six fifty-five, which is in seven minutes. So what significance could the number six fifty-five have in that context?" And off he went to create espresso for people who just seriously shouldn't have been ordering that this early in the day.

I looked down at Steve and Eydie, who were drawing some attention—both positive and irritated—from the queue. I washed

down the last of the muffin with the last of the coffee and got up
off the barstool. I picked up the leashes.

"Let's go, guys," I told the dogs. "Sam has to earn his keep."
I'd have put money on the counter but Sam would have been
mad at me later; he never lets me pay at Cool Beans. He thinks
we have a special relationship. He's probably right, but not in
the way he thinks.

He smiled at me on the way out and I considered that maybe
he was right in the way he thought, but I was wrong. Nah. That
couldn't be it.

On the street, I picked up the conversation I was having with
Steve and Eydie. "Bruno is a big dog," I said. "If someone wants
to take him somewhere far away, like Taylor said, they're not
going to put him in a carrier and take him on a plane. He could
be put in with the cargo, but the people who are taking him know
exactly how valuable he is, and they're not going to want to let
him out of their sight or let the TSA see him at the gate. He's
way bigger than a bottle of shampoo."

I stopped because Eydie had business to see to, and waited
until she was done, looking elsewhere. Eydie is a private dog. She
deserves to have her dignity.

"So if you're transporting a large, valuable dog, how do you
do that?" I concentrated my gaze on Steve, who was investigating a piece of grass that obviously held some olfactory interest.
"You're not driving him to wherever you're going. Too easy to be
stopped by the police in whatever state you happen to be traveling, because the NYPD will put out a bulletin with a picture of
Bruno, and he's hard to miss."

Eydie walked back to the pavement, I did what a good citizen should do, and then we moved on.

"You probably can't transport him by train; he's big and noticeable so you can't transport him by car. A truck seems awfully showy, not to mention that it isn't very efficient and has the same hazards as a car by way of getting seen by the cops." Eydie seemed uninterested, but Steve was pondering the possibilities, mostly about an area of the street where someone had dropped a piece of fried chicken. Two months ago. Steve's nose has a long memory.

I stopped walking. There was only one possibility left. "They're taking Bruno away by sea," I said, not even pretending to talk to the dogs anymore. "That's what's going on. So six fifty-five isn't the time. Taylor wouldn't tell me to remember the time, and she'd just say five minutes to seven. What can six fifty-five be?"

We started walking again. "A ship. Can six fifty-five be a ship?" I got out my phone. Normally I wouldn't think about trying to look something up while I was walking the dogs; it's too easy to get distracted, the dogs can walk into a problem (like the street), and besides, I'm holding two leashes attached to animals who like to move at their own clip. But this time it seemed important enough to risk it.

I considered trying to Google a ship numbered six fifty-five, but it was too awkward and clumsy. My thumbs were far too busy holding on to the leashes. I could see what I was doing, but I couldn't do it accurately, so I checked the time. It was just late enough that I wouldn't be that annoying boss who thinks you're always at their beck and call.

I called Consuelo.

"What's up with Bruno?" she asked by way of greeting. It

wasn't just the urgency of the current situation that made her sort of abrupt either. Consuelo truly believes that we have a fast-moving, dynamic business that's always bustling, like on television. What we really have is a fairly busy talent agency for animals that's paying the bills so far and lives paycheck to paycheck. Like in life.

"That's what I'm calling about. See if you can find a ship leaving from the tri-state area today whose number is six fifty-five."

"Ships have numbers?" Consuelo asked.

"Who am I, Captain Horatio Hornblower? I don't know. I know there's a number that we're supposed to remember and it's six fifty-five. It has to do with Bruno being taken away, and I think it's a boat."

"A ship."

"Sure. Whatever." I could already hear Consuelo clacking away on her keyboard, and she was still at home. In the background I heard Diego asking his mother what she was doing.

"I'm looking up a ship called six fifty-five," she said, distracted.

"That's a stupid name for a ship," Dee answered.

"I don't name them," his mother told him.

"Why are you looking for that?"

We were about a block from the house, and as much as I love Consuelo and Diego, their witty banter was not getting me any closer to finding Bruno. "Hey," I said into the phone. "Remember me?"

But Consuelo was already relaying my information to her son, who started to laugh. "What's so funny?" Consuelo and I asked at the same time.

"Six fifty-five isn't the ship," Diego said. "It's probably the pier."

CHAPTER TWENTY-ONE

By the time I made it into the house, unleashed Steve and Eydie, gave each of them a treat, and refreshed their water, Consuelo and (mostly) Diego had found Pier 655 in Elizabeth, New Jersey, not far from the Statue of Liberty (and if anyone asks you where Miss Liberty stands, you make sure to tell them she's on Jersey soil). And Diego discovered that a ship, the *La Paloma,* was leaving that very day for a long trip indeed—to Taiwan. There was no way to find out if there was a large, scruffy-looking dog being brought aboard at this very moment on his way to make someone very rich.

I called Detective Rodriguez with my story and for once she did not treat me like the slightly loopy relation. "I looked up Tibetan mastiffs last night after you called," she said. "And they're really valuable, especially in Asia for some reason. So it might make sense." She said she'd make some phone calls and find out if Bruno was listed as passenger or cargo on the *La Paloma.*

The ship was leaving in two hours, give or take. I figured my job as Bruno's agent was to ensure that he showed up to the Palace Theater in New York for rehearsal promptly today. So I very gently woke my father (by texting him; Dad is always alert to the possibility that a gig might call) and told him the situation. He was in the kitchen in his robe a moment later.

"You're going to the pier?" he asked. He knows me well and besides, I was putting on my sunglasses and a raincoat because it was sunny but I was going near the water. It made sense in my mind.

"I figure I have to know what the deal is, and besides, I haven't gotten Louise to initial the changes in Bruno's contract yet," I explained. "I'd be a bad agent if I didn't cross all the *t*'s and dot all the *i*'s."

"You're nosy," he said, stifling a yawn. "You want me to come with?"

"No, I want you to watch the dogs and I want you to finish your auditions so we can stop having the senior tour of *American Idol* in my living room every day."

Dad waved a hand dismissively. "Auditions are over," he said. "We're making our choices now." That's what producers say when they want to stall you.

"Make them here," I told him. "I don't want to have to worry about you."

"I notice no consideration is being given to whether I have to worry about *you*."

"That's correct."

Without a word Dad went back into his bedroom and emerged seconds later. He extended his hand.

There was a gun in it.

"Take this," he said. "It's not much, but it'll look like something if there's trouble."

I hadn't even known my father owned a gun. "I'm not taking that," I said. "I don't know anything about using it. Do you even have a permit for that thing?"

He looked at me oddly. "Of course not. It's a prop pistol, Kay. You've seen it a thousand times."

I had, too. In one of the jealous-husband sketches he and Mom used to do (without me at all, for which I was eternally grateful), he'd used the gun to blow black powder all over his own face at a crucial moment. Audiences laughed at the cheap joke, as they usually do. Audiences tend to be good-natured and will applaud the familiar.

I took the pistol from his hand. It wasn't as heavy as a real gun, but it would do. "I'm not going to use it," I said warily.

"That's okay. Just have it. I'll feel better." Dad reached over and touched my hand. "Do something for an old man." He looked up at me and his eyes moistened.

"That's from the candy-shop sketch," I said. "You can't con me, old man."

Dad hugged me, and that was real. "What's this 'old man' stuff, lady?" he said.

I took the gun.

It took a while to find Pier 655 at Port Elizabeth; three people I asked for directions told me there was no such number. But it existed, I found finally, about a quarter mile from where I'd parked my car with the GPS device that had informed me in no uncertain terms that I had reached my destination before I'd started my ten-minute walk to . . . my destination.

There was, to my consternation, no patrol car from the NYPD in sight. Rodriguez had no doubt decided that any information coming from me must have been bogus or incorrect and had gone on to some more fruitful investigation, like Googling Louise Barclay's high school graduation picture to send out as a means of identification. I considered canceling my membership in the Policeman's Benevolent Association, and then remembered I'd taken it out so I could hand the card to any cops who pulled me over for speeding. You can't get out of a ticket by showing your legs *all* the time. Or in my case, ever.

I reached into my raincoat pocket and felt for Dad's prop gun. Not that I couldn't feel its weight just walking around, but I'm compulsive about things like that. Don't judge until you've walked a mile—or a quarter mile—in my shoes.

The *La Paloma,* as advertised, was docked at the pier, and it was considerably less grand than its name—or any other—would lead one to believe. It was a freighter, a container ship, one that is simply a flat surface with lots of plain boxes, usually twenty or forty feet in length, stacked one on top of another with absolutely no character whatsoever. Tom Hanks might have captained such a ship in that movie about the Somali pirates. Except this one had less charm.

Whoever was considering sending Bruno all the way to the other side of the planet on this ship truly did need to be arrested and locked up for a long time. And so did whoever killed Trent, I supposed.

The wind was a little chilly near the water. The collar of my raincoat flapped up into my face and momentarily obscured my view of the pier and the ship. When I pushed it back down again, there was a black SUV parked right near the *La Paloma*'s gangplank.

I was too far away to see who got out of the vehicle, but whoever it was led a dog out on a leash. A big brown dog.

As far away as I was, I couldn't imagine that canine was anybody except Bruno. I quickened my step. I had to stop the move before Bruno was on the ship. I didn't know why, but my feeling was that once he got on the *La Paloma*, Bruno was as good as Taiwanese.

I was maybe fifty yards from the pier and close to running, which I used to do for exercise and now do only when absolutely necessary. I could see the person holding Bruno's leash was a man, but he was wearing a black trench coat and a hat, and between the two his face was not exactly featured.

The only thing I could think to do was yell, "Hey!" I kept running, although the years of not running were definitely showing in my speed and my ability to gulp down oxygen at the necessary rate to keep running. The guy leading Bruno to the gangplank did not look up.

Then the door on the opposite side of the SUV opened, and now I was close enough to see that Louise Barclay had gotten out and was walking toward the man holding Bruno's leash. She reached him and patted Bruno on the head. He seemed generally unperturbed, as Bruno always was, and licked Louise's hand. Even on the way to his own deportation, Bruno was determined to be amiable.

"Hey!" I shouted again. This time I was within earshot, and both Louise and the man looked up at the sound. And all of a sudden, I realized that drawing attention to myself might not have been the absolute best game plan available to me at this moment.

I also realized the man was Mike Goldberg.

He pointed at me, clearly asking Louise either what I was doing there or, in my mind more likely, who the hell I was. She responded, pointed at Bruno, and then put her hands on her hips like Wonder Woman. It didn't have that much of an effect, but I appreciated the attempt at character.

By that point I had just about reached them at the pier, and my lungs had given up all hope. I was gulping in oxygen so hard and fast that it was amazing the sky didn't actually disappear into my mouth. I couldn't really speak. I looked at Louise and said, "Bruno. Taiwan."

"You're not going," she replied. "We don't have a ticket for you. It's just Bruno."

"You can't do that." Then I took a long pause to replenish my respiratory system. "You can't send him away."

"Yes, I can. I can do anything I want with him. He's my dog. At least, until the papers are signed and he belongs to his new Taiwanese owners, the Aedo Corporation."

A corporation? "You're selling Bruno to a corporation?" Was the accounting department going to take him out for walks? How did that work?

"Enough." Mike looked at his watch. "They're sailing in fifteen minutes. We need to get him into a crate and get the documentation for the wire transfer."

"Right," Louise said. "You take him on board and I'll be right there."

"You're not taking him anywhere," I said. I was running on fumes now, but that didn't mean I had no gas left in the tank. Or maybe it did. I was really low on air. "He's not your dog. You stole him. You don't have any receipt for Bruno from a shelter or anywhere else. You have no right to put him on a ship all by himself and send him off to be the pet of a company."

"He's not a pet," Mike chimed in. "He's an investment." Because clearly that was the part of what I'd said that was open to argument.

"Bruno is my dog," Louise insisted, at least getting closer to the point. "He was Trent's dog, and Trent's dead, so now he's my dog."

"Trent's dead because you two put a knife in his back," I said. "You were the only one who had a key, and the door was locked from the inside. You were angry at Trent for having an affair with Taylor. You wanted all the money you could get for Bruno, and you didn't want to split it with your husband, mostly because you were already cheating on him with your buddy Mike here." At least *some* of that had to be true.

Except Louise started laughing. "Cheating with Mike?" she managed to push out through guffaws. "You've got to be kidding!" It was a terrible performance, and she had definitely been cheating with Mike.

Mike, for his part, had not tried to get Bruno on board the ship, and right now did not look especially amused.

"Taylor had a key," he pointed out. Mike was doing his best to seize on the least of my accusations and refute them rather than to take on the big questions, like who killed Trent.

"Taylor's the one who led me here," I informed them, just to see the reaction. Mike looked mildly surprised, as if being told that his delectable dessert was actually gluten-free cheesecake. But Louise looked angry.

"Taylor?" she hissed.

Might as well play it up for all it was worth. "Sure. She called to let me know exactly what pier you'd be on and when. She felt bad for Bruno, didn't want to see him be sent on such a long voyage all by himself to go live with people who didn't even really like him. She wanted me to stop you." At least, that was true of the Taylor in my head. The one walking around in the real world had probably just drunk dialed me and said any old thing that came into her mind.

Louise's eyes turned mean. "You're lying," she said. Okay, she had me there. "Taylor didn't care if Bruno was going to Taiwan. She just didn't want me to get the money. She thinks it's hers because she was sleeping with Trent. Like everybody else."

Clearly, that was something I was supposed to have known (except for the "everybody else" part, which was a non sequitur I didn't have time for right now). It was best in a negotiation like this to make sure any deficiencies in my case were downplayed. So I changed the conversation.

"The one thing I haven't understood from the beginning is what Akra's role in all this has been," I said.

As it turned out, that was the wrong thing to say. Mike's face drained of color, Louise's seemed to lengthen and harden, and that wasn't the worst part (although it should have been).

The worst part was that Mike was now leveling a gun at me. I was pretty sure it was a real one.

"Is that really necessary?" I asked.

"What do you know about Akra?" Mike demanded.

He had the gun in his right hand, which meant he'd had to switch Bruno's leash into his left hand. Bruno looked up, saw Mike pointing the gun at me, and growled for only the second time I'd ever heard him do so.

"Don't get Bruno mad," I warned Mike.

"Put that thing away," Louise insisted. "Someone will see it."

"No." Mike's lips were right across his teeth. "I'm not taking the fall for Trent's murder. I wasn't anywhere near the apartment that night, and I would never have agreed to such a thing. But you bring Akra into the discussion, and that gets serious. She"— he pointed at me with the hand holding the leash—"knows too much."

That was such a cliché, I almost laughed at him, but the gun in his hand wasn't all that funny. I needed options. My right hand was deep into my raincoat pocket, holding the handle of Dad's prop pistol. My mind, trying to process at least some of what was being said, was also attempting to determine if taking the gun out of my pocket helped or hurt my chances for survival.

I decided against it for the time being. Lead with your strength, I told myself.

"Bruno isn't just a valuable commodity," I said. Bruno growled at Mike again. That seemed good. I figured I'd say his name as much as possible to remind him who had always been on his side. "Bruno is contracted to appear on Broadway eight times a week, and Bruno is going to do just that. Right, Bruno?"

"Stop wasting my time," Mike said, thrusting his hand with the gun toward me a little. "I'm getting more than a million for this dog and you think you can talk me out of it with a contract for a musical?"

"I have paperwork that shows Louise doesn't rightfully own Bruno," I said, despite having no such item in my possession. For all I knew, no such document existed on the planet. But Louise and Mike didn't seem to know that, because their faces registered concern more than surprise. "Bruno doesn't belong to you," I said to Louise, "so you have no right to transport him anywhere."

"Enough," Mike said. He looked around. The gun was mostly concealed in his hand, but he couldn't shoot me here and not draw a crowd; there were people scattered around the piers. There were crew members on the ship. Anything he did here would be seen. He gestured with the gun toward a public restroom facility about twenty yards from where we were standing. "Let's go over there."

I didn't move an inch. "You're not serious, are you?" I said. "You think I'm just going to walk over there and let you shoot me?"

"You'll go over there and we can figure this out," Mike said.

"I can figure it out here."

"Get over there." He gestured again.

"Why? You can't shoot me here, and you *can* shoot me there. I like it better here."

Louise looked over at him and out of all the possible emotions she might register when looking at Mike holding a gun on me while getting ready to load Bruno onto a ship headed for Taiwan, she chose to look annoyed. "Will you cut it out?" she said. "We only have a few minutes to get Bruno onto the boat."

Mike's teeth were clenched so hard I considered recommending a dentist I know to fit him for a night guard. "She'll run away if we leave," he hissed at her. "She knows it's not really your dog."

Aha! Finally an actual admission. Should I let Mike know that was the first time I'd confirmed my suspicions about Bruno? No. Better not to further antagonize the man with the deadly weapon.

"You said you had nothing to do with Trent's murder," I reminded Mike. "So if it wasn't you, who was it?"

The ship's whistle blew, which only served to refocus the attention of the two holding Bruno hostage (which was the way I'd decided to look at it). They looked on board. "We've gotta go," Louise said.

"You take the dog," Mike suggested. "I'll make sure she doesn't do anything stupid and then we can decide what to do about her when you get back. The wire transfer has to go down quick, before the ship sails."

Louise nodded her agreement and reached for the leash. Mike reached over to give it to her, still leveling the gun at my midsection, which is one of my favorite sections, and therefore a place I'd prefer not to be shot. The scene was not going as I'd planned, which reminded me that I hadn't really planned it much at all.

"Akra killed Trent, didn't she?" I said. It was a Hail Mary pass based strictly on the way Mike had reacted to my previous mention of her name. Akra's, not Mary's.

Louise took in a breath and hesitated for a second. Mike simply said, "Shut up." But he made a mistake. He took a step toward me and it was clear from his voice and his manner that he did not mean to give me a nice warm hug. My impulse was to pull the fake gun, but going up against a real one it would probably not have the same impact it might have otherwise.

I needn't have worried anyway. Bruno, seeing Mike make a threatening move toward me, simply did what dogs do when they sense danger. In a nanosecond, he reached over from his position at Mike's feet and sunk his teeth into the man's calf.

Mike made a noise like a man whose leg was being bitten by a dog and dropped his arm to his side. In a split second I chose between bolting for the restroom and reaching over to grab the gun. I selected the latter option and disarmed Mike as Louise scolded Bruno for saving my life.

Before I could properly aim the gun at either of them, though, I heard Detective Rodriguez's voice through a bullhorn behind me. "Don't move," she said. It was unclear for whom the message was intended. "This is the New York Police Department." That didn't really clarify the issue. It was also odd, seeing as how we were in New Jersey.

"Can I move?" I shouted. "Detective?"

Even through the megaphone you could hear the exasperation. Rodriguez was a real talent at exasperation; she could go pro with it. "Of course *you* can move," she said. "But Mr. Goldman and Ms. Barclay, you are both under arrest."

I turned around—having been given permission to do so— and looked. Rodriguez was maybe fifty feet away, which made the bullhorn she was holding sort of overkill. She could have just yelled and been heard just as clearly. And she was closing the gap between us rapidly. Within seconds, she was behind me, holding her gun on Mike, who was looking down at his leg.

"I'm bleeding!" he wailed. "He broke the skin!"

"That's the master criminal?" Rodriguez asked me.

"As a matter of fact, I don't think he is," I answered. "So you were just going to let him shoot me?"

Rodriguez frowned. "You had nothing to worry about. There are snipers on both those buildings." She pointed to a maintenance facility and an administration building, each of which was four stories high and close enough that a shot, for a trained sniper like Bradley Cooper, probably wouldn't have been that big a deal.

"And they did nothing because . . . ?"

"Because there was never any reason to," Rodriguez countered. "Give us a little credit."

"My leg!" Mike moaned.

"He is a big baby, isn't he?" the detective said. Two uniformed police officers, both African American and large, appeared with zip strips and started to restrain Louise and Mike, who kept whimpering. Bruno, unconcerned now that I had his leash, yawned.

"Have you found Taylor Cassidy?" I asked Rodriguez. "Akra Levy?"

"Ms. Levy is back at her job with Les McMaster," the detective said. "Ms. Cassidy we have not found. She must be staying with a friend."

"Huh!" Louise snorted.

Rodriguez turned to her. "What does that mean?"

"She'll have plenty of friends to bunk with," Louise sneered. "Like half the seventh fleet."

She was speaking in riddles. "Taylor's in the navy?" I asked.

Louise looked at me and her expression spoke volumes about

my clear lack of a formal education (although I had mostly gone to school in the Catskills). "She's a prostitute, honey. She can find a place to sleep, believe me."

Rodriguez didn't seem at all surprised, but my eyes must have grown to the size of quarters. "A prostitute?" I said. "Not a dog walker?" Okay, so that wasn't my best ad lib ever.

"Yeah, she's a dog walker." Louise rolled her eyes. "That's how she affords an apartment on the Upper West Side."

"So how come she was walking Bruno?" I asked. I'm cutting out the part where I stuttered on "so."

"I'm not talking until I see my lawyer," Louise countered. Spoilsport.

"Ow," Mike whined again.

"Oh, take these two away," Rodriguez said. "We'll question them at the precinct."

"A prostitute," I repeated. It should have clarified matters, but it so didn't.

"Yeah, we knew that. It's what she meant when she told you a woman like her couldn't call the cops. Although she could have. I wasn't going to arrest her for that if she gave us some good information about Trent Barclay's murder."

"Well, Mike Goldberg didn't know that," I said. "Maybe he was threatening her as the time to ship Bruno was getting closer. He didn't want to screw up the deal with whoever was buying the dog in Taiwan."

"Yeah, Mike Goldberg. What did you mean you don't think he's the mastermind?"

"I've done a lot of negotiations," I said as Louise and Mike were led away. "He was too scared when Akra's name came up; I could have gotten him to sign a contract for a talking unicorn at that moment. Besides, he's not the type to get his hands dirty. He's the type who hires someone to get his hands dirty."

"You think he paid someone to kill Trent Barclay?" Rodriguez sounded skeptical. "A knife in the back isn't exactly the normal professional killer MO."

"I don't know about that," I said. We started to walk, the three of us. Bruno seemed as natural at my side as either of my dogs would have. "What will happen to Bruno?"

Rodriguez considered. "Well, the guy who owned him is dead and his wife is going to be charged with a crime or two, one of which might be stealing the dog. We found records from a shelter in Poughkeepsie showing that a dog looking like this one was adopted six months ago by a Leo Mountbatten of New Rochelle. Mr. Mountbatten reported the dog stolen three months ago, taken from his fenced-in backyard while the owner, an elderly widower, was watching *Jeopardy!* on TV."

Oddly I felt my heart sink. "So Bruno will be going back to Mr. Mountbatten?" I asked.

Rodriguez shook her head. "I'm afraid Mr. Mountbatten passed away last month, so Bruno would have been on his own at another shelter anyway, I guess. Do you want to keep him? I'm not sure if you can but once we check the records to see if Mountbatten had any relatives, he might be available."

I had decided when I started the agency that I would never adopt a client. Then I adopted Maisie, who was currently making a fuss in my office no doubt, and swore it would never happen again. But Bruno . . . Bruno had gotten to me. "Can I let you know once the dust has settled?"

Rodriguez looked at me sideways. "Might take a couple of days until I can check those records," she said. "I still have to catch a killer. Why don't you take Bruno until we can work that out?"

It would only be a couple of days. "Sure," I said. "So how are you going to catch Trent's murderer?"

"I'm not," Rodriguez said. "You are."

CHAPTER TWENTY-TWO

"I think he's got it down." Les McMaster looked at Bruno, who had just done a complete run through of the song "Sandy" (and yes, I know it's not in the original play, but Les had imported it from the movie) with flying colors. The three young actresses who had performed the song with Bruno had already left the stage and were back in their dressing rooms with their moms. There was no performance scheduled for today, so everyone who had come in for the rehearsal was now free to go home. Except me and Bruno.

And Akra. She was back at Les's side, holding her magical clipboard and saying "yes" a lot, except when I tried to engage her in conversation. To my eye, she was acting very suspiciously.

"He's ready to go into the show," Les said. "Can he start tomorrow?"

Since we hadn't actually located a legal owner for Bruno, I was his temporary guardian, Rodriguez had proclaimed. She'd asked me to come here and put Bruno through the rehearsal in an attempt to smoke out Trent's murderer, whom Rodriguez now believed was in the theater company. Louise and Mike's stories had been believable, involving Mike being in Maryland that night (verified three times) and Louise having no upper body strength necessary to drive a knife that hard, so neither of them seemed to have been capable of killing Trent at the time he'd been knifed to death.

"Sure. Bruno's ready to go," I told Les. "The problem is that I'm not sure exactly who you're contracting with for his services at the moment, so I'm going to set up an escrow account that you can pay into and work out who gets the money when all this is sorted out. Is that okay with you?"

Les nodded and called back to Akra. He never turned to look at her, just assuming she'd be there. "Do you have that?" he asked.

"Got it," came the answer.

When I'd first seen Akra at the theater this morning, I'd felt compelled to confirm for Rodriguez that Akra had indeed reappeared at Les's side. But there had been no way to covertly call or text without Akra seeing me do so. I was concerned that if she caught a whiff of suspicion, she'd bolt again. Better to do as Rodriguez had asked, and observe as much as possible to report back later.

"Great." Les, in a sweater and khakis, could have been in a Gap ad. He rubbed his hands together and looked around, taking in the stage set. "We're all set."

He walked down off the stage to the front of the house, where I was standing. Bruno was wary of the stairs and sat on the edge of the stage. I moved toward the steps but Les caught me by the arm. "Do you think I'm a good director?" he asked.

What the what? "Everybody knows you're a good director, Les. Where'd that come from?"

Les let go of my arm, so I went up and attached Bruno's leash, pretending it was necessary. Bruno wouldn't run away if the Sofia Vergara of dogs passed by carrying a sign reading IN HEAT AND INTERESTED.

"Not everybody," Les said quietly.

"What?"

"Not everybody. Some people don't think I'm a good director." He sighed. "They think I'm a hack."

Akra, having gotten closer in case Les had mentioned his next desperate need too quietly to hear from her previous perch, clicked her tongue. "No one thinks that," she said.

Les didn't answer but he still looked miserable. I decided it was time to change the subject. I couldn't actually bring up Trent's murder at the moment, so I moved on to something I actually wanted to ask. "I have been wondering," I said to Les. "Why have you been so involved in casting a new Sandy? That's not something a lot of directors in your position would concern themselves with."

"It's because they think I'm a hack," he answered, looking at the floor. Had Les been drinking? "It's because I can't get another job. They wouldn't let me direct *Landfill* because they think all I can do is make nice dances for suburban families."

"You're exaggerating," Akra told him. This was about the other play, the straight play Les had wanted to direct. I'd thought it was a done deal. Dare I ask?

Wait! Landfill? The same as the file in Trent Barclay's hard drive?

It hit me and came out of my mouth. "Trent was going to be one of the producers of *Landfill*."

Akra shot me a poisonous look. Apparently this was a sensitive subject. It wasn't that I didn't realize; it was more in the area of me not caring that it was a sensitive subject.

But Les wasn't listening to me anyway. He was in mid-rant. "I was that close to getting it and then they'd see I'm not just about tap dancing and eleven o'clock numbers," Les said. "It's a brilliant play and I get it like nobody else would. But they won't let me do it." He *had* been drinking. It was a miracle Les had gotten through the rehearsal, but he was nothing if not a pro and he wasn't going to let those little girls see him smashed.

"Why not?" I asked. *I* would have hired him for the play, but then, I represent dogs for a living. And I needed to get him to say it.

"Bad publicity," Les said. "Rumors I'd lost my edge. They said I was drinking. I *wasn't* drinking!"

And then it all came together. Les was about to get the job he'd always wanted, directing an important new play that had Tony Award potential and could open him up to respect and admiration he mistakenly believed he'd never had before. And one little slip-up had caused the rumor mill that is showbiz to go into overdrive. Someone told the producers of *Landfill* he'd started drinking again. Maybe he had; maybe he hadn't. It didn't matter—the rumors had started and that was enough. Les had been cut out of the job.

"Oh my God," I said. "You killed Trent."

Akra's head looked up toward me so fast I was afraid her neck would snap. "How dare you?" she hissed.

"You did. Trent made those comments backstage after the audition for a new Sandy. Right, Les? And somebody backstage heard it and let the word out. They said you were drinking again, and you suddenly became an insurance risk for *Landfill*. You hadn't signed the contract yet, so they just withdrew the offer. 'Creative differences,' right? That's what they'll say?"

Les gathered himself. It was truly an awe-inspiring performance to behold: He drew himself to full height, seemed to sober up before my eyes, and regarded me with a glance that bordered on the regal.

"I have no idea what you're talking about," he said. But then he started up the stairs toward me. "I told you, if I couldn't take a little criticism, I'd have been out of this business years ago."

Idiot that I am, I did not tighten my grip on Bruno's leash. If I had, I would have been able to expect the same kind of protection I'd gotten from him at the pier.

Instead, just as Les was advancing on me, I felt the leash pulled out of my hand. And sure enough, Akra had grabbed it from behind me and was leading Bruno, loyal but not that bright, away.

"I think he needs a walk," she said calmly.

"He doesn't need a walk," I said, as if there were even a hint of sincerity in what Akra was saying. "He went out just an hour ago. He's fine. Akra!" But they were gone.

"I had no reason to kill Trent Barclay," Les said. "But Moshe Berkowitz, now, there was a man who needed to die."

Moshe Berkowitz? It seemed a bad time to mention to Les that Trent and Moshe were the same man. Mostly because Les was standing about six feet from me and I'd prefer that he not make that five feet or less. "Um . . . why, Les?" I tried to sound casual, like I was asking him why he'd chosen to take a taxi rather than the subway when he'd gone to kill Trent. Sorry, Moshe.

"Because he was the weasel," Les said. He didn't look like a happy drunk at all. But at least he wasn't advancing anymore. "Because he stopped me. He came here for one lousy audition with his *dog* and he stopped me."

I could have told Les he was rambling, but would that have had the desired effect? I doubted it. Also, backing up suggested itself, but somehow I felt that if I moved, that would cue Les to move as well. Dammit! He could have gotten away with the crime. I personally had figured Akra for the killer. But no. I had to come out here and do Rodriguez's work for her, and now I was feeling severely threatened by a man on the set of *Annie*. Somehow that seemed wrong.

I plugged on. "How did Tre—Moshe—stop you, Les?" I asked. "It was right after that I heard about the *Landfill* deal falling through." If I'd only known that was the title of the play, this could have happened much sooner. Would that have been better?

Les got a really unpleasant smile on his face. "That's right. Turns out old Moshe was an investor. In *Landfill*. His company was one of the biggest producers of the show. And once he decided I wasn't good enough for his *dog,* he poison-pilled me with his partners. I was perfect for that job, and he got me booted out of spite."

My brain was processing this, but not quickly enough. Trent was Moshe. Moshe owned Swing Productions. Swing Productions was a big investor in *Landfill*. Because I'd brought Trent to

Bruno's audition for Les, and Trent, being Trent, had decided Les was a hack, he torpedoed Les for *Landfill*. So Les went to Trent's apartment that night and . . .

Now that all the cards were on the table, I could give up the pretense that I didn't know Les had killed Trent (I'd sort of given that up when I blurted it out, but I'm not sure whether that had penetrated Les's gin-soaked brain yet). "How did you get into Moshe's apartment that night?" I asked. They so rarely kill you when they're talking. So keep them talking.

Les waved a hand. We were two old drinking buddies and he was going to tell me this great story about how he'd put one over on his archnemesis. "It was easy," he said. "Akra had a key."

Well, that explained it. Wait, whoa! "Akra had a what?"

"A key. She watered their plants once when they were out of town and they gave her a key." Les clearly had been drinking a *lot*. He giggled. Really. "He gave her a key. And she gave it to me." He mimed opening a lock with a key, like that was the really clever part. "And I went in to have it out with old Moshe."

So he stabbed the guy with a kitchen knife? "You didn't bring anything with you," I said. *Where were Akra and Bruno? Was she going to try to ship him to the Far East again?* "You weren't going to kill him when you got there, were you?"

It might not have been the best idea to remind Les that he'd killed Trent. He took a step toward me and his face darkened. "I never intended to do anything like that. I am not a violent man." Which was good news for me, I guessed, except that he looked like he wanted to tear me limb from limb. "I figured sneaking into his bedroom to talk some sense into him would be enough.

Maybe mention that I could tell his wife some things he didn't want her to know. Like that he was paying Taylor Cassidy to have sex with him."

That solved one puzzle: Taylor and Louise had been given house seats to *Annie* the night I was there with Bruno because Les knew them both and wanted, perhaps, to curry favor again with Louise if she'd inherited Trent's share of *Landfill*.

I backed up one step because Les was invading my personal space. I would have run for the door, but I was in heels and Les was in running shoes. Men give themselves all the advantages.

I heard my voice getting louder, but it didn't seem intentional. "So what went wrong?" I asked Les. Clearly if it wasn't his intention to kill Trent, something had gone wrong.

"He wouldn't listen to reason!" Les's jaw clenched and his eyes looked like they were pickled in something stronger than Dr Pepper. His breath was not exactly fabulous either, and I was close enough to notice. "He kept saying if I couldn't direct a dog, then I couldn't direct that play! Like *he* knew anything about the theater!"

I needed to calm him down, and reliving the night in Trent's apartment wasn't going to do it. "Tell me about the play, Les," I said. "Tell me what makes *Landfill* so unique." You can lecture me later on how "unique" is an absolute and there are no degrees of it to discuss. I was busy saving my ass, thank you.

Except it didn't work. Les wasn't listening. He reached over, out of nowhere, with both hands, and got them around my throat. And he started squeezing.

The effect was astonishing. I had been exhaling when he

grabbed me, so I couldn't even rely on the air I'd just taken in for a few seconds to think. Right away my vision started to blur. I think my tear ducts were already reacting to the movement and the sudden deprivation of oxygen.

I couldn't exactly talk, but I could manage to croak, "Why?" I wondered if I'd ever see my parents again. I thought about Sam, of all people, and puzzled very, very briefly on why I hadn't given him a chance when he wanted to ask me out. For a nanosecond I considered why the rule is "*i* before *e* except after *c*" when there were words like "neither."

"He killed my career!" Les was in full rant now and his hands were doing the full strangle. "You're going to tell them!"

I tried to shake my head to tell him I wouldn't (I totally would have), but I couldn't muster much lateral motion. I was rapidly losing what air was stored in my lungs and my head was cloudy.

So when I saw Akra come back onto the stage without Bruno's leash but with two uniformed policemen, one holding each of her arms, and then heard a loud noise, I wasn't really processing the data all that well.

I was monumentally grateful, though, when after the loud report Les's hands fell from my throat and air flooded back into my lungs. I didn't even fall to the floor; I held my ground and stood.

Les, on the other hand, was lying on the stage and clutching his left leg, which was bleeding from the thigh. He pointed toward the balcony and moaned.

There was a man up there with a rifle, raising the barrel up toward the ceiling and standing down from what must have been his station. He looked down toward us on the stage.

Detective Rodriguez emerged from the orchestra pit and surveyed the scene: I was gulping in air as hard as I could, my head woozy. Les was bleeding all over *Annie*'s living room and groaning in pain. Bruno walked over from the wings and licked my hand.

"See?" Rodriguez said. "I told you. The snipers always come through when they have a good reason."

CHAPTER TWENTY-THREE

"Okay, let's see if I've got this straight." Consuelo crossed her legs and took another sip of her beer. She sat in a lawn chair next to the picnic table in my backyard, which had been carefully scoured for any . . . souvenirs the dogs might have left there. The place was clean as a whistle, assuming a whistle is pretty clean but not perfect.

"Les McMaster killed Trent because Trent was Moshe and Moshe was blackballing him with the producers of *Landfill*," Consuelo went on. Diego was on the other side of the yard, throwing a tennis ball for the dogs to chase. Steve and Bruno were all over it, while Eydie lay in the sun, watching her men in their adolescent pursuit of sports. She sighed, but you could tell she was really looking to see who would win.

"But that's just part of the plan," I told Consuelo. "The way it seems, based on everybody's confession, is that Mike Goldberg, who was a school pal of Moshe's, had worked out this plot where he'd steal this dog nobody knew was worth all kinds of money except Mike."

Dad, standing at the charcoal grill wearing an apron with a picture of Shakespeare on the front and the caption, " 'Tis an ill cook that cannot lick his own fingers— *Romeo and Juliet*, Act 4, Scene 2," said, "How did Mike know about Mr. Mountbatten's dog?"

"Mike was Mr. Mountbatten's neighbor from around the corner," I said. "Detective Rodriguez was mad at me for not remembering Mike was from New Rochelle, but once she looked it up, it was clear Mike could see Bruno—or Spunky, as Mr. Mountbatten called him—from his kitchen window. He got to wondering what kind of weird dog that was, did some Googling, and discovered more than he expected. He masterminded the plot to steal Bruno from Mountbatten and set him up with Louise and Trent in the city because nobody would look for the dog there. It took him a few months to locate a buyer on the black market for Tibetan mastiffs and negotiate a deal. But he never told Trent how valuable Bruno was, and only told Louise after Trent was dead to get her to cooperate. He was going to split the money with her."

Mom opened the glass doors in the back of my house and walked out onto the deck. She surveyed the scene. "Does anybody need a cold drink?" she asked. "It's getting warm out here."

Consuelo waved her beer bottle. "I'm good, Mrs. P," she said. "Thanks." Mom didn't get a response from anyone else, so she walked down the steps and went to the grill to check on Dad. She carried a glass of lemonade, which she gave to him when she got there. She doesn't need to ask Dad; she can just sense when he needs a drink and makes it appear in his hand.

"But none of this had anything to do with Les," Consuelo pointed out.

"No. Les had nothing to do with the whole Bruno side of this crazy plot," I said. "Les didn't know Bruno was worth all kinds of money; even Akra hadn't figured that out. When I first brought Trent and Louise to Bruno's audition, she didn't know how to figure her old school chum coming in, but Trent managed to signal to her not to let on. Louise said Trent wanted to see how Les would audition the dog—that they still didn't know was going to be Mike's fortune—without the connection to Les's assistant."

"And he didn't like what he saw," Dad said, flipping a burger.

"That's right," I told him. "Trent thought Les didn't know how to direct Bruno. I'm not sure why, but that's what he thought."

"He thought that because Trent was a jerk." Taylor Cassidy stood up from the chaise longue, where she'd been drinking an iced tea and sunning herself, much to Diego's interest. Consuelo had actually poured some cold water on her son as he undid two buttons on his shirt, claiming he was in need of some cooling down because playing with the dogs was taxing him. "Trent didn't think anybody could do anything right except him." Taylor, who had surfaced after Les, Louise, and Mike and been arrested (she'd texted me from another disposable phone), walked toward Consuelo and me, ignoring Dee's eyes, which never left her.

"Watch yourself," Dad said casually. "You sound like someone with motive." There was a light chuckle all around.

I'd invited Taylor to the barbecue because she'd apologized

for her behavior (like helping to get me blown up), explaining that Mike Goldberg had discovered what she called her "day job," although I doubted she worked the afternoon hours much, through a client and had threatened to expose her to the police, Les, Akra, and me (I thought I was the least of the threats) if she didn't cooperate with his plan to get Bruno out of the country. Taylor's "day job" was of an upscale nature, which didn't so much excuse it as made it harder to argue against.

"Not me. Not Trent," she said. "I just knew him because we lived in the same building. They had to be out during the day and knew I would be in my apartment, so Trent asked me to walk the dog. Said he'd pay cash. I just liked Bruno and I didn't have anything better to do." Bruno noticed the mention of his name and trotted over to be petted because that was what he lived for. He was indulged rather excessively by everyone in the vicinity. "Who's a good boy, Bruno?" Taylor asked. "Who's a good boy?"

Bruno didn't answer.

Dad's cell phone rang, so he handed the burger flipper over to Mom, who handed it to me. I took my place at the grill and watched as Dad took his call. His face showed some interest. It was probably a gig.

Sam Gibson had sent a gallon of iced coffee and one of iced tea from Cool Beans, and I'd gone through most of the coffee myself, so I was wide-awake and ready to grill. Sam had to keep the store open but promised to try to drop by after hours if we were still back here, which I expected we would be.

I'd been thinking about Sam and come to no conclusion whatsoever. But it was certainly in his favor that he had never once been a suspect in a murder as far as I knew. The number of men with whom I was acquainted who could make that claim had diminished seriously of late.

"So wait a minute," I said as I turned a couple of hot dogs. People weren't eating nearly enough of the food, making my station here seem extra superfluous. Dad walked into the house so he could hear his call better. Maybe I'd shut down the grill for a little while until people got hungry. "None of the Bruno stuff had anything to do with Trent getting killed. Instead, Les shows up using Akra's key to the apartment. You didn't have one, Taylor?"

"No. When I was walking the dog, they'd leave one under the welcome mat, which is a cliché but nobody ever looks there." She put a shirt on loosely over her shoulders, which didn't much diminish Diego's interest. Consuelo gave him a look you'd think would discourage a young man, coming from his mother. And it probably would have if he'd even glanced in his mother's direction.

I nodded. The dogs, happy but tired, had congregated on the far side, where there was some shade, and were just lying there panting despite the presence of a huge communal water bowl only a few feet from where they lay. "So Les has this key and he tries to threaten Trent with knowledge of . . . business Trent was doing with you?"

Taylor shook her head. "Never once. Mike was lying about that. I don't even think Trent knew what I do for a living."

Dad walked out of the house and directly to Mom, who had sat on a lawn chair where she could watch me and the dogs at the same time. He leaned down and talked quietly to her. Whatever he said made her smile slightly. She nodded.

"New gig?" I asked him. There was no reason to be secretive about it now that Mom had given the okay.

"Yeah. We'll be on a cruise ship sailing the Greek islands at the end of the month." Dad was grinning from ear to ear. He's happy to be around me and be stationary for a while, but he's never more engaged than when he's working. Mom was getting a little weary of the road, but liked to see Dad so happy (and she does actually like to perform, no matter what she tells you).

I didn't have any Champagne chilled, so we toasted their new engagement with some of Sam's contributions to the party. But something was nagging at me about Trent's murder and I was trying to unknot it in my head.

"What was Akra's interest in all this?" I asked. "Mike wanted the money from Bruno. Les wanted the job on *Landfill*. Louise wanted . . . what did Louise want?"

"After she found out, the money, and Mike," Taylor said. "That was never a question. She'd do anything the guy even considered suggesting. That's why I thought she'd killed Trent, to get him out of the way so she'd have a clear path to Mike."

Diego walked over with a look I'd never seen before. I realized, after a moment, that it was shyness. He was fascinated with Taylor, and she was so in another world from him that it broke my heart just to see that expression cross his face.

"Akra," I reminded myself. "Mike wanted money, Les wanted *Landfill*, Louise wanted Mike, for whatever reason. What was up with Akra?"

Everyone sort of looked at one another for a moment, in one of those tableaux that suggest one person isn't getting it and they're deciding who should be the one to break the news. "Les!"

yelled my parents, Consuelo, and Taylor. Diego was still taking in the wonder that was Taylor and did not join in the chorus.

"Akra's in love with Les?" I said, and even as the words were escaping my lips it was evident to me that I should have known that long before. "Of course she is. And so if Les wants something, Akra wants it. But she was Trent's school pal. How does she reconcile that with his putting the kibosh on Les's dream job?"

"Think about it, Kay," Mom said. "She gave Les the key to Trent's apartment. And then she heard that Trent was stabbed in the back at the time Les was there. Even if Les didn't tell her what happened, he had to give her back the key. She couldn't not have put two and two together. Now she's an accessory. So what did she do?"

"Nothing," I said. I was being tutored in the things bizarre people do.

"That's right," Taylor said. "I mean, I wasn't in on all of it, or even most of it. I was basically Mike's project, and all he cared about was the dog. The murder was a side issue, a distraction. I know for a fact that Mike was pissed when he heard about it because he thought it would mess up the deal he was making about selling Bruno."

Detective Rodriguez had questioned Taylor extensively, but had not yet arrested her for any crime. Taylor said she was hoping the detective would look the other way about her "day job" in exchange for all the information Taylor had on Trent's murder and the illegal attempt to sell Bruno, which the NYPD and the Port Authority Police were calling robbery, fraud, illegal trade, and exporting a dog without a license (I made that last one up). Taylor was pretty sure she could avoid any jail time, and was considering a change of occupation, although not an immediate one. She still had to pay off the student loans she had accumulated while attending law school at Columbia University. Other people might work their way through with a job at Starbucks, but I don't judge.

Dad looked around and saw that everyone had either food or a used paper plate near them. "I'm going to shut down the grill," he said, and after no one objected, he did that. "We have to start thinking about the new act."

"New act?" Mom gets nervous about learning new material. "What's wrong with the old act? The Greek islands haven't seen it."

"No, but there's no Greek material in it. I'll get something together, El. You'll have plenty of time before we need it."

We sat and drank beer, iced coffee, or iced tea for some hours until it got dark and the dogs, happy though they were to be around all these adoring people, needed a proper walk. I walked by Cool Beans, and Sam walked back with us. Taylor had left by then, and Consuelo and Diego were considering doing the same. I got the distinct impression that once Taylor was gone, Diego's interest in the gathering had deteriorated considerably.

Mom, Dad, Sam, and I sat around the wood stove I have back there for a while, until my parents lied about getting tired and left the two of us (plus three dogs) alone in the backyard.

Sam, having been briefed on the complicated saga, looked at me over his bottle of beer. "So you helped solve a crime," he said.

"I guessed. I don't think that's how it's supposed to work." Eydie came over to get a head scratch and was rewarded.

Sam tilted his head to one side, which more than anything

else reminded me of Bruno. "It's not nothing," he said. "People who had done and were going to do really bad things are in jail tonight because of you."

I looked away; that was not a responsibility I especially cared to accept. "They did what they did. They deserved to get caught and punished."

He looked puzzled, as if he didn't understand my response. "I'm not blaming you for anything," he said. "I think what you did was admirable."

"You think most things I do are admirable." That hung in the air for a moment, and I didn't want to milk it, so I moved on. "I'm not a detective; I'm just a showbiz girl."

Sam's face took on a look of mock surprise. "I thought you weren't showbiz," he said. "That is definitely what I was told."

"Well, maybe I am. A little."

Bruno ambled over, having seen Eydie get a juicy head scratch, and lobbied for his own, which he also received. I had the feeling he wasn't going to be leaving Scarborough for a new home anytime soon. But now that Les was behind bars, he also wasn't going to be playing Sandy on Broadway. The producers felt that his presence would attract undue publicity, given the circumstances. They opted to renew Horatio's contract, which delighted Gwen Harper and undoubtedly annoyed pretty much everyone else involved in the *Annie* production. The good guys don't *always* win.

Sam and I sat up for a few hours talking about things other than the events of the past week. Eventually I stopped putting logs on the stove and it gave up, just a few embers sticking around to remind us that we might contain fire but we can't control it.

The dogs all went inside on their own and took up their positions in the house to sleep.

After that, Sam got the idea that I would be happy to follow the dogs inside and he took off, noting that he had to be back in his store in scandalously few hours. He did not try to kiss me and I didn't encourage it. We weren't there yet.

I went into the house for a while and assessed the cleanup I'd have to do in the morning, which wasn't much. But I didn't want to go to sleep just yet so I put on a fleece I bought in Houston some years ago with the logo of the Johnson Space Center on it. I'm not an astronaut, but neither is anyone else who bought the fleece, so it seemed fair enough.

I sat on one of the chaise longues and looked at the sky, which tonight was as full of stars as you can get in Northern New Jersey. My thoughts, naturally, turned to Trent's murder, Bruno's abduction, and the dizzy group of people who had been swarming around them.

Long story short: I didn't reach any conclusions. A lot of people with whom I might otherwise have done business had done some pretty terrible things, and if Rodriguez hadn't sent me to spy on them, they might not have gotten caught. So I guessed that even if I was a horrible person for deceiving them, I had done it for good reasons.

I had screwed up a lot of the investigation. I'd gotten blown up. I'd had a gun pointed at me and a man I knew had tried to strangle me.

Frankly, it wasn't the worst week I've ever had. After all, I'm just the agent.

ACKNOWLEDGMENTS

Every book is a collaboration, and any author who tells you otherwise is either lying or self-deluded. Although I've never run into an author who said that.

This one is no exception. I could not have deposited this story into your hands, your Kindle, your tablet, or your audiobook player without many people doing their jobs and doing them well.

Chief among these is Marcia Markland, who listened to a one-sentence pitch for the series and said, "Sold." Then we had lunch, which is always a pleasure with Marcia. She has excellent taste and is wonderful company. Marcia's two assistants who helped move this project along, Nettie Finn and Quressa Robinson, were also of great help.

Along for that lunch was my ever-astounding agent Josh Getzler of HSG Agency, who had thought of bringing the idea to

Marcia in the first place. What I know about the publishing business is roughly equivalent to what I know about sending people to Mars, so it's always an enormous help to have Josh with me because he knows everything.

Thanks to David Rotstein, art director, for making the cover of this book look so amazing, and to the copyeditor Rachelle Mandik for catching all my mistakes, of which there were many.

Thanks to everyone online who has ever posted anything about a Tibetan mastiff because there is no doubt I have seen your work in preparing this manuscript. But some of those posts were just silly.

And thanks to the people who conduct "haunted" tours of Grand Central Terminal (not "Station!") for filling in a few blanks and being so entertaining.

Last but certainly not least, this book is dedicated to the late Gene Wilder, who was that rare artist who could be hilarious without trying to be funny. But it is also for Copper, who was a very good dog, and Gizmo, who only thinks he is.